Ocean of Fireflies

Other books by J.S. Fields:

The Ardulum Series:

Ardulum: First Don

Ardulum: Second Don

Ardulum: Third Don

Tales from Ardulum

Ardulum: The Battle for Pruitcu

Other Fantasy and Science Fiction:

The Rosewood Penny

Distant Gardens

Farther Reefs

Lofty Mountains

Queen

Awry With Dandelions

Ocean of Fireflies

J.S. Fields

Space Wizard Science Fantasy
Raleigh, NC
www.spacewizardsciencefantasy.com

Cover art by Katie Cordy
Illustrations by Kristine Cordy
Editing by Courtney Brooks
Book Layout © 2015 BookDesignTemplates.com

Ocean of Fireflies J.S Fields.— 1st ed.
ISBN 978-1-960247-32-2

Author's website: www.jsfieldsbooks.com

Warning: This book includes misgendering by side characters; warning for gore, fantasy violence, and body dysphoria.

To every teen who saw themselves in Sorin
And every adult who found an echo of their past
I hope this sequel is everything you need it to be
Be safe on your journeys, and may there always be a princess
waiting for you at the end.

CONTENTS

Glacier
Continen
Gasta Fl
QUEENDOM OF SORPSI
Village of Thuja
Liriodendron Village
Village of Sage
Cedar River
Sea of Tii
Capitol City
Village of B
Capital Cove (Port)
Main Road
Village of Taxodium
Village of
Pseudotsuga
KINGD
EAS
CITY
VILLAGE
CONIFERUS FOREST
MOUNTAINS
HARDWOOD FOREST
GLACIER
RAINFOREST
TRADE ROUTE
GRASSLANDS
BORDER
FARMLANDS
RIVER
Coastal Road

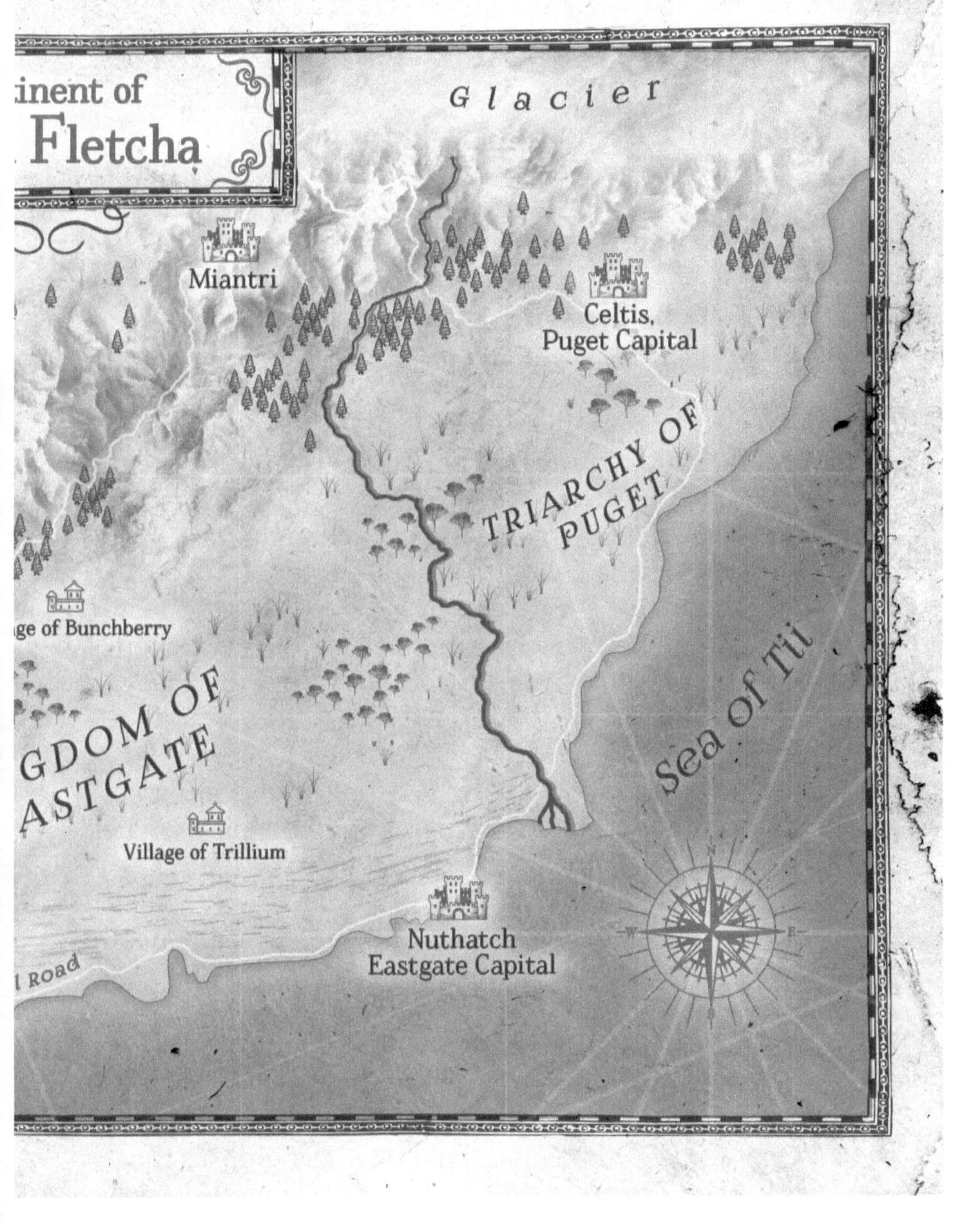
inent of
Fletcha
Glacier
Miantri
Celtis,
Puget Capital
TRIARCHY OF PUGET
ge of Bunchberry
GDOM OF
ASTGATE
Sea of Tu
Village of Trillium
Nuthatch
Eastgate Capital
Road

Guilds of the Three Countries

The Carpenter Guild, held by Sorpsi, encompasses functional woodcraft. Symbol: handplane tattoo.

The Cooper Guild, held by Puget, encompasses woodcraft used solely for alcohol. Symbol: barrel tattoo.

The Glass Guild, held by Sorpsi, encompasses all glasswork. Symbol: stemmed cup tattoo.

The Masons, held by Eastgate, encompasses all stoneworkers. Symbol: three vertically stacked bricks.

The Music Guild, held by Eastgate, is the home to all professional musicians. Symbol: bass clef tattoo.

The River Guild, held by Eastgate, encompasses fishers, boatspeople, and those who work with the waterways. Symbol: black fish tattoo.

The Shepherd Guild, held by Eastgate, encompasses ranchers and other livestock owners. Symbol: picket gate tattoo.

The Smith Guild, held by Sorpsi, encompasses all metal work. Symbol: two crossed hammers.

The Textile Guild, held by Puget, is the home to weavers, dyers, spinners, and knitters. Symbol: cotton boll tattoo.

The Trapper and Trader Guild, held by Puget, houses those who work with pelts, skin, and other animal-derived materials. Symbol: beaver tattoo.

The Woodcutter Guild, held by Sorpsi, encompasses artistic woodcraft. Symbol: leafed branch tattoo.

The Alchemy Guild is one of two unbound guilds and, as such, does not have a primary guildhall in any of the three countries, nor do they have a grandmaster. They are symbolized by a black cauldron tattoo with a beaker suspended above it.

The Witch Guild is one of two unbound guilds and, as such, does not have a primary guildhall in any of the three countries, nor do they have a grandmaster. They are symbolized by a black cauldron tattoo with a daisy growing from the middle.

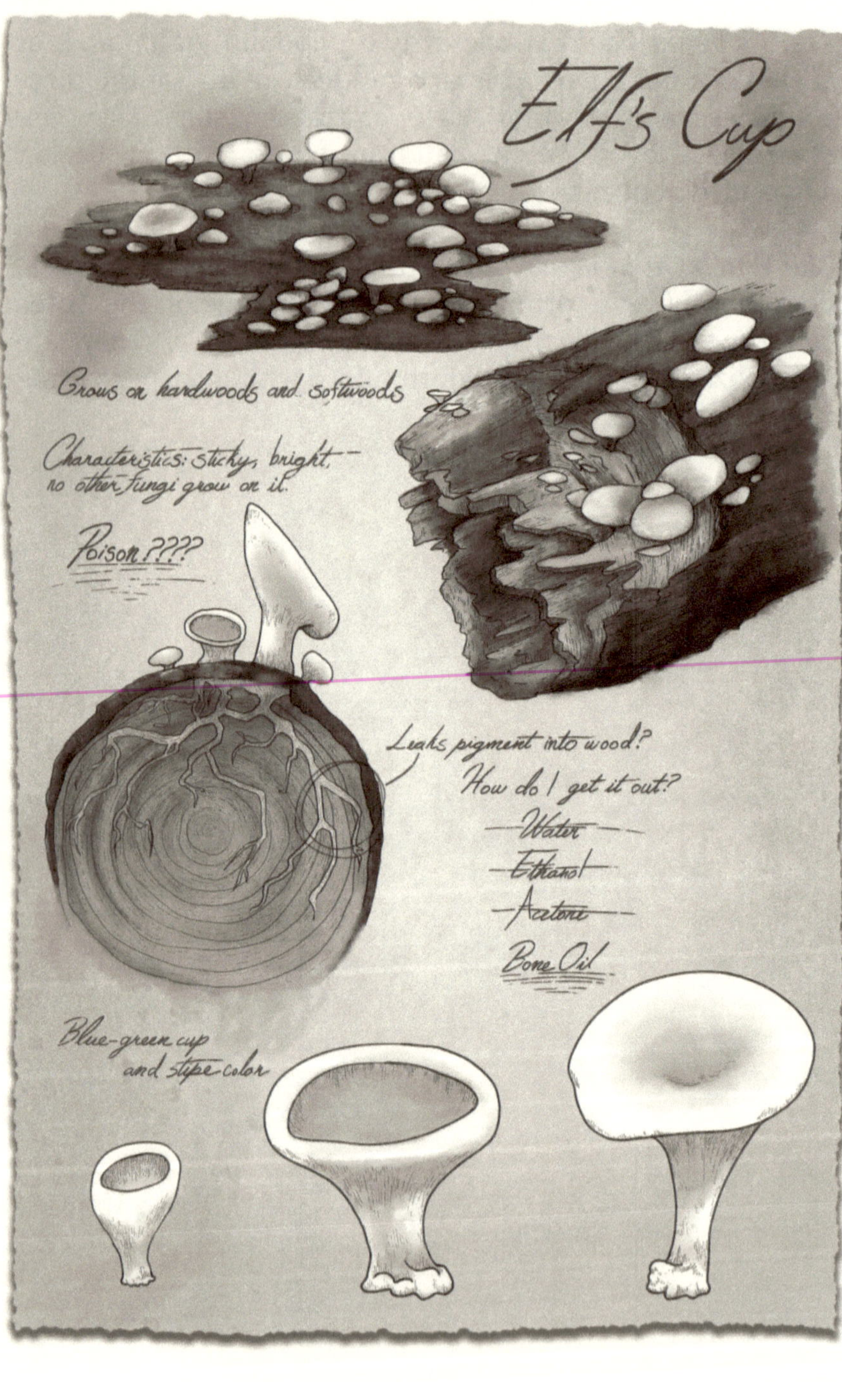
Elf's Cup
Grows on hardwoods and softwoods
Characteristics: sticky, bright, —
no other fungi grow on it.
Poison????
Leaks pigment into wood?
How do I get it out?
Water
Ethanol
Acetone
Bone Oil
Blue-green cup
and stipe color

Flaming
Dragon
Red and blue in wood
No fruiting form ???
Extract makes
Crystals
How long do crystals grow?
Extract can cause Explosion ???
Reaction controllable?

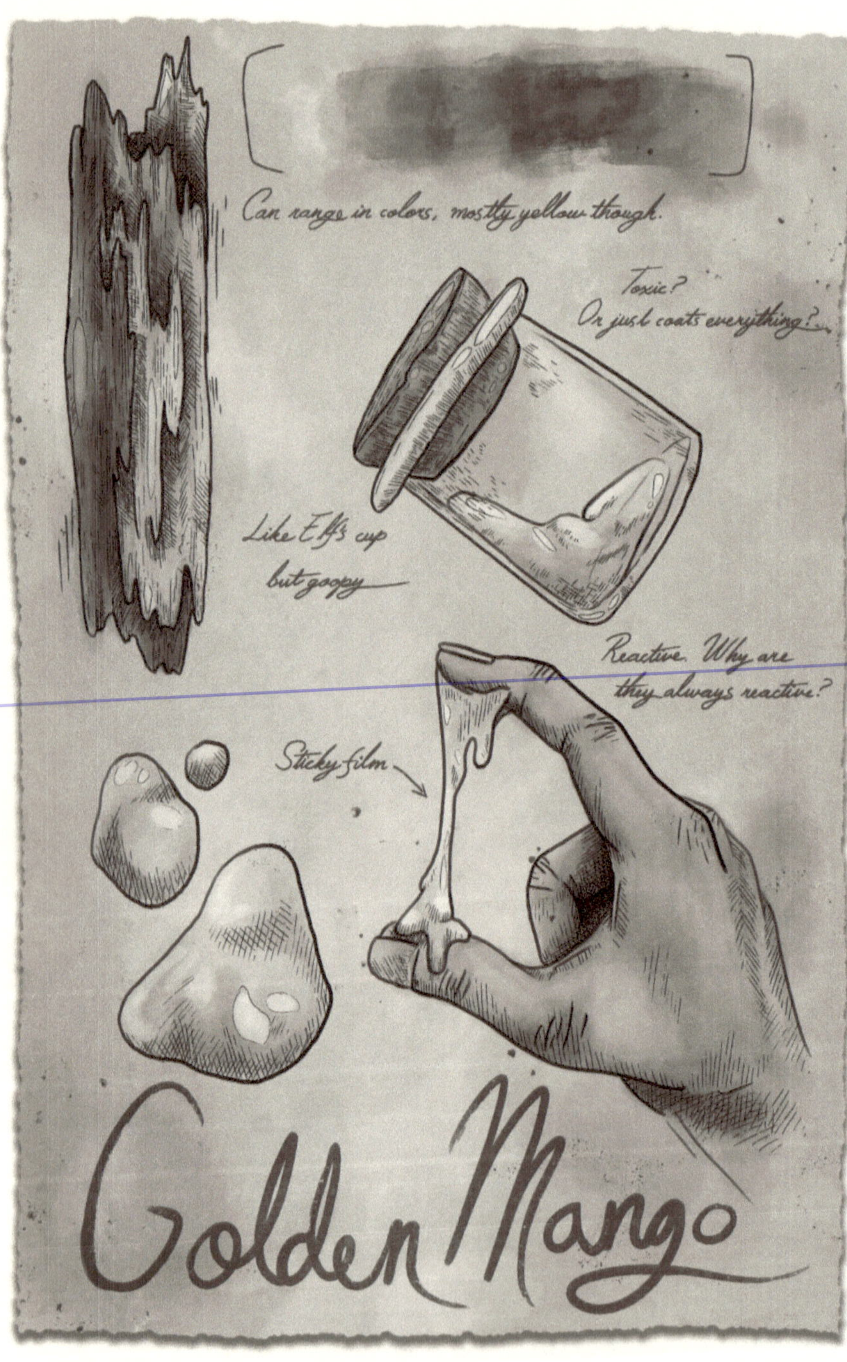

Can range in colors, mostly yellow though.
Toxic?
Or just coats everything?
Like Elf's cup
but goopy
Reactive. Why are
they always reactive?
Sticky film
Golden Mango

Prologue

How long did we sail Tii? Long enough to bring forth twelve generations of children, if not more. Records are hard to keep when there is little to write them on. Long enough for the elders to forget the feel of stable land, dry earth, and silence. Long enough to move past despair at never seeing land again, to an existence entirely of the sea, and ships of wood so old no one had the knowledge to replicate them.

But then, then there was land. Children screamed when we first found Gasta Fletcha. Adults screamed. You screamed, a terrified toddling child whose stars had been stolen from him and whose wooden planks had been replaced with yielding sand. On the ocean, on Tii, the sun would nestle into stars and the horizon always glowed. The forests of Gasta Fletcha, choked with vines and trees, canopied all but the most extreme shores. On the Sea of Tii there had been a world of light, of the known, of the whimsical, giving water.

Gasta Fletcha was cold, spongy, and dark with congealed magic.

And of course you will ask me, why Gasta Fletcha? Why not sail on, as we always had? Would another boated generation have harmed anyone?

This, this is what I need you to understand. The land of Gasta Fletcha was birthed from the ocean for us. It was brought to being by an outpouring of our magic. Gasta Fletcha formed from deep within our elders, from the songs we sang while bailing water and securing rigging. Gasta Fletcha came from our dreams and nightmares, possibly mostly nightmares. But the land was ours. We had birthed it, and we were responsible for it.

The magic, we brought with us. It is magic you will need to survive here. On the boats we'd had limited space and limited raw materials. We'd turned to the world's intangible offerings—tiny creatures, odd beams of light, the power of words. We'd survived by air farming, yes, but we'd survived by magic farming, too, borrowing against a lender with no understanding of the interest. Magic grew from a ghostly religion to a solid home, to Gasta Fletcha. So you see, you cannot ignore magic, for you live now only by its whim.

It has been twenty-six years since we found Gasta Fletcha and every day, magic use dwindles. Your hands are your magic now, your minds adaptable and the forests so very giving. Families are branching into skill sets—shepherds, metal workers, glass workers. The continent has been divided into three parts for better governance, although our borders will always remain open to acknowledge our shared heritage. Old traditions slowly slip away. New ones grow. A few elders still work magic, like myself, but this was a communal pastime of still silence and quiet contemplation. Magic has now feathered away to the recesses of the mind. Magic has become, not inaccessible, but ignored, a vestigial power no longer needed.

Oh, my children. Magic will not care for this. We brought it forth, farmed it like corn, and it will not disappear. Not immediately, not in a generation, not in twelve generations.

Magic will not retire.

We grew this power over centuries, bred it like a hen to continually produce. But what happens to eggs when they are no longer needed? The hen does not stop laying.

Where will the magic go? Where will it amass? I have seen it slip from angry youth, leaking through yelled words and gathering in crowds until a reaction occurs—a wildfire, an earthquake, a snowstorm. The cities are large enough now that another magical congealment could lead to fissures so deep, they might swallow the world whole. Magic has cost and consequence, and our heads are too deep in the sand of Gasta Fletcha to see it.

If we cannot use magic safely then it must be removed or stored. This is why I write to you now, my children and grandchildren. You're wasted in the smithy and fields. Come to me here, on the edges of this world we created. Meet me where we bury the bones of our forebearers. We will use magic one last time, to extract and bind away our greatest gift so that Gasta Fletcha, and our people, may survive.

To: Queen Magda of Sorpsi
From: Thuja Village Elders

Dearest Queen,

Please allow us to congratulate you on your upcoming coronation. Your mother, Queen Maja, was a remarkable leader and we know you will do well by her legacy. Long may you reign!

We are hoping that after your coronation tasks have concluded that you might consider a visit to our small border town, or that you might see fit to send an emissary who could report back directly. Two factories have taken residence in Thuja, the first producing structural iron using a method called puddling, the second a rolling mill for said iron—which we have been told is far faster than hammering. Both are slated to begin production sometime in the next fortnight. Another factory begins production tomorrow—a new textile mill that employs most of the village's youth that were formerly employed within the guild structure.

As a member of the Smith Guild yourself and having not succumbed to the blight that has affected many guilders, we would very much value your perspective on the working conditions of these factories. We were at first enthusiastic for their building—who is not excited for progress—but now have reservations. Far from the family-run, handmade guilds of our recent past, we have concerns around such large machinery with a functionally limitless work life. We also do not care for the dirty air that it produces. Our incomes have improved but is there no way that could happen with the restored guilds? Are the factories necessary? Is there no chance to return to our guild heritage which was slower, yes, but also cherished, and yet keep this more cushioned way of life?

Is it right for us to fear this change? Do you fear it? Should we march, bravely, into this new world, like our ancestors did from their boats to Gasta Fletcha? We hope for your guidance, Dear Queen, in the coming weeks.

With Deepest Fondness,
The Village Elders Of Thuja

Chapter 1 — Oak

"How many of these blasted things are there?"

"Magda please don't yell. The Triarchy of Puget are going to rethink letting us stay here another night before heading back to Sorpsi."

"I'm the queen. I get to yell. You're supposed to answer my questions. Right?"

"I...yes, Queen of the Blueberry Jam nose. No, don't bother to wipe it. Let's just finish eating. My best estimate on the amulets is hundreds, if not thousands. There's the ones your mother made, that hold the stolen guilder skills. There's the ones that were buried by the old king, that kept finding me on the glacier. We have no accurate counts on either."

"I don't like that answer."

"You don't have to like it. You have to understand...no, no wipe the other side. Now you're just smearing the jam. Ugh. Let me help. There. This is worse than when you tried the new imported curry for the first time. Now sit back and please listen. The amulets are a technology. Who knows how many times the methodology was rediscovered? Our mothers weren't the first. Was King Tunbridge the first? I've never heard stories older than him, but I grew up sequestered in the Thujan woods. I could dig through the royal library I suppose. But that would delay more experiments."

"I'm not going to spend my rule of Sorpsi solely digging up old magic amulets. Those things destroyed the Old King and my mother. It's time to end the cycle. I refuse to let their legacy be mine."

"Then don't. Let's focus on the guilders and the return of their skills, then focus on the factories. We are fighting an industrial revolution. I don't think we have time to play with magic. Science and technology already won. Leave magic in the past where it belongs."

I was destined to spend my life smelling of dead fish. The usual culprit, my pyridine bone oil, festered in a long, flat, rectangular dish atop my main workbench. Open to the elements, the solvent fumes stank up the Royal Alchemist's—now Royal *Chemist's*—laboratory. Floating on the bone oil solvent was an oval disc of oak—the surface black from solvent absorption.

The oak amulet—Experiment 75—had just finished its two-minute soak. Whatever was in the amulet was, in theory, now in the bone oil. Theoretical extraction complete, I now needed a separation. I needed to get the skills out of the amulet / bone oil so I could get them back into the guilders, thereby restoring the continent's economy and culture, and undoing the work of two very foolhardy witches. One of which happened to be my mother.

I poured an equal volume of boiled water across the disc. On top of the dish I placed a clear bowl, then wrapped the edges with old cloth. I would not pray for success, because I was a chemist, not a monk, but I needed this extraction to work. It *had* to work. The guilders had waited long enough and if I kept failing and the factories kept being built...

No. I had to focus. I had to focus on the chemistry.

Magic, and whatever was bound to it, was soluble in water. This fact had been discovered and weaponized by the Old King and used to slowly poison Sorpsi. Magic was not *quickly* soluble in water, however, and neither I nor the guilders had years to wait for water to slowly leach out the contents of the amulets.

With luck, the pyridine was faster at extraction. Pyridine was generally a better solvent than water, and I'd already tried all the more standard options: ethanol with varying impurity levels, acetone, and ether. A mixture of water and pyridine? My hope was that the magic and the bound guilder skills would extract from the oak with the pyridine, then move to the water. Water evaporated faster than pyridine, so in the morning I would have magic-laced water vapor that my test subject could inhale and thus, regain their skills.

A long shot? Yes. Worth a try? Also yes.

It was all trial and error, experiment and fail, and try again. What were the working properties of magic, as an element? No one knew. What solubilized magic other than water, which only did so in very minute quantities over vast amounts of time? No one knew. How in the name of every god that had ever been, had the late Queen Maja shoved a load of intangible cultural heritage into a wooden amulet to begin with? *No one knew.* Mostly because everyone involved in the process was now dead. The Queen had sucked the skills from all the guilders of Gasta Fletcha, stuck said skills in wooden amulets, and had completely failed to sort *how to get them back out again.*

The queen was dead now, replaced by her daughter, Queen Magda. My own mother had been caught up in the debacle and was dead too, leaving my brother and me, and Magda, to sort out a disgusting flop of magic. Queen Maja had stolen away hundreds of guilder skills and locked them in the amulets as a way to concentrate her power and the economic might of Sorpsi. But now she was dead, the trade skills of an entire continent were inaccessible, countries without guilds had no economy, and no one was particularly keen on starving to death.

Except that wasn't entirely true, I reminded myself sourly. There were the factories, and the machines, come down from the glacier and land bridge that connected to our little continent of Gasta Fletcha. Machines that could do the work of twenty guilders and would, if we let them, render guild knowledge useless.

I didn't like being useless, personally. No guilder did.

"I hate magic," I said as I leaned against the stained countertop that had once belonged to the previous Royal Alchemist, Master Rahad. The man who almost been my mentor. My head tipped back and I batted at an amulet hanging from the rafters, swinging it until it just tapped the next. The entire ceiling clacked. Hundreds of amulets hung suspended from the rafters, all of oak, all containing the skills from the guilders of Gasta Fletcha. And in the far corner of the laboratory, where daylight never reached, were seventy-five broken amulets—devoid of magic, their contents bled away but not recovered.

All failed experiments. Seventy-five guilder skills that would never be recovered. Seventy-five guilders, lost forever.

I'd been trying for six months.

I had succeeded zero times.

I was very, very tired.

"Master Sorin?"

I shivered at the title. It felt cheaply earned, noting the broken amulets, and simultaneously too expensive, when you considered the magic carnage that had led me here.

A page poked their head around the corner—a youth of indeterminate gender with a head full of neatly parted brown curls. "Master Sorin. Another packet arrived." In a tightly clenched fist, they held a package of parchment tied with string. The paper was even, white, and crisp, the string waxed and taut. Not guild made. Not crafter made. Factory produced. An absolute blasphemy.

"How many does that make this week?" I asked.

"Twelve packets I've delivered, Alchemist. You have three other pages attending."

"Good grief. I've got seven unopened packages already. Tell the other pages to start putting the new packages in one of the treasuries. I'll get to them when I can."

"Does that include this one?" the page squeaked.

I'd been this frightened once, this eager to please. I softened my tone. Giving orders had been Mother's job. How well I'd grown to fill her role. "No, this one is fine. Place it on the table." I pointed to a low bench made of pashako wood. The finish was chipped in five places and I'd never found the time to repair it. "Where is this one from?"

"The Triarchy of Puget. Potentate Jun signed off for the courier and dated it. It took longer than usual to get here because the roads are clogged with traffic. The same thing happened with our spice shipment. It was two weeks delayed, and they've only just finished delivering the wiring for the palace electrical system."

I pivoted away from the page and tried to sound disinterested. With no guilds to contend with, the factories and all the associated international trade that went along with them, were colonizing Gasta Fletcha faster than fleas on a dead llama. "Oh?"

A pregnant silence descended, as I visually scoured the carvings of the upper crown millwork—rows of asters intwined with parrots, the work of a master—and the page remained silent as a stone.

When it became clear the youth was disinclined to leave or continue the conversation, I forced myself to turn back. "Was there anything else? If not, I need to return to work."

"Potentate Jun?" the page said, the words flooding out, a damn crushed by youthful eagerness. "The word potentate means...not a queen or king but the same rank and I was wondering if you and the potentate are..."

"I'm assuming we aren't talking about the marvel of electricity or the tang of paprika?"

"I..."

I'd tried to lighten the mood with humor and had failed miserably. It was fine that the page couldn't give breath to the question so sorely desired. I had no idea how to answer it. Mercifully, my mother had trained me well in avoidance.

"Do you have more errands to run?"

The child withered in the chill of my words. Shoulders fell and the child tore from the room, door left agape.

"Sorry," I murmured. I should have followed. I should have immediately penned an apology, because witches help the poor short-haired page with the loose-fitting tunic routinely pulled away from the chest. The Queendom of Sorpsi had no words for people like us, but I'd quickly learned upon accepting the Royal Chemist position, that it didn't mean we didn't exist. I'd spent seventeen years locked away in the Thujan forest, studying woodcutting and secretly perfecting alchemy. Six months in the outside world and I felt I'd aged another full decade. I knew so little then. I knew so little now, but at least I was aware of my shortcomings.

Back to the table. To the packet. To another amulet. Another looming failure.

"Are you a shepherd?" I whispered to the package and the awaiting amulet inside. "A mason? Trader? An...an alchemist, like I was? Maybe, maybe a witch? Ugh." I'd sent letters to the other monarchies asking them to hold on more shipments until I was ready, so it was very strange that Potentate Jun had sent this one. Especially via courier direct instead of waiting on a trade transport.

"Guess you're the top of my workload now. Hope you're useful." I walked to the table and squatted, eyeing the clump of wood and string with the same level of distaste I had for used finishing rags. Would this amulet be fresh, silvery streaked oak of the newer amulets made by the former Queen Maja of Sorpsi? Those were the ones with the stolen guilder skills and the ones I was working with currently.

Occasionally I also received partially decayed red oak amulets that had been used by the old king, King Tunbridge, generations ago, for similar nefarious purposes. He'd had a problem with women though, if I recalled my stories correctly, or perhaps just thought theirs the better skills to steal. He'd selected women, trained them in skills he'd wanted—archery, swordsmanship, falconry, the usual king nonsense—then extracted those skills and taken them for himself. He'd been a witch and had, according to the stories, done all sorts of things with amulets, including burying a mess of them all over Gasta Fletcha for reasons that still did not make logical sense to me.

So, ancient silliness, or modern magic? What had Potentate Jun of the Triarchy of Puget thought so important to send me?

The cloth fell away with one pull of the binding ribbon.

Oh. It was just—

No.

Wait.

From between two poorly carved amulets of decaying red oak I pulled a dark piece of wood. *Sound* dark wood, not black from soil. Strings of ribbon tangled in my fingers, and

I hastily cut them away with a razor blade. The dark amulet came free in my palm. What...what *was* this?

Of the seventy-five amulets I'd processed in my time as the Royal Chemist, all had been oak. Oak, oak, red oaks and white oaks but always oaks except for the occasional ash someone had clearly misidentified. Aside from the age-related color, it'd been easy to identify Queen Maja's amulets. They'd all had the same sloppy, crafter-carved design of a parrot—Sorpsi's sigil. If the old king's amulets had any crest on them, it'd long ago been eaten by the dirt.

The amulet in my hand was black, so deep in color that it glinted purple in the candlelight. Carved onto its surface were three waving lines, a half circle, a line, and a triangle, the lines of the carvings so fundamentally basic they could have very well been done by a child, and clearly meant to represent a boat on the water. It was warm, like all the amulets, but significantly heavier. In the pile, underneath where it had been buried, was a folded piece of paper that read,

Found in the royal treasury at Celtis Castle, Triarch of Puget, during renovation. Depth in the piles indicates a creation date well before the Old King. Triarchy alchemists confirm the weight is too heavy for wood alone. Further digging revealed two others, all with variations of seafaring vehicles. Consultation with the royal secretary notes their original location as found along the Sea of Tii coastline. We have dispatched men to search the entire coastline for more.

I thought you would find them an interesting problem. It has also been one month since you last wrote. I'd enjoyed our weekly correspondences and find myself unbalanced in their absence. Have you no more questions about bindings and courtship and the trauma of unwelcomed words? Do we not have a friendship beyond mentorship? I'd like to think that we do.

I would love to visit again with you, Sorin. Might you attend Magda when she takes her coronation tour? I could bring the other two mysterious amulets. I am overdue for your presence and I miss you terribly. We are too alike to drift apart. Perhaps you might consider visiting me again at Puget castle? Although the castles of Gasta Fletcha all have similar architecture, their locations on the continent make for very different views. We have an excellent coastline not far from here, with long sand bars and clear blue water. The view puts every old nursery rhyme to shame. I'm certain you would love it.

On the matter of the amulet, I will consult the Puget library for records relating to this symbol. I wonder if you might also take up the case? Together, I believe we would be unstoppable.

- Potentate Jun
Triarchy of Puget

This interior paper, the folded paper that had been just around the amulets, was threaded with heavy cotton, pressed with cream bunchberry petals and specks of dandelion. It felt like Sorpsi's rich heritage, and would decay just as quickly if preservative measures were not taken. So much to save, so much to consider, and when had I even last given thought or voice to Jun's and my mutual burden? Had I ever thought about our budding friendship outside of that burden? Had my focus on the guilds turned me into a selfish friend?

But thinking about Celtis, and magic, bindings and breasts and dead mothers, oh I would suffocate from the weight of it all! I flung the paper away and focused wholly on the new puzzle in front of me. I would write Jun again, later. When I could find time to form words that did not whine. We had known each other all of six months, and mostly through heartfelt correspondence. A response deserved my full attention.

To the amulet. In my hands it was warm, like all amulets I'd encountered—all amulets that held contents, anyway. But this amulet was definitively not wood, for holding it in the light I saw no growth rings, and the weight distribution was too uniform. Uniform, but familiar. What else had I used frequently enough to identify with touch? Fungi? Yes, but they were never this hard. Bone?

Oh.

The amulet itself was made of burnt bone.

Human bone.

And from the weight of it, it was filled with not marrow, but magic.

Chapter 2 — Bone

I had extensive experience with bone, having distilled it down to make the bone oil solvent pyridine, but I'd only ever used animal bone. Especially as wood was far more available. Wood also worked well enough to hold magic, as the swinging amulets above my head proved.

So why bone? Why burn the bones? And why bones from a human? Because the bone *was* human. I had no doubt.

Bone was porous, yes, like wood, but did not interact with water and other solvents the same way. It did not decay at the same rate as wood. Was human bone any different than that of an ox or crocodile? I didn't think so. And with all the countries of Gasta Fletcha digging up amulets for months now, why was this the first bone?

"Master Chemist?" a big, booming voice came from outside the laboratory door. "This is Advisor Alibe. The Soon-To-Be-Queen sends a reminder that you are to be at your final fitting in ten minutes. She has warned of grave consequences should you be late or smelling of fish. The word 'dress' was used as a weapon."

After six months of nonstop chemistry work, I'd have thought Queen Magda well used to the bone oil smell. I hardly noticed it anymore. "I'm coming!" I yelled back, not moving at all from the workbench.

"The Soon-To-Be-Queen wishes for visual confirmation of your movement toward your door. If she had faith in your ability to follow directions, she'd have sent an attendant and not one of her much busier advisors. I do not appreciate standing in the rain."

"In a minute."

"Master Chemist, I have been given permission to physically remove you from your laboratory if you cannot do so under your own free will. I would much prefer to avoid entering, however. The smells coming out are deranged."

'Deranged' was unfair. I'd always thought of the bone oil as more of a pungent, earthy smell.

"Master Chemist!"

"Ten minutes!"

Alibe was Magda's largest advisor, her loudest, and also an avid butterfly enthusiast. He'd been with the palace only a few months and hailed from a continent two days boat ride from Sorpsi's main port—a detail I only remembered because he had, one evening, discussed the history of his island and that his people had cut down every tree decades ago. Being yelled at by someone with generational poor planning and an entomological collection did not create a sense of urgency in me, but his voice did break my concentration.

"The orders were immediate," said a very irritated Alibe.

"It will be longer than ten minutes if I cannot finish my current work. There's still an hour before the coronation." Then there would be four hours of coronation, two hours to sleep, and Magda would be off again—this time on her official coronation tour of the continent. We'd spent so little time together since returning to Sorpsi, yet what could be done? Without the guild skills we had no economy, no country, and no heritage. There would be time to be with Magda, to talk and kiss and...whatever else, once I'd finally solved the crushing issue at hand.

Alibe's voice broke into a sigh. "Master Sorin, please do not make me go back without you. When you are late, the princess yells. When I am late, she throws heavy metal objects. Would you please come out. Now."

That was a fair ask. Magda was hot-headed enough without a looming coronation. Showing up without the target of your errand might lose one their head. "Five minutes, okay? I'll be early. Go back and tell Magda that."

"Master Chemist—"

My voice cracked like a whip. "Go!"

A sigh like a glacial crack preceded Alibe's receding footsteps.

I yelled at him. I'm tired. I shouldn't have yelled. Six-months-ago me would have followed the man blindly into the castle. Six-months-later me ordered staff around like I was the one getting crowned. Perhaps I did need to spend more time outside the laboratory.

Like at a coronation...

I had, in fact, completely forgotten about the coronation. Again.

But I had a human-bone amulet in my hand, burnt nearly beyond recognition.

I had five minutes.

Right. To task. What questions could I answer in five minutes about this bone amulet? Age? Maker?

I held the amulet to my nose. It smelled of dust and old blood, and of course fire. The weight of it pulled at my hand— too heavy for bone alone. Which made sense – every amulet I'd come across had been built to hold. The surface, as I rolled it across my palm, was sticky. It should not have been sticky no matter what the contents, due to the external char from whatever fire had scorched it. I took the amulet to a wash basin to clean it. The surface did not lighten. The towel I used to dry the bone wiped clean and no cotton fibers stuck to the bone. But back in my hand it pulled at my skin in a tacky, unpleasant manner. A touch of fuzz grew in the corners of my vision, thicker when my fingers were wrapped tightly around the bone.

The contents of this amulet had definitely not leaked. It held magic, and plenty of it. The burning had perhaps been meant to keep the contents from leaking through the porous bone, but they were leaking now, regardless. Which begged the question, why bone? It was porous like wood, but wood was far easier to obtain and didn't require murder or digging up corpses. All three countries of Gasta Fletcha had laws against both.

"Gross." I flung the bone to the floor, toward a pike of rags lest it shatter, and wiped my hand on my pants. Magic, and who knew what else. Magic was the carrier in these amulets, the solvent. It was there to move something, or hold something otherwise intangible. I did not need said intangible thing in *me,* especially right before a queen's coronation.

I yelled at the amulet, "Stink up the corner all you like. Five minutes is not enough time to toy around with old magic."

I expected the amulet to stay where it landed but it rolled of course, off the rags and well under my workbench where the darkness of the bone ate the flickering candlelight—dulling it to an ember. From there it kept rolling, inertia never decreasing, simply spinning in tighter and tighter circles until it spun on its own axis like two whirling beetles joined in a mating flight.

"I don't have time for magic!" I said to the spinning amulet.

The amulet spun faster.

"I have to go to a coronation. To *Magda's* coronation—the princess I am quite possibly in love with. These are our last few hours together for months. Could we do this tomorrow?"

No response from the amulet, and no stop to the spinning, either.

"I can't just leave you here! A Master Chemist doesn't leave active magic in a chemical laboratory for an entire evening. Or...ever. Cut it out."

The amulet continued its spinning.

"*Stop*! I've got a fitting, which"—I looked out the window at the setting sun— "which I am late for. A damn queen is being crowned tonight! So you just, just settle down!"

The amulet spun yet *faster*.

"STOP!" I squatted, leaned in, and slapped my hand over top of the amulet.

Fwack.

The bone fell flat to the floor and I held it there to the count of seven. It didn't squirm, thank goodness, but when I brought my hand up the amulet stuck to my skin like a blackberry burr. The fuzz returned to my vision, clouding all but what was directly in front of me.

Again I flung my wrist but this time, the amulet did not dislodge. I flicked it with two fingers, and when that failed, I pressed it against the table edge. Still it would not come free. Finally I pulled, but succeeded only in stretching my own skin. Memories of my last trip to the glacier, of cementing myself to the ice with my fungal pigment powders and having to cut my skin down to bone, rolled through my mind.

"SORIN!" That very irritated, very regal, still very distant voice, was definitely Magda's.

I was out of time. I could not finish my coronation fitting wearing a bone amulet. If the oils of my skin had been enough of a solvent to attach the amulet to me, then a stronger oil should remove it. Right?

I stood, found a dropper of pyridine, and pushed a few drops where my skin met bone. Dizziness from pyridine absorbing into skin came instantly. This I was familiar with.

The amulet dropped to the ground. This was excellent.

The amulet did not resume spinning. My vision range returned.

Had I moved the magic? Absorbed the magic? Did I have time to sort out the difference? Another five-minute delay wouldn't be a tragedy. Right?

"Magic is oil soluble. Have to write that down." I said the words calmly, while simultaneously yelling it into my mind. Chemistry had more rules than alchemy! Pyridine alone was an insufficient solvent on wood amulets. It had been the first solvent I'd tried after the late Queen Maja had hounded me for its secrets. It was part of the equation, certainly, but not all. But bone? It was sufficient for bone, perhaps because it had been made from bone? I'd have to set up a proper test. What oils could I get from the royal kitchen...

Kitchen. Palace. *Coronation.*

"SORIN! I SWEAR AGAINST OUR WITCH MOTHERS IF YOU DON'T GET HERE SOON—"

Magda had to be screaming at me from her window. Grabbing a pair of leather working gloves, I picked up the amulet and placed it on the far corner of my workbench. I tossed my robe onto the floor where a page would no doubt find it and hang it up for me. Tidiness was not high on my task list since moving to the palace. Neither was punctuality, which I'd promised Magda I'd work on. In return, she'd promised I could wear pants to the coronation.

I threw open the door to my laboratory, inhaling long breaths of the cool, damp rainforest air. I could make up at least a minute by running, which I did—my pyridine-filled lungs rebelling against the exertion.

Slap slap, slap slap, my booted feet against the stone pathway.

There was Alibe in royal purple hose and tunic, white hair bunned on top of his head, wrinkled face scowling as he stood in the doorway, frantically gesturing for me to get inside. I ran faster.

Slap slap thwack.

Slap slap thwack.

The extra sound was more than my poor gait. My pants had deep pockets, and the right side now carried a distinct weight. I reached into my pocket as I continued to run across the palace courtyard. Inside the thick cotton, my fingers wrapped around an oval object. It was warm, the texture porous. I drew out the dark piece of bone, grimaced at the burr-like feel of sticky magic on my skin. The weight in my palm felt like a distant echo, like a voice decaying from a distance.

"No thank you!"

I did not wrap my fingers around the amulet. Instead, I pinched the blasted thing between thumb and forefinger and placed it on the bright cobblestone by my foot. The cobblestones were meticulously swept. Someone would find it and bring it to my attention tomorrow. "I hate magic," I hissed. "Almost as much as I hate witches. Get lost!"

Slap slap.

Almost to the side door, the servant's door, the door that would take me on the quickest route to Magda's suite.

Slap slap.

Slap slap.

Slap slap thwack.

This time I did stop. Again in my pocket was the amulet, just as sticky with magic as the last time.

"No!" I scolded the amulet. "Not today, not right now. Whatever is going on here has to wait!"

I tossed it to the ground, where it attracted motes of dirt, the particulate shivering against the bone.

"Stay put," I commanded into the moonlight.

The amulet did not move.

I counted to ten, eyes unblinking. At ten I turned away, only for a moment. When I returned to the amulet I saw only an oval indent in the dirt, and felt a suspicious weight in my pocket.

"SORIN!" came a much closer yell from Magda. Closer to the bellowing princess, the underlying threat was much more apparent. I had no recourse. An ancient magic amulet tailing me like a puppy was less of a concern than Magda's disappointment/murderous rampage should I miss the biggest ceremony of her life. As long as I didn't touch the amulet, it wouldn't leak magic into me. Right?

"SORIN IF YOU ARE NOT HERE IN THE NEXT TEN SECONDS, YOU'RE WEARING A DRESS TO THIS CORONATION!"

"Absolutely not," I hissed back. To my pocket I said, "Don't do anything obscene or I will find the first stone and bash you apart." I resumed my run. I'd just have to go through Magda's coronation with unknown ancient magic in my pocket.

We'd defeated witches, continent-wide conspiracies, and my endless pool of crushing anxiety. This was just one little amulet. Even if it was a problem, it wouldn't be a problem in the next handful of hours. Right?

Dear Sorin,

Forgive me for writing again so soon, and the overly formal tone of the last letter. I hope it has not put you off writing to me. I do not mean to bother, but in the absence of a response I have been contemplating your fungal pigments. I knew nothing of alchemy before your visit to our country, and I am further delighted in the process you call chemistry. I'd like to think I also made a study of the natural world and its elements, when I was young, but I'm afraid my imagination became caught up in history and myth. But the ocean, Sorin, oh how I've fallen in love with it of late, especially the more I read about our continent's founding. You write often of guild legacy, but I wonder what you know of Gasta Fletcha's own legacy, and how we are tied to the ocean? You would adore the history! And on those old boats we had none of the issues you fight against now. Everyone worked together. History was oral, and treasured. There were no factories, no polluted air, no familial legacies and inheritance laws that strip a child's right to choose their destiny. You'd have loved the old ways, as I think I am starting to as well.

On a not-unrelated topic, I have been pondering your goal of restoring guild skills, and the issues with the wood amulets. Your drive to aid our guilders and our economy are noble goals. But I wonder if you are too focused on the immediate? You spent much of your life in a small house and have only begun to taste the broader world. This is not healthy for your development. Think how many elements are out there, unidentified! Think what natural beauty could be yours to find. If you will not think of those things, think of the magic of Gasta Fletcha, and how much more there is to discover!

You have written me letter after letter inquiring about our similarities. I am too small a case study. You require more data. You will not find those data in a workshop in Sorpsi. How many fungi are found on a packed dirt road? How many are found in a sequestered patch of forest? How many exist across Gasta Fletcha?

Might I tempt you with a new puzzle, one that has caught my attention as well? You seek our similarities, so let me propose a new one. Just because a natural wonder is rare, does not make it unique. Magic exists across the continent, as prevalent as your fungi. You can find an elf's cup mushroom in a heartbeat, because you know where to look, but I wonder if you have thought more about magic, about its ebb and flow. About its creation and propagation, and growth. About how and why it remains the secret of the witches' guild and no one else.

Have you ever thought to ask a witch? Have you ever heard of magic farming? Have you ever thought to read the writings of your mother, or the queen? I know you want to repair the guilders, but I believe it is time for a different kind of forage—a forage of knowledge. Do not take your collection basket but rather, take your heart, and your head, and your insatiable quest for the minutia. All the answers that you want, all the answers for the guilds, and Gasta Fletcha, hide in magic, my Sorin. You just need to be brave enough to look.

With all my love,
Potentate Jun
Triarchy of Puget

Chapter 3 — Cotton

"How often you think about the inn at Celtis, Magda?"

"I...often. Do you? Think about it? And why are you asking me now?"

"I didn't mean to startle you! No, sit back down. It's okay. I'm not going to attack. I was wondering more if you'd like to try again."

"Wait. Now?"

"No! You said you had twenty minutes for tea and I'm covered in bone oil and lost guilder skills. In the future. During a time we plan. We could, we could talk. About it. About what happened. I've written to Jun about it and we have had long conversations. I have more perspective now. And a better binder! It has much more give and I breathe better. Puget's textile advancements are...were...superb."

"Why are you sitting so close now?"

"Because neither of us are the same person that went up on that glacier, Magda. How many years have we aged in the last six months? How much longer are we hiding behind youthful missteps? Gasta Fletcha is evolving at breakneck pace, you're about to be crowned queen, and yesterday your hand went from the small of my back to my actual backside while we were walking. I heard you snicker. I winked back. We play at this, then you freeze when we confront the larger issue. So, I'm confronting it. After your coronation, I want time alone with you. Maybe that time could involve a bathtub. We are going to sort this all out."

"Sometimes I swear I don't recognize you at all, Sorin."

"Don't confuse the Sorin that stumbled from the Thujan woods with the Sorin of our youth. I'm building my own life and my own skill. Are you doing the same?"

"That's a lot to ask me over breakfast tea."

"Hence the need for a room and a bathtub. What do you say?"

"I need time to consider it, but a kiss might help speed the decision."

"An excellent idea, My Queen."
"Sorin?"
"Hmm?"
"Wipe that smirk off your face."

I slammed my way through two unnecessary palace side doors, down the hall devoid of servants—Magda hated being waited on—up a flight of winding stairs, until I stood in front of my personal suites, which adjoined the queen's own. Mine had been a consort area at one time, but Magda and I had stumbled around intimacy since the incident in Miantri. Not that I didn't fantasize about it nearly every night. Not that her eyes didn't blaze with that unwavering light when she watched me while she thought I wasn't looking. But there were countries to save and guilders to avenge and who had time to debate gender, much less make another (doomed?) attempt at intimacy?

The winter air nipped at my fingertips, so much colder with the higher humidity. I looked out a narrow window to a clear sky of stars and let the fresh air clear my nose of the bone oil stink. I couldn't afford to be absentminded tonight. I also couldn't afford wayward magic. Blasted amulets.

"Sorin? Is that you heaving out there?"

"I'm...sorry?" I didn't have an excuse. Apology was the best I could do.

"Just get in here." It was a queen's voice that called to me from an adjoining room. It was also the voice of the girl who, ten years ago, had been my best and only friend in the world. "*Now* Sorin. The seamstress still has the sleeve hems to fix."

"Yes, Queen Magda," I called back, taking one final taste of the night air that had followed me inside. And I wasn't heaving. Restoring a continent's stolen skills didn't leave a lot of time for exercise.

I took one step more before Magda once again yelled, "The only people who address me so formally are courtiers and business moguls trying to wheedle permits for more factories. If you call me that again in our private rooms

I'll...something. Ugh. I don't have time to sort threats. Just get in here!"

I'd come as fast as I could...more or less. I didn't move, but I did say "Yes my queen," in an overly loud whisper.

"I swear to Iana if you just said 'yes my queen,' I will scream."

"I said you look pretty in dresses!" I yelled back. I patted down my pockets, noted the amulet still bulged in the right side, lower pocket of my tunic. "Magda—"

"Sorin, get over here *now*. I refuse to do this alone."

I blew out a breath hard enough that a few strands of black curls lifted from my forehead, the opened the door to what had once been Magda's study. I was certain there were books still on the shelves but all I could see now was chintz—the highly decorated cotton fabric—covering every millimeter of space, including being draped down from the ceiling. The pattern had been hand-stamped not three years ago. Now it was made by the bolt and the prints rolled on using a giant steam-powered monstrosity that belched black smoke so high into the air, we could see it across the capital. The textile factory lay on the southern portion of the Cedar River, and for a handful of kilometers downstream the water ran green from the washed-out dyes.

"Yours is over there," Magda said, grabbing my arm and pulling me around an oak coffee table to where an overly long tunic was being held out by a plump, frowning woman.

"Where's yours?" I asked. Magda was back in her leather pants and loose jerkin that she favored and got away with wearing only because no one was going to irritate the sole remaining heir of Sorpsi.

"Already fitted and ready to go. I want to make sure yours is too, before I change. My anxiety is high enough. I don't need your sleeves catching an errant candle and setting the ballroom on fire. You are late, I am irritated, just do as I ask."

I snorted. "Fire? Out of the two of us, *my queen,* I am not the clumsy one."

Magda's glare could have cut through stone. "Sorin you are the very definition of clumsy. Now try on the tunic. No bandolier? I thought you might want it for a formal occasion."

As adults we'd been awkward around each other. Being together in the castle turned us both back into quibbling children. "I've not worn the bandolier since the glacier. I'm no alchemist, I'm a chemist, remember? And I don't think we want my fungal pigments at your party. Turn around if you want me to change."

Magda, spun up for a retort, managed to get a "I've—" before snapping her mouth shut and turning to face the door.

"Thank you." I stretched the sleeve of my oil-covered tunic and tossed it to the floor. The royal seamstress, who'd seen me in my binder multiple times since I'd been installed at the palace and whom had never once commented on it, handed me the new tunic.

"How is the amulet work going?" asked my suddenly very conversational future queen while I dressed.

"Complicated. You have time for an update now?"

"No. And I doubt I will after the coronation either. Could you put it in a letter and hand it to the stable hands before I leave tomorrow? I can read it on the first leg of my, ugh!" She rubbed her palm into her side. "I'm pinched into a horrible corset. If your binders are anything like this then I apologize for the earlier heaving comment. I don't think I can even bend over. I refuse to ever be coronated again."

I smoothed the front of my new tunic over the layers of cotton binding my breasts down to my chest. Chintz was a royal pattern of flowers and very few others could afford the glaze finish. Hence, my tunic was a soft, sky-blue affair with embroidered, but not colored, flowers across shoulders and hemline. There would almost certainly be matching hose somewhere I'd be expected to put on, but fitting those wasn't as large a deal as getting the tunic to not catch and gather on my binder. This was the third iteration, the seamstress and I, at perfecting the fit. She stepped out of the way and I did a half-twirl in front of the mirror leaning up against the fireplace. A nice fit. Tight in the shoulders but loose through the chest and waist. I'd be the object of no one's attention outside of, maybe, a discussion around the quality of the cotton I wore.

"Nice," I said to no one in particular. "I appreciate it."

"Even if it's factory made?" Magda said.

"It is a gift and I thank you for it. My Queen."

Magda growled.

As Seamstress Annez rotated me, then tutted over the minutia of sleeve length I added, "Did you need to approve the tunic?"

"When you're ready, yes. I wouldn't mind your thoughts on my hair. My coronation dress is out of either of our purviews. It's the same Iana wore at her coronation."

That meant it was at least handmade.

The seamstress placed the last pin. "Ready?" I asked.

Magda and I turned in tandem. The jousting bled away as it so often did when we had nothing to do but stare at one another. With a studious face Magda said, "It's very flattering. You look... handsome."

"So do you," I said, although Magda wore nothing out of the ordinary aside from the corset—which was well hidden under her leathers. Yet this was the truest form of Magda, her hair tightly braided with escaped whisps framing her face. She'd have to let the braids out before the coronation almost certainly. Her leathers were worn but clean, her sleeves rolled up to her elbows, showcasing a museum of old blacksmith scars. She wouldn't be in them much longer. Even a queen couldn't wear leathers to her coronation. "I can't believe they talked you into a corset." *I can't believe you're leaving tomorrow morning, for two months!*

"It draws attention from those shoulders," Annez said with a tut. "A princess may have time for a smithy, but a queen does not. Now then. You're both ready. Off with the clothes and I'll make the final stitches."

"Would you give us a moment?" Magda asked, her eyes still affixed to mine. "Your face gives you away, Chemist."

"My Queen, you have twenty minutes before your entrance in the ballroom," said Annez. "Time was wasted when you fought the lacings."

"We just need five. Thank you, Master Seamstress."

Annez took her dismissal with a professional grace, masterfully ducking her way under drapes of cotton on her way out.

A weight settled in my body, wholly separate from the bone amulet.

The door clicked shut.

Magda collapsed onto a pink embroidered fainting couch. "I'm so nervous I could throw up."

Ah, this was pre-coronation Magda, not 'I'm-about-to-travel-and-want-to-clear-the-air' Magda. "I know. I'm sorry I was late. I'm sorry I argued. I'm here, now. How can I help?"

"Want to be crowned instead?"

I stuck out my tongue. "No thanks. You should, though. Be crowned." I knelt, took her hands in mine and smiled. "I mean, how many coronations does one get in a lifetime? Two, maximum, I'd think."

That almost made Magda smile. "It's not just the coronation. I've put off dozens of other tasks during the preparations. I've got two trade delegations arriving at the end of the week to discuss royalty share on four new planned factories. I've just run out of spare rooms for the guilders coming for your trials, and my word Sorin, I have never received this many pigeon correspondences in my life. I know for certain my mother never got this volume. It feels like every villager, mayor, and guilder in Sorpsi has decided to write me personally." She closed her eyes and let out a long breath. "I'll never catch up, even with handing off half the work to Advisor Alibe to prepare for the coronation. I feel like I haven't had a moment to breathe, much less grieve for the guilds. I miss my time in the smithy. I miss the vibration of metal. I miss just working with my hands because at this point there are so many letters I don't even get to write them myself, just dictate. I don't know how my mother did all this *and* plotted the death of the guild system."

I felt that loss just as deeply. But like Magda, I had managed to keep my insides from shattering through a combination of overwork and bullheaded determination. "Villains and witches have more energy?"

Magda kissed my forehead, far more sloppily than needed.

"You're disgusting. That's not how friends act."

"No? I wonder if my chemist would allow me to take a liberty? Especially noting the upcoming travel?" Magda leaned into me, her lips just grazing my own.

I was an oily rag about to combust in a room filled with expensive, poorly made cotton. "Did we have three minutes left?" I whispered. "Two? That's not enough time for talking..."

Magda's eyebrows began to knit together. She drew back. One too many jabs from my side.

"Magda. Come back." I closed the distance between us, pressing the tips of our noses together. "Sorry again," I said with a sigh. "It's a big night. Kiss me."

With a relieved laugh Magda arced down to my ear and kissed the lobe. Her lips then found my chin, then my cheek, and finally we pressed together, like we'd been apart for years instead of a day. Her tongue darted into my mouth—too quickly—before she pulled back and said, "There's so much I want to talk about. Time is not our friend. Don't suppose I could interest you in a side job of being my personal letter-answerer? Your curt demeanor would stem the correspondences in short order. Then maybe we'd have more time for this." Another kiss, this time across my cheekbone.

"Didn't you just call me handsome?" I murmured.

"Those descriptions aren't mutually exclusive."

The door clicked back open. Alibe's thick voice said, "Time is short, Your Majesty."

"And you are still not dressed." Annez slid back into the room, kicked the door shut after her, and had Magda's tunic over her head before either of us could stand.

"Queen Magda, I've one last seam to do on your dress. I'll be back in a moment. Master Chemist, off with the tunic. The left sleeve needs work." Without any warning the seamstress pushed Magda out of the way and lifted the tunic over my head. I'd have fought her, or voiced a protest, but she had the blue cotton halfway out the door before my mind had wrapped around the details.

Which left Magda and I more or less alone, both missing a vital element of clothing. Magda still had on her corset, but the way it shaped her form and buoyed her breasts was far more evocative than just being naked.

Every ounce of humor, every centimeter of progress between us, bled away in that moment.

"Uh. So," I said. "It's uh. Cold."

Magda's eyes focused on a piece of crown molding and stayed there. "Just when I thought we might move forward. I swear we are cursed."

"Nonsense. We could talk. Talk about factories?" I said, determined to keep my arms at my sides. There was nothing to see, and my binder was functioning properly. Magda's corset was half-undone. The situation was more than fair, and we had both grown and matured. We would not repeat the missteps of the inn. "Who uh, owns them? I thought um, tradespeople were putting them up but I suppose they don't have the kind of capital needed, right?"

"I can't have a conversation when I can't look at you."

"So look at me." Bold words, coming from the person who'd melted down the last time Magda paid me this kind of attention.

Magda's eyes dragged back, but stayed on my face and nowhere else.

"Come on," I said with an exaggeratedly floppy hand wave. "It's fine. It's comical. Neither one of us is going to panic. You're a *queen*. Almost."

"You sure about that," she said with an eyebrow raise. "You've got a line of scratches down your arm already."

I shoved my hands into my pockets, wrapping fingers around the persistent bone amulet, which had of course transferred from my tunic pocket to my pants pocket. "You know, your eyes don't have to stay on my face," I told her. "Mine can't seem to stay on yours."

"I don't want to mess up. I don't want to relive another slip up for the next two months, unable to apologize, or explain, or touch you, even if it's just as a friend."

"You won't."

"I will."

"Damn it, Magda. I'm saying yes."

My queen finally looked at me, all of me, with a mix of analytical fascination and hesitancy. A part of her look was feral, too, like our history had, at that moment, been scrubbed from the record along with my tunic. "Say something. Or I'll fill the air with useless babble and inevitably the wrong words."

It probably was unfair to fluster her this close to her coronation. Violin music was already leaking underneath the rooms' outer door. We didn't have time to play 10,000 emotions which meant the only safe topic was factories. Talking about the guilds would disassemble both of us faster than kissing.

"How many factories are there now?"

"I just approved a permit this morning for our tenth in Sorpsi. Eastgate and Puget have easily twice as many. It's hard not to. At a 50/50 split of profits, with the other half going to the factory owners who are mostly native to our country. Sorpsi has generated more tax revenue in six months than any year of my mother's reign. According to Alibe, we are on track to outpace his home country of Pleila by the end of the year in terms of imports and exports." When I wrinkled my nose, Magda added, "Pleila is the largest continent within range of our current ships—three times our landmass. They dominate international trade and don't have a single starving child due to their income and social policies. They're a model for Gasta Fletcha."

"Three times our size and we are about to match income? What?" My jaw dropped low enough it could have hit the floor. "Who is buying all of the output? Pleila?" And how much money was Advisor Alibe making off of negotiating these trade deals? I pinched a corner of fabric hanging just behind my head. "How many dresses does the world need? Or roofing nails, or anything else?"

"Most of our exports are actually timber, not factory goods, but the goods are catching up. We're situated, for the moment, in a very pretty place." Magda eased onto yet another velvet fainting couch and patted the cushion next to her. Clearly factory talk was far less terrifying than being half-naked. Or late for your own coronation. "The world is big and well connected, if not primarily composed of oceans and archipelagos. Gasta Fletcha is remote but also unusually rich with raw materials, which, once people knew we were here, makes us an easy destination. We've barely touched our natural resources, compared to the surrounding island chains. Now that we can produce enough to make trade worthwhile...there are no shortage of contracts when you have no shortage of trees, mines, grasslands, and animals. The concept of factories may have come to us from above the glacier, across the land bridge, but the people of that northern island are far from the first to conceive them. Gasta Fletcha has lagged behind the rest of the world for too long. We could not stay locked to the past forever and the idea of stamping out hunger? Poverty? We'd been looking at the factories as a curse, but I've begun to think otherwise. Opening up Gasta Fletcha has given us all the modern marvels, too—steam power, electricity, silks, and a thousand spices. Each one is a wonder."

We'd done just fine without any of those things before. "The guilds?" I asked as I sat, stunned. "Am I to bring back the guilders just to have their skills be useless?"

Magda's eyes darted away.

If I was spending every day in a lab just to turn guilders stripped of their memories and heritage into guilders with no functional use outside of factory fodder...

Magda's fingers interlaced with my own.

My heart skipped.

"I need to dress the queen," Annez yelled as she barreled back into the room. "Chemist, please move." She laid

Magda's dress tenderly across the back of a larger velvet couch and shooed me away with her other hand.

"Time's up," I said.

Magda stood with a long sigh, then offered me a hand up. "I have to become The Queen of Sorpsi." She guided me to my feet, her grip strong, her fingertips still calloused but oh so gentle.

"You've been one. Far before your mother passed, even." I rested my head against her shoulder and said, "Go on. You'll get your crown, say the speech, then all you have to do is dance with me. Just three things. That's it. Then this is all over."

"And I don't see you for two months."

"We'll survive, Magda. We've done it before."

"Yes, but I don't *want* to do it again."

"My Queen?" This time Attendant Alibe came physically into the room, although stayed well behind a chintz curtain. Orchestral twining swelled behind him, now accompanied by flutes and drums. "It's time. Please knock on the door when you're ready for me to introduce you to the hall."

"Definitely don't forget your dress," I said with a smirk as Magda disentangled our fingers. "Naked isn't the legacy you want."

Annez elbowed me away from Magda then proceeded to yell "Suck it in!" loud enough that every courtier in the ballroom had to have heard.

As the laces tied and the eyelets hooked, Magda managed to breathe, "I wouldn't mind seeing you with fewer clothes again. This was...this was nice, Sorin. Thank you for being here. For being with me. And for attending this—" Annez attached the top clasp and Magda wheezed— "event."

I handed Annez the frilled, floral monstrosity that Magda would wear over the corset for the next four hours. "You're welcome, Magda."

The soft smile Magda gave me turned my stomach upside down. "No final 'my queen'?"

I shook my head. Annez fussed and Alibe cleared his throat, but it felt like the world was just Magda and I surrounded by lightening streaking for the ground.

"Sorin," Magda said. Just a statement. No attempt at a follow up.

She couldn't leave the room like this. She couldn't meet her subjects like this. There was no way we'd be able to dance like this, two solvents evaporating in an air-tight container, ready to explode, combust, and take the world with us.

I broke the tension in the only way I knew how. The way Magda had taught me, during our long trip through the frozen northern forest and across a glacier. "Go, princess. Become my queen. Then after the ball, after we've danced and drank and made absolute spectacles of ourselves, I'll wait up. Wait for you in our quarters. It will only be an hour or two we have but how about we will see if you can negotiate my undergarments better than you negotiate contract deals?"

Magda audibly swallowed. Murder and desire warred in her glare but she said nothing as Alibc led her away, through the door, to the court, the ballroom, and her future.

To: Queen Magda of Sorpsi
From: The Village of Taxodium

Queen Magda,

We are sending this letter via carrier pigeon to arrive after your coronation, so as to not burden you during this joyous occasion. That is the only nicety we can afford at this time. Once you have better settled into your role, we need you to send a royal machinist to Taxodium. This is a matter of urgency.

The rapids of Cedar River have long been a blessing to our town and have attracted adventurers and gold miners for centuries. We housed a River Guildhall before the guilder affliction came to pass, that employed all four major families across generations, from toddlers carrying fish, to grandmothers repairing nets. It is no surprise that as steam power traverses Gasta Fletcha that Taxodium would be, once again, a destination, and we have no qualms with this new technology.

We would like to express concern however, over the repurposing of the River Guildhall into a screw-lathe factory. We are a village of workers, and every villager, no matter the age, has always had a place in our livelihood. Hence the new factory already employs half of our village's able-bodied workers and is looking to hire more. With guilds defunct, our people need income, but this factory is no place for a toddling child.

Why is production needed at this level? Where do these screws go? Is global demand this high? Who buys them? Why is it necessary to employ so many? We cannot meet the needs of this factory with just adults, but even if we could, our families are used to the income from all members. The nimbleness of a young child's hands and the attention of their eyes is a blessing, but it is no blessing when an eight-year-old, used to fishing or clamming, loses their hand to a lathe.

We invited the factory here thinking it would be a small, profitable thing. Your mandate to place it in the guild hall has made production a burden. This factory will cripple that population in the next year if changes cannot be made. We know too little about the machinery to use it safely. We require experts brought in, or regulations made, or anything akin. You give us order quotas to meet that are also unreasonable. Queen Magda, the money is not worth our children. You must rethink your strategy.

With Urgent Regard,
The Village of Taxodium

Chapter 4 — Cedar

"Your hands are freezing, Sorin. Put them under my furs until we're out of the mountains."

"I'm fine. But if we're going to chat in the freezing air, could we discuss why I don't have my own horse?"

"Potentate Jun said they only had one to spare at the royal stables. Are you going to warm your hands or not?"

"The potentate smiled the whole time speaking and never even left the library to look at the stables. It was clearly a ruse. And you agreed we would try friends, first."

"Friends share horses. I think we should...ARGH! Do not put your icy fingers on the back of my neck!"

"Yes, my queen."

"Sorin you're...you're sticking your tongue out at me, aren't you?"

"You'd know for sure if I had my own horse."

Magda's coronation was my first ball. It was my first party. Thinking on it, it was also the first time I'd been in a room with more than twenty people. That I'd made it past the doorway and into the ballroom proper while wearing formal cottons was another milestone in itself.

I'd of course been in this hall many times as a child. Magda and I had once launched potato mash from the backs of forks up to the ceiling in an attempt to hit one of the numerous gold and iron chandeliers—the same that had all recently been converted to electric. My mother, Amada, had found us. We'd then had to clean said chandeliers with sore backsides. But I'd won the contest, which was why to this day one could still find 'Magda is going to be queen so potatoes don't matter' carved into the underside of the wainscotting just behind the throne.

It was so very different now, to be in the great hall, especially at a coronation. It didn't matter that the wooden floor, made from wide planks of soft, red cedar, I'd installed myself the year before Mother had cut me away from Magda and forced me into seclusion. I'd not spent time in the hall since, but aside from a handful of new embroidered banners that dangled from the walls, very little had changed with Magda's reign. The familiarity should have been helpful. The well-fitted clothes should have been helpful. That it was Magda up there on the dais and not a towering queen I hardly knew, that should have been enough to keep my hands from shaking.

It wasn't of course. One could only grow so much in six months.

"Such a beautiful queen," a woman said as she noticed me fidgeting. The group of equally ruffled and laced women around her sighed in acknowledgement. "And you look lovely as well. Which town are you from?"

"M...me?" Iana help me, yes, all five women were now looking at me. My feet had already taken me to the edges of the crowd, and I very much did not need to be this close to the action.

A woman in pastel green chirped, "No Apolonia. I recognize the face. You're her master chemist, aren't you? Master Sorin?"

"Yes." How I managed to get the word out without choking on it, I did not know. "I...didn't know I was...known to the court."

"You are, and you look lovely as well," said another woman whose hair had been teased high enough to just clear the lowest chandelier. "It's an honor to meet you. We all have theories so please won't you help us settle them, how did you meet the queen?"

"Ch...childhood friends," I stammered.

"Fascinating," said the teased hair woman. "I wonder if you might—"

I very purposefully turned my head toward the throne. Magda was still up there, reciting and nodding. The music had not stopped, only bubbled to near bursting as more woodwinds entered the mix. My only escape was one of the green marble pillars on the edges of the hall. Everything was well lit, but the pillars were large enough to cast shadows, and my tunic was dark enough to possibly blend in. There'd be no escaping the noise. "I...am not good. With this." I indicated the ballroom. "I'm better with, um. Flasks and beakers. Pouring. I uh, I'm good at pouring things from flasks into beakers. I'm...going to take my leave now." Following that utter failure of syntax, I backed away from the now very perplexed group of women, found the closest pillar, and tried to talk myself out of bashing my head against it.

"Darling, we didn't mean to press!" called yet another large-hatted woman. The group started toward me but at the same time the music cut out and Magda yelled, "For Sorpsi and Gasta Fletcha!" Applause followed, Magda curtsied—an act I'd never in my life thought I'd see—and music and conversations picked back up. I was mercifully forgotten.

Her proclamation heralded the end of the formal ceremony. The next part would be the dancing. There'd be no avoiding that. Magda shook hands with a few robed elders, stepped from the dais, and was just about to head my way before her silver-robed advisor redirected her to her throne. The chattering stopped. Magda, hands shaking almost imperceptivity, received a small wooden boat (our past, said an advisor in green), a cedar cone (our present, from Alibe, in purple), and a scroll listing all the guilds across Gasta Fletcha (our future, via an advisor in gold). A silver circlet got tucked amongst her straight black hair, which she'd worn loose for the first time since I had known her.

We're going to have to change the ceremony, I thought to myself as Magda once again bowed, managing to keep the items in her hands and the crown on her head. Its jewels glittered in the oppressive candlelight, and I had to squint to keep looking at her. By the time I was able to open my eyes properly, Magda had already divested herself of the artifacts and was amongst her courtiers on the main floor, smiling and shaking hands like they all had a history of playing 'chandelier potato' in this hall.

Magda looked really, really pretty with her hair down. She looked regal. There was still a blacksmith under the flounces and curls but there was also, definitively, a queen. My queen, yes, but a queen to all of Sorpsi who now had no choice but to lean on her advisors, courtiers, dukes, whomever, because no one person could run every single facet of a monarchy.

Ceremonies are the smallest of the changes Gasta Fletcha needs. With the factories established, Magda needs very little.

"Balls do nothing for my mood," I muttered to myself. "Maybe I should try the wine."

What good are guild skills if the factories can provide in half the time? What good is a chemist who toys with obsolete amulets in a world powered by steam engines?

No more standing alone with my own thoughts. Music had started up, and dancing. There were plenty of distractions, I just needed to pick one.

Others need you, more than Magda.

I was clearly very poorly suited for parties. Obviously, Magda needed me—we were longtime friends, Queen and Master Chemist, and almost-lovers. Right? I moved farther back from the main dance but even with the space, the aggressive twirls of the white, floral printed cotton assaulted my skin, my eyes, my nose. Who were all these people? Why did Magda have so many courtiers? What did these people do for a living? Were they traders? Factory owners, from overseas? A shawl of some shady gauze flew over my head and blocked my vision. I tore at it, gasping for breath. I would drown. I would suffocate. I would—

"Sorin? Stop hyperventilating and come dance with me." Queen Magda's voice lilted over the sounds of plucked strings and tapped drums and helped focus my breathing. I closed my eyes and took in one long, mindful breath.

I was not Sorin of Thuja anymore. I was Sorin the Master Chemist. True, I didn't know these people, but the clothes I wore had been made for me. They'd been commissioned by a princess, now a queen, and I was her choice. Her chemist. Magda, being here with me, made this possible. Magda would never turn her back on the guilders, or the guilds of Sorpsi.

I opened my eyes, but Magda had disappeared amongst the swirling cotton and teased hair. The air stung with the incense of cedar trees, not from the floor, but from tiny votives of burning bark that had been suspended from lower portions of the ceiling.

Your time would be better spent in the laboratory.

"Enough!" I said it loud enough that the surrounding dancers turned to me with amusement before carrying on. I would not give in to self-destructive thoughts right now! I needed... Cedar. Yes, cedar. I would ground myself in the cedar floor, away from my too-loud mind.

What did I know about this cedar? I knew I could slide on socked feet from entryway to the first servant's door without falling, and Magda could make it to the first tapestry, a few handspans beyond. I knew that the fourth door on the left led to a small prep kitchen where the head cook would hide pastries for Magda and me to eat. I knew there was a small dish cloth in there too, to wipe away the candied apple filling from our mouths and fingers—a cloth that I always used, but Magda ignored in favor of streaking long, red glazed fingerprints down the front of her much-hated dresses.

Magda wore one of those dresses right now. I had pants. I very nearly giggled.

"Queen Magda?" I called into the crowd that pressed around me. "I'm by the pillar. The...the green one." They were all green marble, but the moment wasn't ideal for longer descriptions.

The song and corresponding dance ended abruptly just as "green one" left my mouth, ensuring that the most awkward parts of my sentence traveled across the length of the ballroom.

Silence followed, a simmering silence of whispers and questioning looks.

I closed my eyes again. They were looking at me, weren't they? Didn't matter. I had pants. I had a well-fitted tunic. I was a master chemist. I was fine.

They are looking at you. You're out of place here.

The thoughts that shouldn't have been mine were so loud. I squinted one eye open and yes, every single courtier *was* looking at me and the one person they should have been looking at was lost somewhere in the chaos of a ballroom. I had a tunic, a blue tunic and it fit and my binder was fine and there was an amulet clenched in my fist which was *not* fine and—

Magda spoke my name again from an indeterminable distance, the word a feather floating through the still, pregnant hall. "Sorin."

The seas of glazed cotton parted. In the very middle of the room, dead center atop a stone inlay map of Gasta Fletcha that I'd pressed into the wood flooring myself when I was just eleven years old, stood my queen.

Waiting for me. *Me.*

Gods help me, I was going to throw up.

To: The Triarchy of Puget
From: Queen Magda of Sorpsi

Dear Triarchy,

Was it a lifetime ago that I stumbled into your castle halls, or only a day? Planning for and executing a coronation nearly stops time. I've drowned in chintz and fruit alcohols, and danced with a young Chemist I'm certain you remember. There are moments, here and there, that I want to snatch from the air and press between paper sheets like one might a violet—to preserve, yes, but to also revisit, untarnished by time.

And yet, much like a violet, I find myself pulled from the field of sun far too quickly. I'm writing to inquire if you, too, have experienced the village discord that has arrived along with the factories? Guildhalls always had their spats, and unguilded tradesmen stirred problems, but I have never seen such a wholesale...response. Rebellion is the wrong word and yet, with every letter that arrives to my castle, it is the word that keeps recurring. I cannot say I blame them, either. It feels like even Sorin and I tiptoe around our own guild feelings, knowing that once we open that dam we will drown in the flood. Guilds were the lifeblood of Gasta Fletcha and it is so, so hard to just...let that go.

To the pressing matter. We knew factories were inevitable. We knew progress was inevitable, and that our continent could not stay forever buried from time. We knew we had to grow our economy beyond the guilds, as the market for those exports was dying even when I was a child. Yet I flail in the thought that it was wrong to officially permit the factories. Should I have turned a blind eye? Fought in words but not in actions?

Eastgate has five factories already, and the last time you wrote me, Puget was going on a dozen. There are eight now, in Sorpsi. There are jobs for everyone who wants them, including low skill jobs for the former guilders. Our port at Capitol Cove, much like Eastgate's main port at Nuthatch, runs every hour of the day. We cannot weave fast enough to support the demand from the trade vessels that arrive. Our water-powered silk mill runs the golden floss of our golden orb spiders from the forest and the fabric produced...we raise the price every month and yet still we sell more. Soon no person on Gasta Fletcha will go hungry. Soon every village will have electric light and steam power, and any medicine they can dream of. This is real progress!

My Master Chemist, Sorin, does not see this as our way forward. Sorin would bring back the guilds and while I want to help the guilders and undo the work of my mother, I do not believe I should undo progress in tandem, no matter how much Sorin's and my heart align. There are also villagers that agree with Sorin, although they may be a loud minority. Please tell me, my friends, where do you sit on this matter? How have you wrested with it? What conclusions have you drawn?

I look forward to seeing you in the coming weeks as I make my travels.

With love,
Queen Magda of Sorpsi

Chapter 5 — Leather

"How long do you have?"

"An hour? The King of Eastgate arrives tomorrow, and I should be well-rested."

"Why come out at all then? There's no moon and the clouds have covered the stars. There's nothing to look at but darkness."

"Am I not allowed to look at you?"

"Magda, you...of course you are. Come here. Sit here, next to me, on the log."

"Here?"

"If you want to freeze to death, sure. Or come sit right next to me. Put your cloak around us both and talk. What's wrong?"

"Nothing is wrong. It's just...hard. Being the queen-elect is hard. Balancing everyone's requests and needs is hard. No matter what decisions I make, someone gets the short stick. What would you do, Sorin, if you were forced to pick between two mutually exclusive paths? Both with benefits and drawbacks, but both economically feasible?"

"Is this a metaphor or a real question?"

"Hah. Amusing, but it is a real question."

"I didn't get a good grounding in economy growing up, Magda. I'm not sure I'm the one you should ask. I thought you hired new advisors?"

"I did. They're competent, but what...I mean what I'm trying to say is, what if this decision affects the land, but me too? What if it affects those I care the most about?"

"I think...I think you do what is best for your people. You have to. You're the queen. That's your job. Without people, you have no country. You have to ask, what do the people need? Right now, they need the guilds back. They need livelihoods. They need their sense of self. I know that's what you want too, and it's what I want. I don't see the conflict."

"I'm sorry. It's too late at night for philosophy, isn't it?"

"It's certainly too cold for it. But I'm glad to have this time with you, regardless."

"I've been looking for you," Queen Magda of Sorpsi said, eyes so intent on mine that we might as well have been back in her study, half-dressed and flirting like time had no cost.

"Green...pillar," I replied. I patted the column behind me for unnecessary emphasis.

Magda started toward me. Puffy dresses scattered, slippered feet slid on the fresh shellac that I had not applied, and now wondered who the castle had brought in to do a job I could have done blindfolded.

Magda wore a modest skirt paired with a maroon and brown chintz jacket and a beige shawl with amanita mushrooms printed across it. She hadn't had a jacket earlier and it certainly would not have been part of Iana's coronation garment. A last-minute addition for comfort, or had a seam torn? It was too near the design of Magda's favorite hunting jacket to have been sheer chance.

No more time to wonder about inane details. In two breaths Magda had crossed the floor and now stood in front of me with her bemused smile. The hair her maids had so patiently brushed and parted now frizzed and haloed in the damp evening air. She did not look near-feral, like the Magda of my youth, but rather ethereal—a wind-touched goddess of Gasta Fletcha itself. A reincarnation of Queen Iana. Her dark eyes both demanded and reassured, as she offered me a hand covered in important royal rings.

This close, she wasn't just pretty. She was breathtaking.

"My Queen," I said with a cross of my ankles and a bow— my best attempt at blending a curtsy with the traditional men's greeting. Here at least, Magda couldn't get upset about formalities. "You honor me."

"Master Chemist," Magda said with a head nod and not-at-all-subtle wink. Behind me, a courtier snickered. "You promised me a dance. Shall we move to the center of the floor and give the courtiers a reason to gossip?"

Two months of nightly practice and I couldn't remember a single step now Magda stood in front of me. "As you like, Your Highness." I placed my hand in hers and waited for the crowd to spread farther, or for Magda to just barrel her way through, like she always seemed to.

Those closest were disinclined to move. They'd come to see their new queen, and the closer they got, the better view they had, I supposed.

"The skin on your hands is softer today. Been working with oils?"

"Y...yes?" I wrinkled my nose at her. We were both terrible at small talk. "Every day. Have you been...writing...laws...a lot? Or, contracts?" What did queens do when they weren't secretly witches bent on continental domination?

Magda chortled but did not move.

We had not practiced the lead up to dancing. What else could I say to fill the required discussion? "Your crown is really bright." Bright was not the right word to use. Those were sapphires, and they'd probably come from Queen Iana's original crown. Which is why my next attempt was, "Are they old?"

Magda's free hand went over her mouth, squashing a smile.

Could we not just dance?

"Mag, rather, Queen Magda?" I asked as I tugged her toward the room's center. Magda's hand remained firmly around mine, her ring bands digging into my fingertips, her blacksmith grip unshakable.

"Mmm."

"Your dance? Is there a set time limit for my babbling?"

"Mmm?"

I canted my head and caught the haze to her eyes. Oh. She was just as lost in memory as I'd been a moment ago.

"This is our first ball together," she said, looking up at a chandelier.

"It is," I said. Best to keep my answers brief. Magda didn't need an international incident on her first legal day as queen. And there were a lot of unknown faces in the crowd. There were courtiers, yes, but I recognized a handful of trader colors as well as the semi-vacant stares of a few guilders. Compoundingly interesting was that the person closest to my right elbow had long hair, a flat chest, a pronounced bump to the throat, and wide, wide hips. The clothing was equally mixed, with a too-long tunic over a bushy skirt.

"It shouldn't be. Damn it Sorin, it shouldn't be!" She squeezed my hand and her skirts rustled, like she'd stomped one of her delicately shoed feet. "I'd have invited you to every single one of these balls growing up, if your mother would have let you out of the woods."

The courtiers were whispering for the wrong reasons, and the few servants in my field of view exchanged glances. The person behind me, in the tunic and skirt, bit into a lower lip.

Prickling spread across my skin, not the kind that itched but the kind that sprang up from a warm bath after a chilly rain. "I'm here now," I said, and moved into her. The smell of lemon from her shampoo drowned out the cedar. Our hands stayed together, and my head rested on her shoulder. "Let me know when you are ready," I said into her neck.

Magda's breath caught, loud enough she could have passed it off as a hiccup. "I...right." Her fingertips skated across my shoulder, up to my ear, then looped through a loose, dark curl that fell across my eyes.

"This isn't dancing."

"Right." Magda projected the word across the ballroom before lowering her voice and saying, "We're going to make up for lost time. I've put as much as I can on hold until the end of this coronation. Alibe is holding all the village letters now too. Dumping them in the library, I think. I don't care. We are going to dance."

Finally, we had our opening back to the main dance floor. Magda pulled me through the parting crowd to the center of the ballroom, into the smell of cotton and wine. The servants were busy in this section, refilling cups that were barely half done. I waved an oncoming one away before words left her mouth. The last thing either Magda or I needed was alcohol.

"If you don't mind, I'll lead," she said as her right foot instinctively began the steps. "And ack, your fingers are icicles on my neck."

We couldn't both be awkward. "I apologize for my hands but I don't think you want them lower when they're this cold."

"Sorin!"

I almost fell out of step as I replied, "You started it!"

The intensity of the strings picked up to near deafening levels. There'd be no talking over it. With no option but dance, Magda and I started into the steps proper. Back of hands, bend the knees, side step, hop. There'd be a bow at the end but I always forgot when that was and had to wait for Magda to initiate. I was better at the closer work, when we came together and touched cheeks. When my sneaked kiss on Magda's jaw would make her forget her counts and our thoughts would sync while dance steps fell from alignment.

Step, heel. Step step. Twirl. Bow? No, not yet. Another step. Now the bow. Thank Iana no one had ever suggested I lead. Step, hell. Step step. Step heel. Step step. Now a bow. Then a twirl.

The music stopped as abruptly as it started.

Magda's head bobbed. I quickly bowed again. We stepped apart. The first dance was just us. Now the courtiers would fill in as well. The second dance involved partner changes, but Magda had already informed both her dance instructor and the court that we would not participate. Being the queen had to have a least one decent perk.

There went the music. Slower this time, but the same steps.

"Chemist," Magda said with another deferential head bob. "Shall we continue?"

I let her pull me back in, until my head rested on her shoulder and her arms wrapped around my waist. "You're doing alright?" she whispered as other couples filled the dance floor. "The clothes are appropriate?"

"I could do without the embroidery and lace, but the hose are functional," I replied. "It's never been about the clothes. I saw another dressed like this as well, or close."

"There are four, I believe, in different states of mixed dress. Two traders from South Sorpsi that have been helping transition the smith guildhall and two from the ship that docked last week." She said after a pause, "You were never alone."

"I'd rather not revisit my Thujan woods imprisonment right now," I said, my voice muffled by both the string music and her chintz collar. Although...foreign sailors at her coronation *and* people who are actively destroying guildhalls? Was the guest list that short?

"Would you be up for politics?"

"I'm sorry?" I moved back enough that she could see my nose wrinkle, but kept up the steps. "You just said we were leaving that behind tonight?"

"It has been brought to my attention that there are items we still need to discuss, that need to happen before I leave tomorrow." Her eyes went pointedly to the amulet-shaped bulge in my pocket. "It's hot here. Let's move back, shall we?"

"Magda, we can't—" My heel brushed someone's shin but Magda had me back in her arms a breath later, leading me to the edges of the ballroom where we were not supposed to be.

"You're supposed to dance in the middle, so the other high-ranking nobles see you. Placement matters. Being visible matters. The dance instructor hammered that into both of us."

I sidestepped, but though it had been years since her smith guild apprenticeship, Magda's arms were still as thick as my thighs. Even if I'd had the strength or skill to drive the dance, no one told Magda what to do. That'd been apparent since we were toddlers.

"We did our duet appearance. They can get on without us for a few moments," Magda said. The music ended. The courtiers applauded. Magda had danced us behind her throne, to a dusty patch of ballroom where the candlelight dissolved. Her hold on my hands loosened, but she did not step away.

"What's this about, Magda?"

"Politics. Just for a moment. Because I don't want to spend our little bit of private time after the coronation talking business. My advisors tell me you got another shipment of amulets. From the Triarchy. From their treasury, specifically. They've been asking about ours for years, asking for visits, asking for inventory. I find it very interesting that they're now sending us items from theirs."

Who had told her about the deliveries in the first place?

"You brought me behind your throne, in the middle of your own coronation, to talk about deliveries and amulets?"

Magda's hands went to her hips. "There's only so much coronation a person can take. I've let it take up too much time already. I haven't had an update from you about the amulets in over a week. I just want to know what Jun sent you and if it suddenly produced any success?"

Behind the throne was quiet, and dark, and private. Under different circumstances, rather under the same circumstances but a very different question, I'd have thought about demanding a kiss. But her tone was a strange mix of demanding and hopeful, and I wasn't sure at all how to interpret it.

"We only have a few moments, Sorin. Could you update me? I need to know if you've succeeded with the amulets. Can you...can you bring back the skills?" She swallowed. Hard. It was hope then, after all. That same jagged, horrible stone that sat heavy in both our bellies, crushing us with the weight of not just guild history, but our own history as guilder children.

"It'll spoil the coronation." *It could very well spoil the time after the coronation, too.*

Magda snorted. "Excessive drama will spoil the coronation. I just need an answer. Please. I'm drowning in this, the same as you. Either fan the flame or extinguish it but I can't continue to simmer. Nor can Sorpsi."

"I am not dramatic!" Although I couldn't finish the sentence without bursting into laughter. Magda joined me, our shared giggles loud enough to allow Magda's purple-robed advisor, Alibe, to locate us and head in our direction.

"I'm sorry," I said, wiping a tear from the corner of my eye.

"You are not, but that's fine. Now out with it, before Alibe takes us both back to the dance."

I slid my hand from Magda's and tapped my right pocket, a distinctive bulge *thunked* behind the fabric. "No success as of yet, but a new data point. This amulet is made of bone. I need to do more tests. Jun did say the treasury has more of them."

There are many more amulets like this for you to find.

Had I drunk wine? My overactive imagination had a history of anxiety, yes, but it had never given me such aggressive auditory hallucinations.

"It sounds more like another wrinkle that this country does not have time for. But you brought the amulet here?" Magda asked. "Why? Can I see it?"

I shrugged. "It didn't give me an option. And I'd advise against holding it. There's active magic."

Magda held out her hand anyway. "Explain. Show me."

"Magda—"

"It's not a request, Chemist. Time is the one resource I no longer have in abundance."

"Fine." From the depth of my left pocket, I pulled the tacky bone amulet.

Magda took it and turned it over in her own palm, studying the surface. "You don't think it's just burned wood?"

"No, it's burned bone. *Human* bone. What do you make of the carvings? Have you seen the boat icon before?"

Magda handed the amulet back to me. "Human seems a stretch. And your carving could be weathering or chicken scratches."

"I..." I took a deep breath and said, "Was the amulet sticky when you touched it?"

Magda shook her head. "No. Are you sure this isn't just an Old King amulet that got burned?"

"Your highness?" Advisor Alibe pressed from his invisible vantage point. "It's time to return."

I suppressed a foot stomp. "Yes, I am sure it is bone and sure it is filled with magic. This is a problem."

Magda sighed, and it sounded like the guilds of Gasta Fletcha extinguishing. Again. "But is it our problem? Does it have to be? The Old King's are enough. Our dead mothers are well enough. Nothing has changed with your results, which is all I needed to know. There's no change, and no hope, and we just have to move forward with that. Put the amulet away and let's return to the party."

"What are you talking about? There is always hope, and I'm nowhere near running out of hypotheses. Especially not with a bone amulet to try."

"Just put it away, Sorin."

I put the amulet back in my pocket but still grabbed her wrist when she started back toward the main floor. "I *can't* put it away. It's following me. There's a sigil carved into it, the bone, *bone*, grabs at my fingers. It spun on its own accord and I think I solubilized magic. There's actually a lot to discuss if you—"

"Sorin. Leave it be. I don't"—she blew at an errant strand of hair—"I have to move on. Wounds have to heal eventually, right? They cannot just seep forever. This bone amulet is just another distraction from you, and from Sorpsi, and our future." She intwined our fingers and took a step forward. "Dance with me again?"

Do you really need to follow her? There are other things that require your attention. Magic things. She wants to move on. But you know you can't.

Magda and I often had opposing views, but we were mostly adults and could work through them. A bone amulet wouldn't keep me from dancing with my queen. What a ridiculous thought.

Dancing wastes time.

You don't have time.

You have to solve the amulet question.
You have to do it now. Now now now now.

What in the world was wrong with me? This wasn't anxiety, this was like a really annoying parrot inside my head that wouldn't...

Oh.

Oh no.

The bone oil. The amulet stuck to my hand. The solvent had moved the magic. It'd moved the magic into *me,* or at least, the essence of whomever had been trapped inside. Maybe the same person who whose body the bone had come from in the first place. Oh Iana help me, what a horrible mess that there was no time to explain.

Except.

Except.

It wasn't just a mess, was it? It was also a key. A success. A path forward that I'd spent the last six months searching for. The essence of whatever had been in that bone amulet was in me. I'd move the contents! I had succeeded! *Finally!*

"Are you alright?" Magda asked. "Should we step outside instead?"

"I'm alright," I said, nudging her forward. "Lead me out there?"

That earned me a smile as a now much lighter Magda wove back into the center of the crowd.

The amulet stayed heavy in my pocket as I followed, a sticky, magic-filled reminder of the work to come. As much as I wanted, as much as I treasured this moment with Magda, the ball had lost its magic. I'd make it through the night, but once Magda departed then it was right back to my laboratory because the only magic I cared about now was whatever I'd managed to inject inside myself, and how I might be able to replicate the methodology and save the guilders of Gasta Fletcha.

To: the Queen Of Sorpsi, or whatever she might call herself
From: The Glazier Family, Pseudotsuga Village, Southern Sorpsi

I demand an update on the progress of the guilder skills. My village demands an update. I understand the grandness of this undertaking, and that with the factories you could abandon it entirely, but I know that you, a Master Smith, would never do this. As misguided as your mother may have been, she brought you up in guild tradition. Are you walking away from that now? Rather, are you walking away and burning it all behind yourself?

I understand many villagers pushed for factories and for the wealth they offered. However I, like many others, now see their downsides. I am certain you see their downsides. Yet it feels as if you are leaning into the factories, not away from them. And then we get word that perhaps your chemist has found a way forward. Which is it?! Why do you toy with us like this!?

My wife passed last month. Our five children are strong and thriving, but the work in the textile factory chokes their lungs and stoops their backs. I have taught myself to hold a pencil again, but writing is a marathon act, and one that my eldest child must frequently aid with.

We cannot live like this, Queen Magda. Leave us behind and let us die, or send us to the factories for a different kind of death, but do not let us linger in this barren place of mind. Are we obsolete guilders, or factory fodder? Do our children work to strengthen Sorpsi, or are they being sacrificed for it? If you return our skills, will there be any place left in Gasta Fletcha for us? Are we to return to the past, forge ahead to the future, or dally here forever, in a no-man's land?

Make up your mind. Hurry your decisions. Sorpsi has dispatched poor rulers before, and is well capable of doing so again.

With disdain,
Maslina Glazier

Chapter 6 — Wine

"How are you settling in, a month on?"

"As well as a chemist might, I suppose. I've cleaned a bit."

"I noticed. I never thought I'd see the floor of Rahad's laboratory. Have you thrown much away, or just organized?"

"A bit of both. Old bottles have gone to new uses. A few books I recognize as Mother had them, too, or volumes very similar. I've not had a chance to read them."

"Mmm. But today is warm and the humidity low. Do you have plans?"

"When a queen saunters into your laboratory and asks if you have plans, I believe your answer must be 'no.'"

"I'm just making conversation!"

"Oh? Well in that case, why don't we take a walk?"

"To the royal forest?"

"No. I walk there for work. Right now, I need to visit the old king's statue."

"That thing? Why? I'm set to tear it down next month."

"I wanted to stand there with the girl I once chased around that decaying limestone base, tugging on her pigtails while she shrieked and stuck out her tongue. Take my hand and go walking with me?"

"Magda? Did you hear me?"

"I did. I'm sorry. I...that's...you've changed, Sorin. Do you think I have as well?"

"I think your changes came long ago, Queen. Mine were a bit delayed. Cleaning up an old laboratory, cleaning up after our mothers, there's time to think. There's time to catch up on all the growing I missed. There's time to think. Think about all the things I don't want to miss out on."

"And...I'm sorry you've got me off balance. Let me try to find my voice again. What, uh, what shall we do at the statue? He's missing his arms now, the king, and half his

face has all but melted in the now-caustic rain. Very fitting. King Tunbridge's vision was an abomination, and our mothers took that vision and snarled it into something so horrible that even after their death, it still threatens our continent. There is no reason to have a monument to greed. We could replace it with a spirit house, like they do in Puget, for Tii celebrations. But if the statue holds fond memories for you..."

"No, you're right. It was memories I was chasing, not the statue itself. Maybe, if you want, we could find a place to make some new memories."

I'd had too much wine.

That had not been my plan. Everyone toasted a new queen, so one glass was a forgone conclusion. The second glass had been from a cask of Magda's favorite vintage and with her eyes hawk-focused on me throughout the night, I couldn't decline.

Cheese had followed, then chocolate, enough to sober me into believing a third glass was feasible. It was not. As the party wound down and it became acceptable to leave the hall, walking in a straight line was also no longer feasible. My mind kept suggesting that there was an alchemical recipe for soberness, but alchemy, or magic, on three glasses of wine, was not a good idea. The alcohol had silenced the magic voice in my head, however. That was one thing gone right at least.

I did not have far to walk in my drunken state, as Magda's and my adjoined rooms were one hall away from the main ballroom. As always, the first push of my room door served as a reminder that Magda *could* be thoughtful, she just rarely had time to be. The adjoined three-room suite had been my mother's, back when she'd frequented the palace. She might have slept there—the mattress on the bed had no divot—but it was clear she'd used the room for staging and storage between travels. She likely had never used the room for sleeping off alcohol, as mother never drank. She had used the room to plot taking over the entire continent to protect me from Magda's mother. I hardly used the room at all, generally falling asleep in my laboratory after a long day of chemical failure.

This time sleep was in order, even if only for a few minutes. At least until Magda arrived. I stripped from my clothing, save the band of cotton that wound across my chest, and pushed aside an adult-length marquetry panel to access my wardrobe. Mother's favorite parrot adorned this panel as well, inset amongst weaving vines and purple blossoming orchids. I'd had it out a few days prior to see the back, where both our names were burnt into the frame. The purple and the blue-green of the parrot had come from my fungi, and I'd cut at least ten of those orchids myself.

In fact all the panels were collaborations between Mother and I, the collection spanning back to my earliest work with pigmenting fungi. I'd not yet looked through them all yet but a fortune in master woodcraft sat here, waiting for Magda or I to sort out what to do with it. Maybe we'd sell it. Maybe we'd burn it. Maybe it would linger in this room forever, a monument to a woman I'd spent most of my life trying to get away from.

You don't think about her much, your mother. Not unless you are in this room. Are the panels your inability to move on? Gasta Fletcha waits for you, well past the castle walls.

"Guess I'm sobering," I muttered. Where were my favorite linen clothes? The Royal Seamstress made a habit of replacing my shirts the moment she deemed them no longer serviceable—which to her meant anything other than pristine. Hence it was no surprise to rifle through the tunics and pants in my wardrobe and find nothing I recognized. I chose the baggiest tunic available—I'd become more comfortable with my body in the intervening months but still had no desire to show it off to every passing servant—found a matching pair of breeches with crisp iron lines, and was very close to pulling back the sheets in my overly large palace bed, when a familiar weight manifested in my right pocket.

"I have never wanted a pet," I said to the bone amulet, peeking down the fabric to make sure it hadn't multiplied or morphed into some new horror.

Now you're just being impertinent. Did you ever stop to ask why you might have a bone amulet in your pocket? Especially if you've already absorbed its contents?

Before the voice had been my own—that subtle, jabbing inner voice that too often led to me scratching at my arms or hiding in the smallest, darkest corner I could find. This time it came out as Mother's voice, almost as clear as if it had been spoken aloud. And it had not come from the bone in my pocket, nor within my mind, but...almost like it had dripped from the cool, damp air.

I wrapped my hand around the amulet. It was once again warm to the touch, the surface buzzing with magic.

A ghost? A sending? A memory?

"Who are you?" I asked the damp night air.

Who do I sound like?

"You're not my dead mother, so stop it. Are you the owner of the bone? The skills of a guilder?"

I am not a trapped guild skill, or the echo of a long-dead woman from the Old King's reign.

An indirect answer. "Okay then." I held the amulet up to my face. "Are you a witch? A familiar?"

No.

"Unhelpful." I flopped onto the bed, amulet still in my hand. "Whatever you are, I have had my fill of tricks. Your tactics are tiring. I've enough to do to unravel the mess the witches made. You can leave haunting well alone."

Haunting was never my intent.

The voice, so distinctly my mother's, was uncharacteristically melancholy. If Mother had ever been sad, she'd certainly never shown it. Not until that last day, anyway. I'd forgiven her a lifetime of forced seclusion and moved on. Whatever the voice impersonating my mother hoped to achieve, it wouldn't be through guilt. "So what *is* your intent?"

I was wondering if you'd like to go on a trip? An adventure?

"With an enchanted bone amulet that sounds like my dead mother?" I sat up and placed the amulet on my knee. "I can't go anywhere until I fix the guild problem."

Adventurers often find unexpected answers on their journey.

"What does that mean?" I leaned over the amulet like I could dissect it with my eyes. "Do you know how to help? Are you, a bone amulet, the key? If you have specifics on how I can replicate this process with the wood amulets, I would very much like to discuss."

Mother's voice did not return.

"Hey! We were talking! Why are you here!?"

Still no response.

"If you've got enough magic to torment me then you've got enough to tinker with the amulets. Help me extract their contents. Help me restore the guilders and the lifeblood of the continent. Surely you have to want something, too? What is it?"

A curtain rustled in one of my adjoining rooms, but the voice did not speak again.

"We could do a trade," I said, now sounding desperate and drunk. "Help me with the guilder amulets and I'll...go on this trip with you. Assuming it doesn't involve anything illegal. Okay?"

I thought, just for a moment, that I heard *I'm sorry* brush across my ear. I started to respond, thinking I might actually talk sense into the talking amulet, when a BAM BAM BAM hit my door.

"*Please*, come back," I whispered to the night air.

BAM BAM BAM. "Sorin! You decent?"

Magda would of course, be more drunk than me. Magic would have to wait. Again.

"The door is unlocked and ajar," I yelled through the suite.

"Still polite!" Magda yelled back.

Amulet back in my pocket I stomped, very purposefully, back to the receiving room to find a disheveled Magda leaning against the door frame. She'd lost her shawl, stripped the bottom hem of her dress (almost certainly on purpose so she'd never have to wear it again), and her hair was more mane than well-oiled curls.

I leaned myself against the edge of a fainting couch as my legs were still not entirely trustworthy. "How goes the dancing?"

"It's been hours. I'm done dancing. Can I come in and sit? Remind me to contact the leather traders. Royal slippers leave a lot to be desired. Hand sewn guild ones can't make it through a night like this. I wonder if machine-made can?"

It most definitely did not feel like hours since I'd last seen Magda. "You're a guilder. That's blasphemous. Sit." I lifted a set of three marquetry panels from the fainting couch and kicked the carved, lion foot leg. "Are you officially relieved for the night? Or will Alibe The Purple be back to herd you?"

"Don't be like that. He's new to the role. All four of my advisors are. I didn't keep any of Queen Maja's advisors. They were old enough to have served Iana and they never stopped mom. This group has backbone. They'll advise but they're help direct, too. Alibe wants what is best for Sorpsi and he had ten years of advising the president of Pleila before coming to us. Checks and balances and experience. That's what makes a good monarchy."

"Is it?"

"It is when the queen has to undo her fool mother's attempt to concentrate power while also ushering a country into the industrial age. Every single candle in the palace will turn into an electric light while I'm gone, Sorin. I cannot even conceptualize that! Electricity could be magic, for all I understand of it."

"I'm less concerned about electricity and more about Alibe," I muttered.

"Don't be. His international knowledge is useful in the trade negotiations as we build out the factories. He's secured a number of contracts for me as well." Magda had her slippers off before her rear hit the cushions. "And to answer your question, the advisors have gone to bed. The coronation went later than planned. I'm surprised you're still awake, although I do appreciate you waiting up. I'd hate to have missed this time with you. I-oh damn. I've got another blister." Magda's fingers prodded the arch of her right foot as she winced. "Do you have water? We could both use some."

Did I care who she'd been dancing with after I left? Maybe? I brought two cups to the couch filled with water from a hand-carved crystal pitcher that sat near the far wall. Its bottom stamp marked it from the Glass Guild. That also made it an antique.

"Here."

"Perfection. Thank you." She finished her water in one long drink. I did the same and then with a much-exaggerated sigh I slumped down and helped her with her socks. Her feet were indeed swollen and blistered—far more than the touch of extra dancing would have done.

"How much time do we have?" I asked.

Magda squinted up at the ceiling like she could see the moon through it. "Two hours? Two and a half? Hopefully long enough for my foot pain to ease. Right now, I don't think I could walk to the stables."

"Two hours is better than none. But what were you doing yesterday?" I asked as I prodded her swollen foot. "This can't all be dancing."

"Last minute fittings. And careful there. They hurt you know. This is what five solid hours of dancing looks like. Have some sympathy."

"It has not been five hours," I insisted. "You're drunk."

Magda took my chin and turned my head toward the window. "Look. It's dark enough outside to see the foxfire."

"I..." She was right. Looking out the window, late afternoon had phased to deep night in the span of a few hours. The faint green glow of foxfire—normal foxfire—dotted in from the surrounding forest.

Magda poked my side. "I may be drunk, but I'm not the only one."

"Ow. It was only three glasses." That I'd never had more than a sip of alcohol before was an irrelevant data point.

"Sleepy?"

With Magda sitting this close? Not anymore. "A little," I said. "The alcohol has thrown me off balance." I paused to gauge her mood, then added, "As did a talking amulet. It isn't what I want to talk about, but I think it is what we should talk about."

Magda frowned, but quickly pivoted. She held her alcohol much better than me, apparently. "It's talking? To you?"

Magda's role in the amulets is limited. There is no need to overly burden her before her coronation trip.

I poured myself another glass of water, hoping the voice would wash away with the alcohol. It had, however, cemented that Magda did need to be told about the amulet. Bone amulets were bad enough. Witch voices and...whatever was happening with the thing in my pocket were way outside the bounds of a coronation night. I finished the water and returned to the couch, but sat instead on the sheepskin rug just under it.

"We don't have a lot of time, especially if you're not in danger. There's...another difficult conversation we've been putting off. Perhaps it's time for that one?" Magda slid from the couch to the sheepskin rug and pressed her forehead to mine. I met those deep, dangerous eyes that had held me willingly captive since our collective childhoods and shivered.

"I'm leaving," Magda whispered. "For two months. For the past six months we have danced around that evening at the inn. I refuse to leave you now with that still on our minds." She had my hands now, clasped in hers, the rough, scarred skin catching against my own.

I'd thought about night incessantly. We'd trusted each other enough to remove our clothes, to gather together on the oakwood bed, and to begin an exploration. But Magda had thought my gender an issue of semantics—a situation requiring lip service but not understanding. She saw me as a woman in that moment, and I had been so battered, so naive, so very hurt, that I had been capable only of storming from the inn. We had yet to revisit either the conversation, or the intimacy.

"I was too harsh, in the inn," I said as I sank into her unblinking gaze. "I was hurt but I could have handled it better."

"It was my mistake, Sorin. I'm sorry. I'd like to think I understand better now, about your breasts, your body, who you are as a person."

I shook my head. "You do, but even back then you were honestly trying. Everything was so raw still, the wounds still fresh and weeping. Every wrong word was a cut to the bone because my skin was as thin as a child's. Mother keeping me locked away in our forest house did not toughen me to the world. But I have scabs now, and scars, ones I'm as proud of as any from woodcutting or alchemy. I've also had too much time apart from you. Pushing you away wasn't the answer, no matter how much I hurt. And coming back here to the castle, these past six months, ignoring everything I feel for you to focus on one crisis after another isn't the answer either. We're both guilty of that. Now you're leaving for two months. *Two months* when we've only just started to find each other again."

"It isn't fair," Magda said with a nod. "But my time, our time, isn't likely to get easier."

"I know. That's why I want to do this, first." I touched my nose to her cheek then slid up, slowly, deliberately, until my lips just brushed the soft skin of her temple.

"That's all you wanted to do?" Magda said with a hitch in her breath. "Two months is an awfully long time."

I kissed her again, across the bridge of her nose. "Of course not."

She dropped my hands, but only for a moment before queenly composure took over. "How hard are those scabs? Have you truly healed from that night at the inn?"

I dredged up every ounce of confidence I'd been building for the past six months. "You don't have to treat me like poorly constructed lace anymore." I winked at her. "I'm a master chemist you know. To a queen."

Magda had both my wrists in one hand then, the other around the back of my head. Then we did kiss—a hard, deliberate kiss that was equal parts frustration and longing. Magda tasted of the coronation's rose wine and the longer I let her hold me there the more the cinnamon oil in her hair intoxicated me. We kissed until we both had to gasp for air, until I thought our lips might bruise and Magda's fingertips might permanently weld to my neck. She moved to my neck only after I let out a whimper, but the respite was only long enough to catch our breaths.

We kissed in so many ways, in those last few moments of deep night. We kissed with the tentative exploration of youth. We kissed with the explosive passion of teenaged liaisons. We kissed slowly, with lingering tongues and soft sighs, like a married couple reuniting after a long trip away. We kissed because even as children giggling and sharing a bed in the palace, staring into each other's eyes and whispering our secrets, this was one desire neither of us had been brave enough to voice. We'd been torn apart by time, by our mothers, and by our own youthful missteps. But right here, in this moment, every kiss was both an apology and promise. And I prayed, in my head, to Queen Iana, that Magda's grip on my wrists, and her hold of my neck, and the fierceness of her lips to mine, would never, ever slacken.

To: Queen Magda of Sorpsi
From: The King of Eastgate
Priority: URGENT

Dear Queen Magda,

Of course, the deepest congratulations on your coronation. We look forward to your visit in the coming weeks. This is the purpose of my letter. Previously you wrote an intent to take the coastal road to our capitol on the Gulf of Tii, at the base of the Nuthatch River. I would instead like to recommend Midland Trail which, while not paved, is currently under less duress. It cuts through our thickest rangelands, but the dangers of the herds should be low noting the lack of Shepherd Guilders and concentrated animals. In this way you will also avoid denser concentrations of villagers.

I wonder if Sorpsi as well, is experiencing the same discontent as Eastgate? Steam power is efficient and fast, cotton gins are a marvel, and we've commercial traffic in the Gulf of Tii in unprecedented amounts. No guild could output like this, Queen Magda. But no guild was ever so deadly, either. Are you, too, inundated with letters and petitioners around the maimed children and broken workers? How do you reconcile that with the increase in revenue generation? For the first time since my reign began, I can feed our entire population. We've built four new roads and a hospital with operating theater. A theater, Queen Magda! Our people had crossed kilometers of rangeland into Puget for surgery before. For our people, the people of Eastgate, the quality have life has never been higher. We are not, however, without growing pains.

This is a welcome, if not hard transition for our people, and Eastgate is not making it gracefully. To my original point, for your safety and those who travel with you, please keep to the rangeland trails.

We look forward to welcoming you,

King Rodolf of Eastgate

Chapter 7 — Paper

"Mumphda," I managed when my lungs needed more than a temporary respite. I had a growing ache in my lower body that would only escalate should we continue, and I doubted we had time to explore more than each other's lips.

The Queen of Sorpsi nipped my lower lip and scowled. "You started it." She did pull back, slowly, as she searched my face for distress. "All okay?"

"Yes." I said it with a smile as wide as a sunrise. All I wanted was to kiss her until daybreak. Which...was almost here? Another glance out the window did not show foxfire but rather the streaks of a mango-colored sunrise.

"We're out of time," I said, my words sadder than I wanted to be in this moment.

Magda started to say something, the words almost formed on her lips before she drew back and let her queen mask slip back into place. "I know that tone. I know that look. What is eating you, Sorin? The amulet?"

I hated this moment, more than any other I'd encountered. I hated that I'd grown enough to not argue, to not plead that the kisses continue. I hated that it was just as easy for me to slide back to the Master Chemist role as it was for Magda to be a queen. The best interest of Sorpsi would always be between Magda and I, and I both hated that, and understood the importance of it. "I appear to have solubilized the magic. It came out of the bone."

Magda's eyes turned sharp, but I saw that glint in them again—the remembered joy of hammer on steel, the rhythmic pounding of a smithy. "Really? That sounds like a success, if only partial. Although, solubilized from the amulet to where?"

"Me."

"Explain."

I recounted the unpacking, the stickiness, the spinning, and the experimental pyridine wash. "And now I think I've got whatever was in it, in me. But!" I tried to push a brightness into my voice that I didn't entirely feel. "That's my first success! Today, after you leave, I'm going right back to the laboratory and starting a new set of experiments. Maybe by the time you return I'll be restoring skills to every guilder who wants them. Wouldn't that be amazing?"

I'd expected at the very least, a grin. Instead, Magda pursed her lips and stared at me like I was a pending experiment. "It would be, and I appreciate your enthusiasm, but I'd like to talk more about what is currently inside you."

I waved my hand. "Extraction technology is well established. I'll get it sucked out later and locked back away."

"But what *is* it?" Magda pressed as she crossed her legs and chewed her lower lip. "None of our previous amulets interacted this way. The ones from the Old King leaked, slowly, over generations into the ecosystem and the ones our mothers made are inert. If we assume for the moment the one you hold is a different beast altogether, that gives us three generations of amulets. This one, bone, then two rounds of wood. One set of wood was made during Queen Iana's time, buried by King Tunbridge, made a mess of our ecosystem, etcetera. We've now dug up most of those. The other wood ones were the ones made by our mothers, all of which we think we now have in your workshop."

"Laboratory."

"Yes. Laboratory. And we've gone and stored the dug-up ones from Iana and the Old King in your *laboratory* as well. Have any of them, any single one, had a carving on them?"

"No. Some are decayed, others water-worn, but no intentional carvings."

"Right." Magda tapped the amulet in my hand. "Different material, different ornamentation. No active magic. What do you think on age?"

A rap came from the door. Alibe's voice said, "My Queen. Your horses are ready."

"I promise to explain in written correspondence," I said as I stood, offering Magda a hand up. "You've another ball to attend, in Eastgate."

Magda scowled. "A coronation tour is not critical if you've got rogue magic talking to you. Let's take the time to make sense of it."

"Alibe is very persistent and even an hour wouldn't be enough time to make sense of magic. Go. Fulfill your coronation duties. I'll carry on with the chemistry and update you as I go."

Magda stomped her foot, her queen veneer cracking. "An hour it isn't enough time to offer you the official title of consort either, or ask you to marry me, or navigate the minefield that would be us trying to make love. But it's my coronation tour, and my horse, and I decide when we leave. So of the options just presented, which," Magda said with an emphatic slap to the floor, "would you like to tackle in the next few moments?"

I swallowed. Hard.

"I didn't mean..." Magda closed her eyes as her head fell back. "That was a lot. I'm sorry."

Interestingly, she'd not even mentioned amulets in the choices.

"Sorin, I—"

"*Marriage?*"

"Well, likely a lot more kissing first," Magda returned, wiping at her forehead with her sleeve. "Generally, a proposal comes next. Which this is not. Not yet."

"My queen?" Alibe called from behind the door. "An estimate of your departure time please?"

"Five minutes!" Magda yelled back. Quieter, to me, she said, "Unless you'd like me to make it longer?" Her eyes darted to the bed.

Iana help me. How badly I wanted to lead her there. We definitely didn't have time for the kind of discussion Magda had in mind. "The amulet?" I said.

Magda's shoulders slumped. "When did you become so pragmatic?"

A smile quirked in the corner of my mouth. "I'm not. I'd just rather rush a magic conversation over whatever would happen on that bed."

"When I'm back," Magda said. "I don't want to talk about magic, or guilds, or Sorpsi, for at least two days. I want you, us, in a room, doing whatever we want. Deal? Magic now, beds later?"

"My Queen, that sounds lovely. To the point, since Alibe will be knocking again any moment. Bone is porous enough to hold magic but isn't as plentiful as wood. Perhaps these came from a time that wood was less plentiful, although Gasta Fletcha has always been choked with trees and liana. Perhaps bone was chosen for a darker reason, along the lines of the Old King? Except he used wood. So...before King Tunbridge maybe?" That *was* an interesting theory.

"Your theory makes sense if we look at amulets as a technology. We know the Old King was lazy. That's why he stole skills to begin with. He couldn't be bothered taking the time to learn them on his own. Why would we think he developed amulet technology? Ugh. I'm not sure why we even care about it, to be honest. It's flawed technology at best. Six months of resources and time we've wasted on it already. Six months of guilders living in a horrible in-between. Sorpsi cannot move forward, nor can it move back. We are stuck!"

"No, we aren't. We could also assume that he found the bones, or a bone amulet," I said, nearly cutting Magda off as thoughts of a far-off marriage were buried under the excitement of the theoretical. "He, or his alchemists or witches, copied the practice to wood, which was far easier to obtain with many fewer questions." I rolled the amulet across my palm, considering. "Alchemy is as ancient as Gasta Fletcha."

Magda settled into thought. "Perhaps as irrelevant as well. We moved on. Do we care about the broken technology of our ancestors?"

"*I* do," I said.

Magda held up her hands. "Might I suggest broadening the search outside of alchemy and magic? History, maybe? Rahad likely had all our alchemy books already in his worksh —laboratory. You can raid our library for historical accounts of Gasta Fletcha but your mother kept her own library, didn't she?"

"The only books we had were on woodcutting," I said with an eye roll. "Rooms and rooms of them, a good half of which I wasn't allowed to read because Mother thought the techniques too advanced." But Jun had suggested reading too, right?

"Too advanced for her heir?" Magda asked with a raised eyebrow. "Is amulet creation not, in fact, the cutting of wood? There is no Bone Guild. Or maybe there was. Go back far enough and maybe some of those woodcutting books cite older techniques?"

"You think this is some sort of master-level guild secret?"

"I think you spend too much time in your laboratory trying to fix a technology that never worked to begin with. Do you have another theory?"

I had a million theories, but Magda seemed to be driving to one of her own. "I've been more concerned with the magic of it." And the voice in my head, but Magda had already moved passed that. No reason to bring it up. "There could have been texts in my home, yes. But my house, Mother's house, was burned to the ground by her witches last year. There's likely nothing worth finding."

"You've not been back, have you? Since the kidnapping?"

I found a very interesting place on a nearby marquetry to study while I mulled how best to answer.

"I'm not blaming you," Magda said, her voice soft again. "I don't want to push. It has been brought to my attention, however, that we cannot just ignore our mothers. As much as we would like to leave them buried in the glacial ice, surrounded by an explosion of magic. A broken house is not so hard to go back to, with time. Right?"

"With time, yes. I don't know if there has been enough—"

"We can't just stay here all the time, can we?" Magda let out a long sigh. "Being isolated never did you or I any favors."

"Some of us were far more isolated than others," I muttered.

"As your now official queen"—Magda tapped the tiara on her head— "I recommend you get away from the solvents and amulets for a while. Maybe Jun's bone amulet is a wild goose chase, but at least it's better than running up against wall after wall."

What was happening? "You want me to stop the experiments? What about all the guilders I just saw at the ball? How many more are in the castle, or the surrounding town, waiting for me to start in-person trials? How many factories do we want to get a foothold? Every day I can't restore the guilds is another nail in their coffin. I just had my first success. I can replicate it, I'm certain!"

"The guilds are already dead, Sorin."

"My Queen, should I send the horses back to the stable?" Alibe asked.

"One more minute," Magda said in return.

I still couldn't speak. Magda had said the words so matter-of-factly that it took me a moment to process them.

"I need to...what?"

"I didn't want to talk about it. Not until after the coronation. It's a hard conversation to have with the most dedicated guilder I've ever known. It's hard to say the words out loud, even to myself. I know how they cut. I know how we both bleed. It's time to cauterize, not just for us, but for all the guilders. We have to move on."

"You're *wrong*." The guilds weren't dead. I had the amulets hanging in my laboratory. We had guilders staying at the palace who were willing to work with my experiments. The guilds were *delayed*, not dead.

"I'm not." She stood and offered me a hand, which I refused to take. Magda was a master smith of the blacksmith guild. She'd seen the guilders wandering aimlessly on the glacier, had found Master Rahad's frozen body with me. She knew the damage the loss of skills had done to our guilder population. She knew the destruction to Gasta Fletcha's economy. How could a queen, a guilder queen, say something so callous?

"You're giving up," I said. "I've hundreds more amulets. Maybe thousands. Experiments take time to refine. It hasn't even been a year."

Magda tried to pull me back into her. I backed away until my rear hit one of the doors to my adjoining room. "Sorin. Please."

"You're giving up!"

"Sorin, the guilds were dead before our mothers did all this. They knew that. They saw the revolution coming. We were naïve but we can't afford to be anymore."

"Our mothers were witches!"

"I'm not arguing that. They were also, in a way, practical. Handmade skills cannot compete with mechanization. Trade outside of Gasta Fletcha is increasingly important to feed our growing populations. We cannot remain an isolated continent accessible for a handful of months whenever the land bridge thaws. We have to change, or we will be left behind. The factories can do good for Gasta Fletcha! Think of what a quadrupled national budget would buy. Food. New buildings. Hospitals in rural areas. Schools."

"We already have those things."

"We don't have enough. Especially not with the guilders broken and wandering." More softly she said, "You've only just started to look at the wider world. Don't be constrained by the ocean. There' are thousands of island chains out there, and they all seem to want to do trade with us. Beyond trade, think about the variety of people. Here there are, what, a handful like you? Across the world, there could be thousands."

I sank to the floor and buried my head in my hands. I felt Magda against me a moment later. Her fingers stroked the disaster of curls on my head while she continued to speak the most blasphemous things, couched in bitter sweetness.

"No more work in that laboratory, Sorin. Not on the wood amulets. Get the magic out of you, yes, but then go to Thuja. Reconcile the past. Rediscover your fungi! You've not made extracts in months. Do you not miss them? We can meet back here in two months. We can talk more then. We have a date planned, right?"

I shook my head, dislodging Magda's hand. "I will not give up on the guilders."

"My darling, I am not requesting."

I had not, until that very moment, considered what it meant to be so close to a queen. Being friends with a princess? That wasn't so bad. Princesses were bossy, but not untamable. Now that Magda's mother was dead, Magda had no higher authority. I could not appeal to her mother or mine to change her mind. She was my queen, I was her subject, and no number of titles, master, consort, or otherwise, would ever overrule the one she wore.

I wiped at the tears welling in the corners of my eyes. "Please do not make this decision. Not yet. Give me these two months while you're gone. Please."

"I'll have the stable hands pack your horse, too. You can leave at midday, after you have had rest. Do not make me lock you from the laboratory, Sorin. Promise me the only reason you will return before I get back is to gather essentials for your trip."

How could I possibly make that promise? I'd have taken any help then, even in the form of a disembodied witch, but the only sounds I heard were my tears *pit patting* on the over-polished cedar floor.

"Sorin?" Magda's voice cracked with warning, and, I hoped, at least a little heartbreak for the guilds.

"There's a pending experiment. I have to take it down in the morning before I leave or there may not be a laboratory, or a castle to come back to." I set my jaw and looked at her. "Chemistry isn't bound by queenly dictate."

"No more, Sorin. It has to end, or there will always be one more experiment, one more theory. We need a clean break so we can move forward. Promise me."

Blasphemous. How could I promise such a thing? "I don't know if I can."

Magda tilted my chin up with a finger, forcing me to look her in the eyes. "You must. Our future, Sorpsi's future, isn't in those amulets. I won't let you, or Gasta Fletcha, stagnate. Let magic go. You never cared for it anyway."

"The guilders' skills matter! The guilders matter!"

"So do all the other people on Gasta Fletcha. They don't deserve to starve while we continue to expend every castle resource on recovering what was already a dying trade."

"I..." My fingernails would have been in my arms again, if Magda hadn't cupped my hands in her own. Her words made sense. They did. But I could not reconcile them. Losing the guilds was losing a piece of Gasta Fletcha and a piece of myself. I already had so many lost pieces. With the guilds gone, would any of us ever be whole?

"Master Chemist," Magda prodded. The first budding rays of sunlight snuck in through the window, casting curls of shadow across the queen's face. "Promise me."

How could I say it? I couldn't say it. I *wouldn't* say it!

But I did say it because in the end, Magda was my queen.

"I promise." The words burned from my tongue down to my belly.

"We can talk when I'm back, alright? About anything you'd like. For as long as you'd like. I can show you the letters I've been getting. We can go over budgets and market reports. It's more complex than guilds, Sorin. Running a country is difficult. My job is to make the hard decisions."

I'd given up my fungi. I'd given up alchemy, to focus on the guilders, and Sorpsi, and rectifying the damage caused by our mothers. "What is my job?" I asked her from the floor as she stood. "What is my purpose, if not to save the way of life that defined both of us?"

"I love you, Sorin," was all Magda said in return before slipping out the door.

Hey ~~Sis~~
Hey ~~Brothe~~
Sorin,

~~Summer on a glacier reminds me of you. It's normal,~~
~~and not unusual, yet people get hung up on it anyway.~~
~~Except in this case the 'people' are just you.~~
~~You have yourself together now, right? A few months~~
~~with Magda and are you two still tiptoeing around who is~~
~~a top? Are you ever going to write me back?~~
How are you? It's been a long time. I've been traveling,
not as much as I'd like. The Triarchy of Puget has passels
of people up here trying to dig amulets, to send to you I'm
guessing. Without the magic from them the climate
is...normalizing I suppose. It's getting warmer. Parts of the
glacier that were safe to cross are now packed slush. The
ground in general is softening, although we're used to
permafrost, so to be expected.

Have you ever been to Rhenna—the northern continent?
There's a small land bridge you can walk across in the
height of summer. ~~Of course you haven't, because you~~
~~never left that house. Fuck Amada. She deserves to be dead~~.
It's pretty country. Flowers. Trees. Sun. I've never gone
past the first border town but it's all just people, like us. No
guilds that I can see, and machinery everywhere, powered
by steam. I've never seen a hint of magic though. You'd like
it.

Back to the glacier. That's why I'm writing. ~~Again~~. I
should have written earlier, maybe catching you before
you got too tangled up in the palace and your new place in
life. ~~You were supposed to write to update me on the amulet~~
~~work you're doing with Magda so I know what is going on,~~
~~remember!?~~ I'd like a few updates. In return, here is mine.
I've been digging amulets, too.

It started by digging a hole to answer the evening call of nature. I found a burnt bone amulet. It was right at the start of the land bridge to Rhenna.

The Puget diggers hadn't made it up this far, so I left it well alone and dug another hole. And found another amulet of bone. Then another, then another. I found them along the border between Gasta Fletcha and Rhenna only. Always at the border path, never beyond. The few times I ventured away from the border I might happen upon a regular amulet, but the bone ones were only at the edge of Gasta Fletcha.

What in the name of Mother's magic is going on?

Are they leaching magic like the old amulets? I don't know. I collected them with gloves and haven't looked at them since I shoved them into my satchel. They're magic and this is your business, Chemist, not mine. You're the one who makes bone oil. I know you have to stay in Sorpsi, at the palace. Returning the guilder skills is probably all you think about. I'll bring the amulets to you. Give me a week. I may arrive at the same time as this letter, I don't know.

~~Every guilder child learns how to write. Exercise that skill and let me know you're coming? Damn it, I don't know how to write a damn letter.~~ No need to write back. I'm headed your way in the morning, with a satchel of old magic. I'd rather not bring them all the way to the Capitol City, however. I think I'd like to go home. I've not been there since I was a boy, but I dream about that little wooden house most nights. Maybe I'm sentimental. Maybe I'm old. Maybe it is childish to yearn for a home that clearly never wanted you. Regardless, please meet me there, Sorin. If it takes you time to get away, I'll camp or stay in the house. Just don't take too long.

Love,
Sameer

Chapter 8 — Paper

"Will it be appropriate for your needs?"

"Magda, the rooms are huge. You could fit my entire laboratory just within the bedroom itself. What am I going to do with all this space?"

"Have you pulled away any of the dust cloths? Go on. Try one."

"This is silly, I...oh. OH. One of mother's marqueteries! I did the back bracing for this one when I was five. I helped her cut the tree for it as well. The woman in the center, she was one of the founders of Gasta Fletcha. That's her boat in the background. We put more time into that boat than the rest of the marquetry together. Mother had at least three books open, trying to sort what the colonizing ships would have looked like. I...I don't remember the story at all."

"I don't either. It's not part of any Gasta Fletcha fairy tales. My governess never made me read any books on the continent's founding, either, outside of we used to live on boats, then we found Gasta Fletcha, and settled it. Interesting. I guess I never thought to ask. We came from boats, as the marquetry says. That's what I know. It's a shame your mother's library burned with your old house. It sounds like she had books in there that would serve a new queen well. Anyway. What do you think?"

"About the marqueteries? Or the bed?"

"...both?"

I did not sleep in those last few moments of morning, after Magda left but before the day began. Instead, I seethed.

It began as pacing, violent and fast, around the outermost circumference of my rooms. When that failed to quell my rage I turned to stomping, then finally punching a half-done marquetry of the Capitol Castle. It was not my worst choice of the evening, but the force of my knuckles did send the panel to the floor via a small end table. Both ended up in splintered bits, the noise satisfying but insufficient.

Magda was abandoning the guilds.

The Queen of Sorpsi was abandoning the guilds!

I could defy her. Break the promise and work on the cure for the next two months. Surprise her with my success when she returned or slink away in failure. Either way, I would shatter the fragile trust between us. I could, maybe, save the guilds, but I would lose Magda. I would lose Sorpsi.

And I...Argh, why did tears have to flow so freely? It'd taken Magda and I a lifetime to reach this moment, of palaces and dances and kisses we didn't have to steal. I could not lose her. But I could not lose the guilds, either. What I needed was backup—a cooler head to talk guilder sense into my queen. I needed my brother, Sameer, which meant there was a much-put-off letter I needed to write.

I threw open the door to my rooms and managed two furious stomps into the hall, when yesterday's page crashed into my hip.

"Master Chemist!" A silver tray covered in letters clanged onto the floor. "I am so sorry!"

"Where are you headed?" I asked as I helped the page gather the fallen paper. In the pile were wax stamps from the Kingdom of Eastgate, the Triarchy of Puget, and many more I did not recognize. Some letters had no stamp at all, just a glob of smashed wax imprinted with a child's thumb.

"Library. It's where all the letters go until Her Majesty returns."

"Is it? I suppose she did mention that last night." I eyed the sloppily stacked tray, the child's half-flattened hair, the shadowed eyes, and decided it was an excellent time to practice the same kind of reckless decision making my mother had once employed. It was also the best place to find parchment and pens for my own letter. "I'll help."

"Thank you!"

From the offered tray I took two handfuls of letters, then followed the page down the stairs to the main floor of the castle. From here we wound through a labyrinth of corridors I'd seldom gone down until the hall ended in a wide alcove.

The Royal Library had once had a double entry door—that was clear from the rusted hinges that still clung to the door frame. I had no memory of what said door might have looked like. It had been removed well before Mother first brought me to the palace. The interior had been designed for royal comfort across several generations. The upholstery across the couches and chairs did not match, the curtains on the stretched windows were covered in dust. The books, however. The books were tidy, the shelves they sat on clean and dry. One large oak slab table ran the length of the room, covered in ample candles. The side of the table closest to me was covered in letters with broken seals. All were addressed to Magda.

It was on this table the page unceremoniously dumped the tray. "There's too many to stack, as you can see, Master Chemist. I don't know what we will do when it overflows. They'll go to the floor, likely. There's too many to read anyway, don't you think?"

"Mmm," I said, placing the letters I held onto the very edge of the polished wood and sifting through an older stack with my other hand. "How long have they been coming in like this?"

"Since before you and Queen Magda left for the glacier. They doubled after Queen Maja's death. They doubled again after Queen Magda signed the trade deal with Pleila, the island two days off our southwest coast."

Alibe's island-continent? What did we have that a bustling hub like Pleila needed? Hastily made factory goods? A soulless guilder population?

"Have you read any?" I asked without thinking.

The page's eyes went wide with horror. "Master Chemist I would never! I swear!"

"My apologies." I pushed a false smile to my face. "I meant, have you ever caught some of the text in passing? Are any of them already opened?"

Relief bloomed across the child's face. "Yes. Queen Magda would open one or two every evening. They're in the piles, but they get quickly buried."

"Thank you." I pressed a small coin into the page's hand. "Will you tell me when you have more to deliver?"

"Of course." The coin disappeared into one of the many folds of the page's tunic. The weight of the metal changed the drape of the fabric and the page bunched shoulders and shifted, trying to hide now apparent breasts.

"I understand," I said to the page. Really, I ought to have had better words. What had I wanted to hear, at this youth's age—the age when people saw me not as a person, but as an inevitability?

"I have cloth I can share with you. Come by my laboratory tonight and I will show you how to wrap it."

Ah, there were the tears I was all too familiar with. The page nodded and left, soundlessly except for the faint *pit pat* of salt water on wood.

If only my problems were as easily solved. I counted to twenty before letting my anger move back to a boil. I pushed letters down the length of the table, flipped apart stacks until I found a broken seal and read the signature line. Domingos of the trade ship *Fair Winds*. The text above negotiated a freight price on metal screws to the island of Pleila. Below it was another opened letter, signed by another trade ship captain, this one with a counteroffer on cotton bolt shipping. I dug further and found three, four, five more with the same back and forth of negotiation. Two letters from the very back of the table contained contracts, signed by Magda, for the export of raw lumber from Sorpsi's forests for eventual burning to smelt iron. A third requested a quote for eight acres of forest timber to be delivered to a shipyard in yet another country I'd never heard of. The price given in return would have fed the Village of Thuja for a year. But without the forest surrounding it, the Village of Thuja had no way to exist. Our food had come from the forest, the same as raw materials for building, medicine, and cooking.

"What are you doing, Magda?" I asked the stagnant library air.

At this time of early morning the library windows were heavily shuttered, allowing in no sunlight. A few stray candles burned low in their holders. The nearest I took and set upon the table. Perhaps I could soften the wax on the seals, remove, read the letters, and reset the wax? Was that lie any better than continuing to work in my laboratory?

A man cleared his throat so aggressively that I spasmed, my hand knocking over the candle, sending wax and flame down among the letters.

"Damn it!" I patted at my tunic, but I had no loose clothing to drown the flame. "Do you have wool?" I asked the voice behind me. "Water?"

A thick purple cape ribboned over my head and down over the table, as expertly laid as a maid with a bedsheet. "Master Chemist, I assume you are lost?" Magda's perpetually purple-clad advisor stood with his arms crossed in the library's doorway, face dripping disapproval that I definitively deserved.

"Advisor Alibe. Is Magda off?"

"The Queen and her contingent have successfully left the palace grounds. I am curious, however. The Royal Chemist does have her own quarters, does she not?" Alibe edged past me, into the library, and pushed the shutters apart. The glow of the sunrise had not yet hit the horizon, but I could feel the promise of it, like the tick of a bomb set to explode. "It is my job to sort these letters and keep Sorpsi afloat while the queen travels. It is your job to take a trip to Thuja, is it not?"

"How did you...I am not a she." It was not good practice to wear the tight cotton of my binding overnight, but in this exact moment, I was pleased with my painful, potentially rash-inducing oversight. I was not pleased with how Alibe knew my travel plans, but not my pronouns.

Facing me now, Alibe pulled a folded letter from a pouch on his belt and tossed it to the table. "Respect goes both ways, would you not say?"

The letter slid from its pile toward me, stopping only when it hit my fingertips. "I didn't open any."

"No, but you took advantage of those that were available. Why not read one addressed to you?"

Looking down, the letter at my fingertips was indeed addressed to 'Sorin of Thuja.' The ends were sealed with pine tar, not wax, causing the thin parchment to rip as I pressed along the seam. "How long have you had this?" I asked as I read Sameer's messy, overly edited text. More bone amulets. A meeting at Mother's house, or what remained of it—the same place Magda had wanted me to go. "Why wasn't it brought to me?"

"Queen Magda asked for all letters to be held until after the coronation. I can follow orders, Chemist. Can you?"

"How long?" I demanded.

"A week," Alibe said with a shrug. "No more. I do apologize for the misspeaking. That is my fault."

I barely heard his apology. It was only one day of travel to Mother's house from Sorpsi's capital. Sameer might still be there if I left before lunch.

And the library, said the voice that was not my own. *Your mother's library.*

It burned with the house, I silently mouthed, head turned enough that Alibe could not see. *My red pigment exploded the entire building.*

You don't know that. You never went back to check. Magda wanted you to go back, too, remember? If you go to Thuja to test the bone amulets, you're still doing what she asked. You're not breaking her rules. You both win, right?

I drummed my fingers against the amulet from the outside of my pocket. It was no more asinine to argue with old magic than to argue with one of Magda's foreign-born advisors. Neither likely had my best interests at heart. *Bending the edict of a queen to suit my scientific curiosity doesn't really engender trust.*

Will you let her tell you what to do for the rest of your life?

"Master Chemist? I'm going to ask you to leave."

"The library is always open," I said with far more indignation than befit my age.

"Not when state secrets become a curiosity. When Queen Magda appoints you to her advisory board, I will ensure you access. Until then, please return to your laboratory."

A rooster crowed.

I did not have time for political games, or arguments with the incorporeal. I snaked passed Alibe, scooping my arm around a tall stack of letters as I did so and sweeping them onto the floor.

"Pettiness does not become you, Master Chemist." Alibe bent to collect the letters, the cracking of his joints managing to sound as exasperated as his voice. I continued toward the exit, pushing Sameer's letter into my pocket along with a handful of other, unopened ones from the very edge of the table.

"Those aren't yours, Master Chemist!" Alibe called after me.

"Come and take them," I said in a voice that sounded dangerously like my mother's.

To: Queen Magda Of Sorpsi

Dear Queen,

As discussed, our iron smelting operations are limited only by our fuel. We are prepared to offer you one quarter of all iron produced for any load fueled entirely by your wood. In previous correspondences, you suggested four longboats could arrive to Pleila as early as summer, two months from now, but you are also entertaining a competing offer to sell to a shipbuilding company on another island. We will meet this offer and exceed it, please let us know your price. In addition, and at whatever cost you charge, would it be possible to expedite the first shipment? Pleian iron is the highest quality on the northern hemisphere and demand far outstrips supply. In exchange for timely delivery, we would be willing to negotiate a percentage of sales of the remaining iron, an offset to cover your shipping costs, or imported Pleilan labor to aid in the forest logging. We are willing to dock at any shipyard of your choosing, although you will have far higher margins should we port at Sorpsi over Eastgate just due to the distance your Thujan trees would need to travel. We understand you have not yet suggested Eastgate's port, however traffic has increased there and at the Puget port in recent months. We merely wish to let you know we can be flexible.

With that in mind, while we understand the need for more commercial vessels to haul Sorpsi's new trade goods, an inquiry into our competitor shows the wood currently is to be used for long-term passenger vessels. Queen Magda, surely investment in iron is more important than cruise ships!

I look forward to hearing back from you as soon as your schedule permits. This message is being sent with its own page, on its own boat, so that correspondence may pass between us as quickly as possible. Please send your response back along the same channel. We would also accept a response from your Advisor Alibe, with whom we have had previous dealings.

With highest respect,

Anodiwa Moyo
Head Chancellor
Pleila Central Government

Chapter 9 — Oil

"You traveled alone, Queen Magda? That's unexpected."

"My guards are in your kitchens. As well they should be, the fried cui is delicious. Thank you for preparing this meal. It's welcome after three days on the road."

"Eastgate is always delighted to welcome another monarch. However, I'd thought we'd be welcoming two."

"I am no longer ten, King Rodolf. Queens do not get prodded about their love lives."

"Who told you that? My wife would be doing it herself if she weren't with her ladies in waiting, finishing up the details for tomorrow's ball in your honor. Lords, Magda, what do you think we talk about in the evening, after we're done with the meetings and inspections and other tedium?"

"There are bigger issues to discuss right now. The factories—"

"Aren't going anywhere. The guilds may or may not recover, but it won't be with this generation. The continental economy is booming. Now is the perfect time to focus on the personal. A queen needs an heir. You can avoid making eye contact with me all you like, but you'll get the same talk in Puget."

"Sorin and I did not part on the best terms. My chemist will be the last guilder to give up the past. Sorin worked tirelessly for the recognition."

"It is Sorin the Chemist, yes? Not Sorin the Woodcutter or Sorin the Alchemist? It sounds like a part of Sorin has already accepted the necessity of change and the inclusive inclination of progress."

"You're not concerned about what may be lost if we completely abandon the guilds?"

"I am concerned moreso about the legacy of Sorpsi's rulers. King Tunbridge was yours by monarchy, and your mother is yours by bloodline. Iana was yours as well. Which legacy will you follow, Queen Magda? Will you consume Gasta Fletcha, or usher it into a brighter future? As you *ponder the answer to those questions, please also consider how you will apologize to the Queen of Eastgate for not bringing her a most unusual dinner guest. Sorin has been the talk of this court since you two returned from the glacier."*

Alibe had not gotten up. He waved me off, still on his knees, still floundering in a sea of trade deals and bargaining. He'd come for the letters, eventually, because Magda was his queen and he'd sworn to serve her. I had gone before he did so. I did not wish to make a habit of lying to my queen, but precedent had been set, shots had been fired, and it was a long day trip back to the Thujan woods. Once again, things were being kept from me. Once again, I was in the dark while queens decided my future. Not again. Not this time. I was Sorpsi's Master Chemist and I would be happy to be Queen Magda's consort but not if it came at the cost of Thuja, or Sorpsi, or the Gasta Fletcha continent. The guilders had to come first. Our people had to come first. I just had to get Magda to see that, too.

My satchel filled with wood amulets clacked against my hip as the passenger ship bobbed on the low waves of Cedar River. The river was not the most direct route to Thuja but it was the fastest, at least historically. I'd traveled to and from the Thujan forest to Sorpsi's capital frequently as a child, with my mother, on this ferry, and knew the routes well. With luck, Sameer would still be waiting for me at Mother's house.

Unlike my travel, my packing had been poorly planned. I'd brought more amulets and vials of pyridine than food or traveling gear, but I'd grown up in Thuja and could purchase supplies from any number of families in the village. I'd not given up space for my fungal powders, but the packets were shoved into my pockets instead of bound on a bandolier across my chest. In my back pocket next to the bone amulet were the four letters I'd taken from the castle library. I was not yet angry enough to read them.

Instead, I leaned against the rail of the trawling ferry and stared at the passing countryside. The last time I'd come this way the roads just outside the capitol had been dirt that turned to thick mud in springtime. The northern trail had been almost feral, prone to bandit attacks and mudslides.

I was two hours outside the city walls now and the road that ran alongside Cedar River's bank was paved with white stone that flickered orange in the unrelenting sunlight. Carts ran along the road—now doublewide—carrying bricks and large metal components. The wheels were even rubber, the wheel spokes identical and unremarkable. Factory made components, to be used to make yet more factories. What would this one take from us? Glass blowing, perhaps? Woodturning? The last shreds of our dignity?

"What do you carry?" I called out when the river meandered closer to shore and a cart driver happened to glance my way.

"Pieces for the spinning mule. For processing yarn!" the woman returned. "One of these takes the place of a thousand spinners!"

One cart, and half the Textile Guild had been rendered useless.

It's hard to watch your soul locked away. But you will set it right.

I turned riverside, so no one could see me speaking to myself. Logs floated downstream, too close to the little boat for comfort. I could not remember a recent windstorm big enough to take trees that size down, but I'd spent a lot of time in laboratory, too. "Why do you care about the guilds?"

I'm no guilder.

"I repeat my question then, along with *who are you?*"

Nothing deserves to be locked in a prison. Nothing deserves to be ignored and forgotten. The guilds gave you economy and civilization and you put them away as easily as a child discards a toy. How long until you burn down the factories for whatever new god you invent? You can stop the cycle, Sorin. You can turn back the clock. You can free Gasta Fletcha. You can free me.

"For a dead spirit that won't give me any concrete information, you seem very sure of my willingness to help. I have a small chance at returning about seventy-five percent of guilder skills."

You minimize your importance.

"No, I'm no longer an isolated forest waif who has nothing better to do than romanticize the guilds. I'm a realist."

You're withdrawing from your task because you fear losing the queen.

I turned back around and crossed my arms. "Shut up," I mouthed. "I'll do what is right, and so will she."

Is that what the letters say?

The damn letters. I'd been a fool to bring that kind of temptation with me.

"Cedar River Pointe!" the captain called out. "Any to disembark?"

"Aye!" I raised my hand and moved to the stern. Cedar River Pointe was a well-built and now well-neglected dock that had lost use when Thuja finished construction of its own dock—somewhere in my eighth year. It was a twenty-minute walk from here to Thuja's boundary and another hour to Mother's house. If I jogged, I could do it in half the time.

I jumped just as the boat brushed the bank. From here the forest would be solidly coniferous and the terrain much steeper. Historically there would have been a precipitous temperature drop upon crossing the river, as the Old King's buried amulets had caused dramatic climatic differences across Gasta Fletcha. With those dug up, the only change was a drop in humidity.

The road on this side of the river had gone overgrown with disuse. I waded through ankle-deep sedge, and into a sea of ferns, moving as fast as the undergrowth would allow. The forest started just beyond.

I was one foot out of the grassland, just stepping into the overstory, when the duff around me lit with a green glow so faint, anyone not looking for it would likely overlook it. At night the light would be blinding, but the sun had yet to hit its zenith and the path cut a wide enough swath through the trees that parts of the horizon were visible. The foxfire dotted the forest, primarily on the ground but occasionally racing up standing dead trees. Mostly, however, it spiraled through the forest beyond, well away from the worn trail.

"I thought we were beyond this nonsense," I muttered.

Gasta Fletcha knows you, the voice said. *Gasta Fletcha* chose *you. You question. You interrogate. You experiment for the joy of discovery.*

"I have moved beyond the crushing weight of destiny and birth rite. Go away."

The foxfire flashed green, a light so brilliant I was momentarily blind in the late afternoon light.

"I'm busy!"

"Do you have food?"

I snapped the top from a fungus in my startlement. But this was no ghostly apparition, rather a boy, no older than ten. He wore the short pants of a child, his feet were bare, and the sleeves of his shirt tattered to the elbow. He was pale and sallow colored, his brown hair coated in a fluffy white film.

"No, I'm sorry," I said, removing my hand from the foxfire. "I'd planned on buying in Thuja."

"Can I eat that?" He pointed, as much as he could. The first two fingers of his right hand were gone to the second knuckle.

"No, and I'd advise against eating any fungi unless you know them well. Would you like my cloak? It won't help your belly but come night it will help with the chill." I unclasped my ermine-hooded cloak and handed it to him. It was far too hot for it at the moment, and by nightfall I'd be at Mother's house. Even if none of the structures remained, I could burn the wood debris for heat.

"Are you a queen?" he asked. He worshipped the cloak as he clasped it about his neck, letting the fir massage his paper-thin skin.

There was a time I'd have lost the contents of my stomach with those words. Life wasn't so much of a fight, anymore, or there were large things to fight for. I knew who I was. Those

I cared about honored who I was. The words of a boy could not harm me. They could, however, further delay me. "I work for one. I'm Sorin, and I grew up with the Master Woodcutter Amada, in these woods."

"What do you do now?" The boy had swaddled himself in my cloak despite the heat, his mangled fingers gripping one outside hem.

"Chemistry. I'm in a bit of a hurry but would you like to walk with me to Thuja? I can give you coin for a meal there."

He scowled, which was quickly followed by a racking cough that sounded like it came from the bottom of his belly. "Thuja? No. Thuja's all cotton factories and log mills. I want to head to the Capitol City of Sorpsi. There's a new factory there hiring, in metals."

Log mills? For the Thujan forest? Already? The date on that letter had been no more than a month ago. "Are they operational? The log mills?"

He shrugged. "Next week, but I don't want to wait. The textile mill is moving, and they've got new machines and don't need so many people. They want only people with fingers." He flexed his broken hand.

"What about the local guildhalls? They're always taking apprentices and you don't need all your fingers for the River Guild. Or the Trappers and Traders. The masters have lost their skills but there are still libraries to study from and apprentices to learn under."

Another round of coughing came from him, and his words that came after wheezed from his lungs. "Guilds are dead. Thanks for the cloak." He turned and went back the way I'd come, the rich weave of my cloak a stark contrast to the thinness of his frame. The whiteness in his hair was a sticky fluff, like cotton. I'd seen it on the clothes of factory workers who delivered to the palace.

I also knew cotton was dusty and guild families often chose to work outside when they could. Older textile guilders, usually those well retired, developed coughs like that boy's. Cotton Cough, called by doctors as byssinosis.

I resumed my jog down the trail, fuming as I did so. That boy was too young for Cotton Cough. He'd have had to work every moment of daylight for years to develop that level of lung disorder, or be subjected to dozens of concurrent looms.

But that was what was happening, wasn't it? If the spinning mule could do the work of a thousand spinners, and the boy had operated one...that was unfathomable amount of cotton dust in his still-growing lungs. I would bet the machine had taken his fingers, too. Ten-year-olds were not known for their forethought of movement.

Ten-year-olds had no business working in factories. Even as a guild apprentice, he'd not have been old enough to work machines unattended.

"He's an anomaly," I said to myself as I drew one of Magda's unopened letters from my satchel. "He has to be an anomaly. Right?"

You already stole them. You might as well open them.

The seals were bound to break open in my bag at some point, and the voice was right. I'd already committed treason. Reading the letters wouldn't be any worse.

With hands vibrating from my run, I broke the seal, flipped open the folds, and read.

To Queen Magda of Sorpsi from Liriodendron Village. This letter represents a formal request on behalf of the village elders for oversight of the steel furnace that has been constructed in the middle of town. The railway system that brings hourly deliveries of pig iron has cut the square in half. The heat from the furnace has maimed half of those who work it, and the converter into which the molten iron is poured requires constant maintenance—particularly the air flow valves. We know steel is of critical importance to Sorpsi and we have added continuous shifts in the factory as you previously requested. As Liriodendron is a small town and the furnace now employs the bulk of the population, we would appreciate oversight into its operation. If injuries continue at this rate we will also need additional medical help, and additional workers.

Half of the workers had been maimed? Did that mean half the town? Or just half of maybe a small workforce? No guild had ever been that deadly.

I read the letter again, this time noticing there was no signature. A wise choice if one was rebuking their queen. "Half the workforce," I said out loud. "That's completely unsustainable. Magda needs to know, immediately." She'd be in Eastgate by now, for another three days. I could get a pigeon in Thuja to bring her the letter directly. If I signed the outside she'd certainly open it—even if just out of rage for me opening her mail.

I could forward two letters as easily as one, so I carried on. The next letter was also from an unnamed villager, this one seeking compensation for the death of their three daughters to a spinning jenny that had just been replaced by the new spinning mule for spinning cotton fibers. The ages of the girls were not listed. They could have been grown, and unmarried, or youths, like the boy. If they were children, *young* children...

The third letter came from a town I'd not heard of, in a country not of Gasta Fletcha and inquired yet again about lumber pricing and port shipping procedure. There was no need to forward this one.

The final letter... was addressed to me, dated from just before the coronation, and written in Magda's handwriting.

> *My Dear Sorin,*
> *Would you believe this is the tenth time I've tried this letter? Forgive me for its delivery. I thought it best to have a page deliver it after my departure. I've written to Eastgate and Puget, and the royals are in agreement that the amulets should be destroyed. All of them. The guilders can still work factory jobs and factories are the way forward. The amulets represent too much risk and play with magic—a force you and I agree should not be trusted. I will not repeat the sins of my mother, and King Tunbridge. It's time for a fresh slate.*

I would ask you to gather any amulets you have, and any you receive between now and my return, in a central location. When I'm back we will arrange a bonfire and burn every one. Magic and guilds are a waste of time and a distraction. It's time to move forward, for Sorpsi, and for us. It isn't fair, and it isn't right, and it will break both our hearts, but there is no other way forward.

Once the amulets are gone and both you and are freed from their heavy history, I'd like to discuss what path you and I might chart together. I have a speech, and a ring, and an expensive bottle of Sorpsi wine but I know you do not like surprises. So I'd like to ask you now, while you have time to think, if you would consider marrying me?

Love,
Magda

I stopped dead amongst the dew-covered ferns, mouth agape and a furious rage boiling inside me. Iana help me what was I supposed to with a letter like this? Destroy the amulets? Give up entirely on the guilds? Immolate Sorpsi's past like a funeral pyre but not bother to mourn because the Queen of Sorpsi had proposed to me?!

A wedding is a distraction, said the voice.

"She didn't mean it that way I'm certain, but you're right. Magda has always been brutally straightforward."

Your goal is the bone amulets. Your brother. Your mother's house.

"My *goal* is to do what is best for Sorpsi, especially if you refuse to tell me who or what you are. Until you relent on that, we have no business together." And the letters had not been more damning than foreboding. I had enough rope to hang myself with if I jumped too hastily to a conclusion. I needed more data points. "Sorry, Sameer," I said to the air. He'd have to forgive me more tardiness. It was twenty more minutes by foot to my old house, an hour if I follow Cedar

River. Most factories needed water to operate their steam powered machines. I could send Magda these letters, but it would be better to send her my own. I needed to see the factories. I would send conditions directly back to Magda if needed. I could stop this nonsense. I could talk sense into her.

You think she does not know? She has hidden from those letters the same way King Tunbridge hid amulets.

"I understand her position on the economy, though not her tactics. She would never condone what is happening to the children, or any mass deaths."

There was no need to justify myself to a magic amulet, and Sameer would forgive me my tardiness. He'd forgiven me everything else, anyway. If the factories were this dangerous, Magda needed a first-hand account.

Every moment you delay, more people die. You waste time trying to convince monarchies who began this process in the first place. It is your skills Gasta Fletcha needs, Sorin of Thuja. You must head toward the problem, not continue to run parallel to it. Find your brother.

In many ways Magda had just as sheltered a life as I had. "Thuja first," I said to the bodiless spirit. Then I changed course, to the damp bank of the Cedar River, and followed it north, to a future I never hoped to see.

Sameer had waited this long. Another day would do no further damage. And Magda I would not give up on. Not yet.

To: Sorin of Sorpsi
From: Potentate Jun of Eastgate

Dearest Sorin,

This is my third letter to you in as many weeks. I still hope for a response. Did you receive the bone amulet? What do you make of it? Have you attempted an extraction with your miraculous bone oil?

I'm traveling with the royal entourage from Puget to attend Eastgate's ball for Queen Magda—although we will be having our own for her within the next fortnight. Coronations are few and far between on our continent, and the celebrations are always excellent. After the Eastgate celebrations end, I thought I might come find you in Sorpsi and see your laboratory, and your progress with the bone amulet. We could go after to the seaside and I could tell you all about the stories I've read. I've learned how to build boats! I'd love to get your advice on the woods to use. Perhaps joinery has progressed since the continent was founded. I'm sure you would know!

Shall we say next week? Afterward I would love to take you on a trip of your own. Have you sailed, Sorin? We could sail together on a boat of our own invention!

Please send your response pigeon to me at Eastgate Palace. I will be arriving there this evening, and am sending you this pigeon en route.

With my love,
Potentate Jun

Chapter 10 — Wood

"My darling king. Queen Magda. The Triarchy is scheduled to arrive within the next two hours, although Potentate Jun may be behind by a bit as the potentate took a separate horse. Is everything sorted for tomorrow's ball?"

"As long as the pastry chef finishes in time, I see no issues. You're sweet to check in, but you opened the door so hard you toppled the tea service."

"Hah, so I did! I'll get a man to come clean it. Apologies, Lovelies. While you've spent the day arranging flowers and whatnot I've been dealing with the cotton mill fire fallout."

"One of your factories had a fire?!"

"You look so shocked, Queen Magda. There's no reason to be. Even a guild hall has burned on occasion. Factories are new and filled with problems. Your only worry right now should be pastries, right? There will be plenty of factory politics for you to manage once you're back in Sorpsi."

"I have no business with tea if my subjects are being burned alive. I should head back. Coronation parties can wait. Factories need a level of oversight that I—"

"Magda. Queen Magda. Sit down next to my husband and drink your tea. There is always a fire to put out or an argument to resolve. Progress is not painless. But let me ask you, can Gasta Fletcha survive without the factories? Think before you answer."

"I don't have to think on this. I know it cannot. Even if Sorin got the guilds restarted, many of the guilders died in the later years of my mother's reign or traveled up the glacier and across the land bridge to avoid capture. Even if we restored the skills of every guilder left on Gasta Fletcha, we could not properly restart our economy. Factory produced goods from overseas were outselling guild goods long before I took the throne. Factories and international trade are our only way forward. That doesn't mean people have to die though."

"And I agree with you. The factories will need oversight, and regulations, and certainly laws around them. We cannot know what to legislate without more information, correct? Would your chemist not agree? Also, you must see the amusement in a leader of Sorpsi valuing worker lives. Historically this is not your strong suit. Now Magda, don't scowl. It was only a joke. Please drink your tea."

The forest died two kilometers from the riverbank. Bunchberry and birdsong abruptly gave way to ferns and tall sedge in a sharp line clearly made by saws. And there were…simply no more trees after that. The terrain dotted with hills five kilometers in the distance, but all I could see directly ahead of me were waist-high stumps and piles of branches too small to be worth milling.

It smelled of wet grass, and trampled aster, and death.

"Magda already started the logging," I said. "She started the logging and she didn't tell me. *She didn't tell me.*" It wasn't as if I owned the land. Technically it was Magda's, to do with as she'd like. But I'd grown up almost entirely in the Thujan forests. Seeing them reduced to shattered bones burned more than the fumes from my bone oil on a hot summer day.

The bone amulets will help, the voice said.

"Can they regrow trees? Can they melt down factories?"

Magic makes many things possible.

"Magic destroys."

It was not magic that did this.

I snapped. How could I not, surrounded by carnage and lies? "Shut up. I don't have the space in my head to argue about the merits of magic right now."

The voice, miraculously, went silent.

I trudged on, following the river north until a stone foundation came into view. There'd been a mill here as recently as last year—Mother or I had purchased flour monthly for the entirety of my memory. There'd been a handful of homes too, not enough to call a town, but enough that if a storm came through you could find shelter for the night before returning to Thuja the next morning.

All of the infrastructure had been stripped down to build what appeared to be a ramp and loading dock into the river. Logs so fresh cut, the ends beaded sap and tar lay stacked in pyramids next to the dock while a group of men and women with hook-tipped poles loaded the logs, one by one, up the ramp and let them loose into the riverway.

"Stay back!" one called out as I approached. "Logs don't always roll the way you want!"

"Are these all from Thujan forests?" I asked as I gave the piles a wide birth. "There's thousands here, surely."

"Pressing farther north every day." A woman—maybe— set down her pole and jogged up to me. Sweat stained her shirt at the neck and armpits, but the cotton was noticeably dry on her torso. Hard manual labor in a binding was a special kind of torture I knew too well. It wasn't just the breathing that suffered. The low-quality cotton I'd once worn could rub my skin raw or raise horrible rashes in high humidity. There was no pain as great, however, as having no binding at all. "We finished breaking down the old mill last week, but the miller and his family moved to Thuja. It's about thirty minutes from here by foot, if you're after bread."

The miller had lived this far out of town to keep his prices low and because he'd thought cities a terrible place to raise children. Mother and he had discussed the merits of feral forest children ad nauseum. "He took the whole family?" I asked. "Has Thuja grown enough to overcome his costs?"

"He'd two toddlers with him. Hold on. Hey Marc?"

A tall, willowy man—again I was unsure due to the lacquered nails on an otherwise burly and hairy frame— joined us at the edge of the log yard. "Break?" he asked.

"In a minute. The miller's oldest two were on a logging team, weren't they? The one that had the cedar fall?"

Marc let out a long sigh. "Yes. Half the crew got crushed either when the tree fell, or when it rolled. Miller's kids included." He looked at me, then at my chest where the fabric of my tunic had frustratingly gathered. "Were they friends?"

"Crushed?" I asked, although the word came out muffled as I clapped a hand over my mouth. "They were barely ten, not even a year apart. What were they doing working a logging crew?"

"There's better money in trees than flour. The big logs we send down to Sorpsi to export round to Puget, where they go on another boat to somewhere else. The smaller goes by cart to Thuja for the steam-powered factories. But none of these new jobs are particularly great for the little ones. You should see Thuja's textile mill. At least out here we get sunshine and fresh air. Those kids are all but chained to their machines."

"They're *what?*"

"Best to see for yourself." Marc took off his grass-woven cap. "Besides all that, I'm really sorry for your loss. We wouldn't normally take a break all at once but it's hot, and you're family. We'll give you time to look around."

"I...I wasn't the miller's family." I kicked at the foundation just in front of me—what had likely once been part of the mill itself. A broken mill, and dozens if not hundreds of broken children. How could things have changed so fast?

"Wasn't saying you were with the millers."

"I...oh." I puzzled between Marc and the woman while their sunburned faces set into soft smiles.

Marc clapped a hand on my shoulder, his nail lacquer glittering in the sunlight. "You look surprised."

"I know I shouldn't be." How many people like me had I met since joining Magda at the castle? A dozen? Each one so distinctly bright, their nail lacquer, or glittering earrings, or adorned binders shining an unmistakable signal of their personhood. Well, blinding for anyone who was looking. I hadn't been, before. I was now.

To the woman Marc said, "Okay to break?"

She nodded, and Marc yelled, louder than any human I'd ever heard, "Lunch everyone!"

After the whoops and cheers died down, Marc turned back to me and offered another familial smile. "You need anything else? Food? Water? Clothes?"

"Those clothes come from money," said the woman, eyeing the embroidery on my blue tunic. "She's fine."

"Not she," I said automatically.

The woman nodded. "I know, but what else do we have? Marc's been toying with a plural but the other loggers get confused. What would you pick, if you got to make the decision?"

While I had spent endless hours debating language semantics with myself, I'd never thought to include Magda or say, the young page who frequented my laboratory. That had been an oversight. How could people like me become a visible part of society if there was no way to talk about us?

Although to be fair, I wasn't necessarily keen on talking about it with strangers, either. "I...have mostly avoided the issue. Magda's been great about moving my name around and—"

"*Queen* Magda? No wonder your clothes are fine. You're Master Chemist Sorin, aren't you? I'm Nya. It's an honor to meet you!"

Nya grabbed me in a hug before I could make any sort of reply. Marc wrapped arms around both of us and it was simultaneously the most uncomfortable and affirming human contact I'd ever had.

"Am I famous?" I gasped from somewhere near Nya's sweating armpit.

"Are you famous? Talk about a ruling body, you're the queen's right hand! And you're, you know," Marc released us and Nya stepped back, pulling at the binding under the tunic.

"In between?"

"Yeah! In between. Flexible. Open to options. Natural but surreal, like foxfire, or fireflies. The continent is changing at breakneck speed, but this is one revolution I can get behind. Thank you, Master Chemist, for being *you,* so that the rest of us can just *be.*"

"I...You're...welcome?" I was wholly unprepared for anyone to know my name, much less have an intuitive knowledge of, well, being me. The emotions flipping around inside my belly didn't make my fingernails go to my skin, but they did make me distinctly...uncomfortable? Embarrassed? "I uh, I'm meeting my brother in Thuja and I shouldn't be any later. Thank you for answering my questions. I'll um, take just a moment here and then be out of your way."

"The Master Chemist of Sorpsi gets however much time the Master Chemist wants. If you need anything else, holler." Nya leaned in and whispered, loud enough that Marc could hear, "And if you do settle on a way to refer to us fireflies, will you send out a pigeon or something? 'She' and 'he,' you know how they cut. If Gasta Fletcha can embrace steam power, railroads, and photography, there should be a place for a little language addition, don't you think?"

I could broach that to Magda in the next letter, right between demolished forests and marriage proposals. "I agree, but it may take some time." When Nya started to frown I added, "It's important to me, too. To all of us. I won't forget. But I do uh, have to get on my way."

"Royal business?" Marc asked with a grin.

Back to safer territory. "There's always an intrigue muddled up somewhere. Just like the gossip says." When had I perfected lying? Iana help me I didn't even recognize *myself* anymore.

"Of course. Travel safe, Sorin." Marc gave my shoulder another hearty slap before heading back to the dock. Nya followed with a wink.

I did need to get back to task. But I couldn't leave without first acknowledging where I was. I was already bowing under the weight of Nya and Marc's familiarity. How much more damage could a remembrance do? I stepped into the center of the foundation, where the millstone lay cracked into three pieces. Here I closed my eyes for a moment, remembering how the miller's two oldest children had helped me collect my fungi just last summer, and how after we'd made ourselves sick on blackberries from a thicket we'd stumbled into on the way home.

I didn't want them just...forgotten. Forgotten, or consumed even, by the march of industrialization. Magda had to be told. She could make laws maybe, that kept children from the factories. And once I restored all the guilder skills, the factories could be torn down.

Although. A betraying thought skittered through my mind. People would *want* to tear down the factories, wouldn't they? No one wanted dead children but if the children were kept from working...

You have so very little control over these changes, Sorin.

"I don't need your empathy," I snapped, the moment of quiet contemplation ruined. "And I'm done here. I've got more than enough for a letter to Magda. It's time to press on to Thuja."

I left the logging camp with a final wave to Nya and Marc and continued following the river. The second small town I remembered was likewise defunct, this time merely abandoned instead of deconstructed. It had been a small fishing village, but with the river now absolutely choked with logs from another logging camp farther upstream, fishing had likely become impossible.

Another twenty minutes through clearcut forest brought me to Thuja. I didn't recognize my surroundings until my feet hit cobblestone and the familiar smell of the fish market wafted to me. Although the fish stench was much diminished this time, replaced, or overlayed, by the musty smell of cotton seed oil—a natural byproduct of harvesting and processing the boll. The river would take me directly past my old home so, like the mature adult I had become, I lingered along the main Thujan thoroughfare. All the small shops remained—the bakery, the milk maids, the tanners. But in a five-shop wide footprint, where formerly trees had grown, was Thuja's very own factory, complete with a steam engine powered by the Thujan forests.

I did not need to see the cotton boll sign swinging by the double-breasted door to know what processing took place there. Across the roof of the factory and in a wide arc around it spread white fluff that could have passed for snow in another climate. It spun in the air too, when disrupted by a passerby. As I drew closer, the low hum I'd first noticed upon passing the city wall grew to first a steady clang, then a metallic whirring.

I could write a letter to Magda with second-hand accounts and heresy. Or I could see the issues myself. A firsthand account would definitely be more persuasive and there was no way Magda had seen this factory in person—or any outside the capital. She left the castle less frequently than I left my laboratory.

The noise as I approached almost had me turn away. My ears certainly would ring for days afterward. My lungs already strained against the thick cotton air. I'd thought to just open the door and walk in, but a wide, firm woman blocked my entrance.

"Business?" she asked when I tried for the handle.

"Curiosity? I'm Thujan, from the woods just north of here. I can hear the factory from there and have heard about the jobs. Could I see the machines?" Another effortless lie.

"We're not hiring," the woman responded, arms still crossed.

Isn't she pleasant? said the voice. *I wouldn't care to invite her for tea. Or Tii.*

"I just want to see the machines. I've never seen anything large enough to make this sort of noise."

"The doors open when the workers leave and not until then."

I pivoted on my heels and saw no windows on the sides of the building. Two short chimneys rose from the roof, belching clouds of fluff. "How do they see? How do they breathe, the workers?"

"You are instructed to leave the premises, or you will be arrested. The workers have to make their quota. Shipment is supposed to leave in the morning, per Queen's orders."

I had to swallow my incredulous laugh. It had been months since I'd been treated like Sorin the Perpetual

Apprentice. The moment here, with this woman, felt as surreal as a lucid dream. A village woman, no matter how large, did not frighten me. Not anymore.

"Eugene!" the woman yelled. "We have a trespasser!"

A *thunk* came from the west side of the building.

My hands went to my pockets, balled and sweating. But the nervousness bled quickly away. I felt for the largest pouch, the one that contained the crystal-forming fungal pigment. I worried the drawstring open with my fingers, careful to make sure nothing came in contact with my skin.

"You were asked to leave," said the bear of a woman who came around the building's corner. Her blond hair was short, her arms massive, and her gait reminded me of the walking palm tree encounter I'd had with Master Rahad just six months prior—ominous, and a little comical.

"I'm not defenseless," I said, drawing out my pouch. "I only want to look. I have the right."

The woman at the door slapped me just as Eugene grabbed my right arm.

Eugene yanked me from the threshold. I raised my free arm up, the pouch of Flaming Dragon fungus crystals aimed to tip over at the next movement.

You'll take down the whole factory if you aren't careful. You'll destroy your entire village's livelihood and possibly kill the people inside. You need to control the reaction.

Control had never been the hallmark of my fungal pigments. *Do you have ideas?* I yelled into my head.

I could help.

Eugene reached for my pouch as her fingernails drew blood on my other arm. Her grip was worse than a vice but not as bad as the roiling contempt she wore across her face. "You ever been held down in a river?" she snarled.

Can you make it just the door? I asked.

Can you imagine it just being the door?

Yes?

I moved my free hand around my back to keep my pouch from Eugene's meaty hands. "Open the door or I will blow it apart."

"This isn't a negotiation." Eugene gave up on the pouch and cuffed me on the side of the head, sending me sprawling onto the white ground. Before I could check to make sure no crystal had gone loose, she hauled me to my feet. I could feel the bruise forming on my cheek but so too could I feel the crystals, sharp and spined, growing between my fingers as they escaped their leather prison. Uncontrolled, they'd pierce my skin and make quick work of my bones.

Focus on your goal. Visualize the outcome you desire.

Ridiculous, and creepy, but I had no other help. My heel found Eugene's foot and while she didn't let go, she did bellow and loosen her grip. The doorwoman left the threshold to come to her aid, and it was in this moment that I threw the tiny crystals in my hand, over her head and at the door, making sure to visualize *exactly* where the crystals should end up. They'd lodge in the door, not my skin. They'd bond and grow and shatter the wood in a controlled, nonviolent reaction.

In times past it would have been more than the door that would have exploded. The crystals would have continued chaining and forming and eventually taken down the whole building. This time, miraculously, they lodged firmly in the wood door and first splintered, then blew the wood apart. Shards of cheap alder flew at the three of us, one piece grazing my upper thigh and separating fabric and skin there. But that was all. The remaining crystals in my hand did not grow. The shards lodged in the doorframe did not morph. The reaction remained stable.

That magic could be useful, could be *tamed* by just my visualization, was an utterly foreign concept. Potentially a useful concept to mull in the future. Not now.

"I said I'm going in."

"My goodness," said a new voice from behind me. "What in Sorpsi is going on here? Sorin, are you alright?" The familiarity of the voice tugged at my memory. One of Magda's advisors? No, the voice was too throaty. A guilder? Unlikely, with the familiarity and that 'master' hadn't been attached to my name. Honorifics were important, even in broken guilds.

"Sorin? Are you alright? Are these two bothering you? Shall I have them flogged? I know this isn't my country, but rank has to travel at least a little, right?"

Eugene and the doorwoman exchanged confused looks, but snapped to attention all the same.

I turned around...and came face to face with Potentate Jun. The potentate wore a royal traveling cloak with the Puget crest embroidered widely across the back, and a thin silver circlet glinted in the waning sun.

"*Jun?*" I said, letting my hands fall to my sides.

"You still can't go in," Eugene said, the words lacking any steel to them.

"Do you know who I am?" Jun demanded.

"From the Triarchy of Puget?" said the other woman, just as confusedly as her compatriot.

"Yes. And this is Sorin, Master Chemist of Sorpsi. Stand down."

The two guards shared an incomprehensible look, then stepped aside and bowed. *Bowed.* "We didn't realize it was you, Master Chemist," said Eugene. "And of course we didn't recognize you at all, Potentate Jun. Our deepest apologies."

"We didn't get notification there was to be an inspection," said doorwoman. "We didn't prepare. We received no notification from the palace and the queen always sends a pigeon two days before an inspection. We were only trying to prepare the export materials. Pleila just offered double their previous amount. The queen wanted to take advantage of the offer."

"Magda's been here?" I asked. "Queen Magda?" I wanted to ask what Jun was doing here, too, but that would have to wait.

Eugene's head shook. "No, but her advisor has."

"Interesting," said Jun, noncommittally. "The crystal additions will be amusing for the next inspector."

I'd bet the entire royal library that inspector had been Alibe. "And you *passed* inspection?"

Again the two women looked to each other, before doorwoman answered, "We have always made any required updates but yes, we have passed."

Jun nodded at me before saying to the guards, "Then there should be no issue with a surprise inspection, right?"

"Of course not, Potentate." Eugene stepped aside. The other woman followed.

Jun pushed open the door and said with a wide, warm smile, "After you, Sorin. I'm glad my horse threw a shoe and I had to detour on the way to Eastgate. I hope you don't mind the help?"

I let out a long, low exhale that bled away the stress of the ball, the mill, and the boat ride all at once. "Gods, I missed you, Jun. It's really wonderful to see you again."

I reached out a hand to shake, but Jun simply pulled me into an embrace.

I stayed there, in that moment, hugging Jun and holding my breath, etching the warmth of Jun's breath and the softness of Jun's grip into my mind. I could almost feel Marc and Nya's arms around the two of us as well, solidifying the four of us into...something. Something big. Something important.

Then Jun spoke. "Would you be willing to share why you blew the door off a factory?"

"Huh? Oh." I pulled away and shivered at the now cold air between us. "I saw a boy without fingers. I wanted to see the conditions inside."

"Do you think the advisor that inspected the facility didn't report properly to Magda? Or the report got lost?"

I thought about the pile of letters on the library table. There was also a solid possibility Alibe had not reported the factory conditions to Magda at all, and distracted her with a better trade deal. And thinking back to the maimed boy in the forest, if Alibe had implemented any safety changes, they'd clearly not been enough. Or her advisors had not drawn her a full picture.

"I'll be sure she gets a detailed report in my next letter. Do you, um, do you want to come in with me?"

Jun's head shook. "Unless you think you might need saving again, I need to see about my horse. Where are you staying tonight? Shall I meet you there? Your mother's house perhaps? I know the house is burnt but the longhouse, perhaps?"

It was good to know the longhouse still stood. Puzzling that Jun knew, but the road to Thuja from the main Eastgate road did go close by. It was very possible Jun had stopped there on the way to town. The potentate had made no mention of Sameer, however. Had he not yet arrived? "That will work. I will see you in the evening. I've a letter to write tonight so please don't worry about arriving after dark."

Jun nodded and headed off toward the town smithy. I pressed past the doorway into the haze of the factory.

The sounds and movement of the explosion had not disturbed the workers, but it was easy to see why. Inside the machines were far louder, and the visibility nearly nonexistent. Coughing, I made my way to the first row of machines, all spinning cotton across multiple spindles, being hand-fed bolls by girls not yet old enough to bleed.

I put my hands on the shoulder of a pigtailed girl, who jumped at my touch. I yelled "May I ask you questions?" but she shook her head and covered an ear with one hand, the other still threading cotton to the machine. That hand, like the boy in the forest, was missing a finger—hers a pinkie gone clean to the final knuckle. Dried, red staining soaked the white fluff under her feet and I could see spatter marks on the metal rigging.

The girl's eyes turned, worriedly, to the door. Again I tried to speak to her but she turned away, both hands now back to work. I picked my way down the line. The next girl had all her fingers but her hair was shorn on one side, and she was missing an ear. After her was a boy nearing manhood, his back hunched and his legs too wide apart to have a stable gait.

I needed to speak to them, because Magda needed to know. I needed the machines turned off or I'd get no answers. But Gasta Fletcha had no guilds related to steam power, and as such I had no idea of how electricity worked. The entire concept had only been explained to both Magda and I within the last month, and my queen had outright laughed.

Disintegrating the factory would set the town to chaos and Magda would have that to deal with instead of the real issue at hand. Instead, I walked up and down the rows, squirreling away as many fine details as I could. Less than half were children, and all the workers were uniformly missing fingers or, in a few cases, limbs. The youths had sloped spines and crooked legs, and every worker sneezed or coughed regularly.

I'd seen enough. No guilder child would have ever been raised like this. No sane person would rob a youth of their entire future for a few years of labor. I raised the neck of my shirt to cover my nose and set off on the shortest path from town, toward Mother's old house. The two guards did not follow, merely waved, their faces still masks of confusion.

Factories, steam power, mass production, they were not sustainable, nor were they ethical. We'd had a perfectly working economy and livelihood and factories were a step backward. And if I couldn't fix the guilders we would have to find another way to revitalize the Gasta Fletcha economy because the factories, every single one, had to be destroyed. With or without Magda's consent.

To: Import Captain, Thistle Landing, Pleila Island

Captain, we need you down at the docks as soon as possible. I've got a steamer ship filled up with Sorpsi's logs that were meant for our fuelwood, but the captain says he got a better offer and unless we can match it, he's turning around and headed farther down the island chain.

I can't compete with the amounts he's talking about. Shipbuilders have deeper pockets and truly, we could burn tiny branches for fuel if needed. You want to try to negotiate, or you want me to tell the captain where he can put his giant trees?

- Kahoda Vad, Dock Master

Chapter 11 — Fungus

"Magda really wants to leave tomorrow morning?"

"Yes, right at daybreak. I thought she might want a day to sleep. Iana knows I could use it. But when she gets overwhelmed her first step is always to fix anything and everything she can. She thinks she can fix the guilds, the damage of our mothers, Sorpsi and Gasta Fletcha, if she rides tomorrow morning."

"You could stay for a while, couldn't you? Our introductions were cut short, but I see the way you look at my shirts. I have tailors I could introduce you to, and fiber blends that will ease your breathing. I know the strain of difference when you are young."

"Potentate Jun, thank you for the offer. I wish...maybe I can travel back in a month. But I worry about Magda, Queen Magda, traveling alone. Not due to safety—she could take any bandit that came at her—but because I don't think she will sleep or eat without oversight. I've known her too long."

"I understand. The Lady and Lord of Puget are similar. I feel like I'm the only adult in the triarchy, sometimes in all of Puget. The crush of items to deal with is ever expanding. I now handle all our international trade deals, as well as guildhalls and finances. Sorting out this debacle of magic will fall on me as well."

"That's an unfair burden."

"People like us have had to learn to ration our energy and time, and our rage. But we have the evening, right? I want to hear everything about you, Sorin of Thuja. I want to understand that fresh woodcutter tattoo on your neck, and the magic of your mother, and to hear about your bone oil wonder. I want to answer your questions about our festival of Tii and why we celebrate the founding of Gasta Fletcha. If there is time, I'd like to ask you questions about magic. I'm afraid I don't understand enough about it to prepare for the weeks ahead."

It was deep in the Thujan forest that I found another rubble foundation, even more familiar than the last. The forest had already claimed what remained of the wood framing, but the hearth still stood, and Mother's cast iron pots still hung just above the fireplace. The wood framing of the house, the furniture, the clothes and tools and memories, had exploded due to a combination of chemical fumes and careless kidnappers—a memory I was not keen on revisiting.

Returning to Mother's house, my house, had always been inevitable. I'd never thought I'd find it welcoming. The ease may have come from what wood I could find being half-covered in elf's-cup fungus, or that the longhouse we'd used for storage still stood as pristine as the day I'd left.

I saw no signs of Jun, but to be fair I had no idea how long it took to reshoe a horse either. It was my brother I expected to see.

"Sameer?" I saw no footprints in the duff, nor camping equipment. The longhouse was far enough from the house that the explosion had done no more than dent the cedar plank. If Sameer had arrived before me, it was the only shelter in sight.

The door creaked as I pushed it open, an artifact of the humidity and disuse. Six old marqueteries still lay propped against the wall, covered in old cloths. A small writing desk I'd made myself of yellow cedar sat in the opposite corner, dusty but still stocked with paper and ink. The bookshelf above it was still stuffed with decaying books that Mother had thought essential I read, and I had studiously ignored. Who had time for reading when the world was filled with fungi to explore?

"Sameer? Are you here?"

Large footprints arced in the packed dirt floor, and a half-open duffle spilled blankets by the near wall. Perhaps I'd missed him in Thuja. He'd be back before nightfall, certainly. I had letters to write while I waited.

I'd a respectable three paragraphs down, mostly detailing disfigured children, when a voice I did not want to hear said, *You work well with magic.*

"It was a desperate moment."

There will be many of those moments, moving forward. Especially if you want to destroy the factories. Magic is your ally.

"Magic is completely unreliable and doesn't follow the rules of the natural world. Please be quiet so I can write this letter."

Magic has rules, you just don't understand them. You fear what you don't understand but expect everyone to have intuitive understanding when they don't understand you.

"This isn't how you win me over to your magic cause," I spat.

I'm appealing to your logic. You've toyed with magic your whole life. You've worked it into your fungal mythology, even. Have you never asked why the foxfire lights for you? Why the amulets are drawn to you?

"I am a chemist and I'm not listening to you anymore. Whatever spirit you are, you can wait at least until I write this letter."

The time for patience is running out.

"I would progress more quickly if you shut up."

"Sorin?" Jun's voice called from outside. "Good grief Sorin, are you in there? Please tell me you aren't sifting through the rubble of the house."

"In the longhouse. Hold on."

I opened the door to Potentate Jun, still in mud and cotton-covered boots, short chestnut-brown hair braided along the hairline and patchy with cotton fluff. A grazing horse, tied to a nearby tree, was equally bleached but did appear to have all of its shoes.

In the quiet of the forest, in the bones of my childhood, contemplation was inevitable. The last Jun and I had been in each other's presence had been right after I'd inadvertently murdered the queen of Sorpsi, and had to deliver the bad news about the state of the continental guilds. Jun was one third of the ruling body of Puget, the northern-most country on the continent. Jun was also the first person I'd ever met that wore a cloth binding across the chest. And now Jun was here, in my forest, at my longhouse, and we had...not all the time in the world, but an evening at least. "I'm really glad you're here, Jun," I said. "Thank you for your help at the factory. And the bindings you sent. And for writing to me even when I was too busy to write back."

Jun smiled. "You're dear to me, Sorin. Although," Jun said with a shiver, "it's freezing! Shall we start a fire? And have you finished your letter? I've got a woman coming by tomorrow to collect it. Your urgency was palpable and I doubted you wanted to wrangle a feral pigeon."

Iana bless Jun for her consistent thoughtfulness. "Thank you, for the courier and the thought. I need a bit more time with the letter but of course I want you to stay the night. Although"—I pointed due south—"don't you have a ball at Eastgate to attend? Magda says royalty is never late." I could hear the overeagerness in my voice that Jun might stay, and decided not to be embarrassed about it.

Jun waved a gloved hand. "You haven't responded to the last three letters I've sent and I know you can get caught up in that head of yours. This house isn't more than a ten-minute walk off the main road from Puget to Eastgate. It will be easy enough to start off in the morning. Besides," Jun winked, "I have questions. It's true my horse threw a shoe but we only left the trail and found the longhouse due to a foxfire trail. You're the only one I know who can make foxfire glow like that. I'm wondering if you know why that happens?"

As a youth you were as porous as bone. As porous as oak. You carry magic just as well.

"Ugh, I am a *chemist*," I said. "I am not interested in the mechanics of leached continental magic. The foxfire can bugger off." Although speaking of nighttime, where was Sameer? I'd had a long day of travel and as much as I'd wanted to see Jun again, I needed to get my letter to Magda sorted. I would take down the factories without her approval, but it would be so much easier if she and I were on the same side.

"I believe magic does not want to leave you alone, but that's a conversation for another time. We once again have the evening and so much to catch up on. To help settle your nerves after that factory tour—I can only imagine what you saw—why don't we tackle a chemistry problem?" Jun patted the satchel at her—their?—hip. The sawyers were right, we couldn't keep playing at pronouns forever, but I simply didn't have the brainpower at the moment. The plural would have to do.

Jun spread the bag opening to reveal two bone amulets. Both clearly heavy with contents as the straps strained against Jun's shoulder. "What do you think? Shall we do chemistry? I've wanted to watch you work for months now. Magda sends updates so I know some of your progress." They thrust the bag to me. "I confess after our last chat I did some reading on magic. I'm utterly smitten on the history, the way of life, the very concept of it all. Have you found much on it? What do you think? To that end, what do you think of these artifacts? How much magic do you think resides in each? How does one even *quantify* magic?"

Your key to releasing the guilder skills is in that bag. Between these and the ones Sameer has brought, you will be able to completely change the course of Gasta Fletcha.

"I just want things to go back to how they were," I whispered.

Jun continued. "These are the ones I wrote about, from the treasury."

I lifted one of the amulets from the satchel. It sucked at my skin the way the other had, pulling at me with the weight of the magic it held. It had the same boat carved onto the surface. I quickly tossed it back to the bag.

"Everything alright?"

"I don't know? It's best you hold onto it, for now." I offered back the bag, which Jun did not take.

"You don't even want to look? You don't want to take them back to your laboratory?"

With a long sigh I said, "I'm not even sure the laboratory will be there when I get back. Magda has been full of orders recently."

Jun sat on the edge of the desk, crossed their legs, and rested their chin on their palms. "Royalty are not always the best informed on subjects of science. She may also simply have no more interest, or time to dedicate to them. I'm one third of the triarchy of Puget and even I feel pulled thin sometimes. Magda must be like a spinning top with her duties. But"—Jun tapped the bag—"I'm royalty, and I'm here. I want to see what you've found. I've made a study of amulets since meeting you. I think I've fantasized a hundred possible outcomes just on the ride here, of what these new ones could be. These are fascinating amulets, Sorin. We don't have any record of their making. There could be anything inside, along with the magic. There could be...dragons!" Jun giggled, a noise I'd never heard them make before.

"I suppose," I said, letting my imagination stray to the absurd. "Or faeries? Oh, I know! Therere unicorns in them!"

Jun dissolved into laughter and I followed suit, our giggles silencing the birds and sending the foxfire around my feet to light.

"Oh, oh my dear chemist. Here, let me catch my breath." Jun sucked in a belly full of air and continued. "Maybe they don't have dragons, but surely they have something wonderful. They could be the key to unlocking the guilder skills, too! Or setting magic free and unbound across Gasta Fletcha. Or maybe a tie to our past, to a simpler time. Historically magic was our only tool. Did you know that? On the boats, before our ancestors found Gasta Fletcha. Our festival of *Tii* celebrates the spirits and the forming of Gasta Fletcha, but if you read back far enough it's not spirits they're celebrating. It's *magic*."

"And magic really isn't that far from unicorns."

Jun grinned. "Quite right! And in case we want a herd of dragons, I even brought a few wood amulets, just in case you needed more. Do you have your bone oil? How long does it take to make? I'm certain we could find a rabbit or cui carcass around if needed. Should we prepare for flying lizards as well?"

The idea of actually extracting sobered me. "I...there's no guilders. It does no good to release the skills to the air. There are too many variables, Jun, and we've got a longhouse and a dirt floor. Just like with dragons and unicorns, we don't want to be underprepared with magic. Who knows what additional factors the bone amulet could add?"

"And you have absolutely no curiosity around that? The Sorin I know would be itching to experiment. And that Sorin certainly did not cower from queens."

"I... They're good points." I loved chemistry, and puzzles, and being around some who intrinsically understood what it was like to have a strip of cotton choking the air from you at any given moment. But no chemist worth their salt reported data from just one experiment. If I was going to defy my queen, it had to be for a properly set up and executed experiment.

"I don't think I have an experiment in me tonight but if you give me time to prepare, I could do one in the morning— an experiment that will take your breath away."

"Really? Alright then!" Jun hopped from the desk and dumped the contents of their pack onto the dirt floor. "The longhouse is dry enough for camping. I have food to share if you don't. Why don't I stay the night before heading on and you can fill me in on life with Magda? Or life as the Master Chemist?"

"We've never had more than an hour together. It would be nice to ignore politics and maybe discuss... our similarities?"

Jun's smile was brighter than a sunrise. "Oh, I'd love that, Sorin. In the morning?"

I nodded and we finished setting up our nighttime routines in silence. The sun had dipped below the treeline and it would be too dark to travel the forest trails now. Sameer would have to overnight in Thuja.

"Why did you bring the bone amulet with you?" Jun asked as they brushed unseen dirt from their bedroll. "Especially if Magda told you not to toy with it?"

"It didn't give me an option," I replied with a yawn.

"Any idea why?"

You know why.

I hauled off my boots and scooted down into the bedroll. "Because magic follows me around like a lovesick schoolboy who won't take no for an answer. I can show you in the morning."

"I suppose that's fair. You act like magic had a choice in all this though."

Flippantly, and with absolutely no regard for the secrecy the voice was trying to achieve, I said, "Apparently it chose me. That's a choice, isn't it?"

I once again had Jun's complete attention. "Did it choose you? Or were you in the right place at the right time, with the right Mother and the right level of isolation? Do you truly believe it chose you? Has...has anything lead you to this conclusion?"

"Can we just sleep?"

Jun laughed and extinguished the candle that was now our only remaining source of light. "Message received. It's late. I'm sorry. Goodnight, Sorin. In the morning, over breakfast, before we get to the bone oil and the bone amulets, I'd love to hear how things are going with Magda as well."

It took me a few minutes to realize Jun hadn't asked about the guilders at all. By the time I started to ask why, Jun was already snoring.

* * *

The morning was unusually dry for Thuja, with no dew clinging to the patches of elf's cup growing along the edges of the longhouse. I'd arisen before Jun, checked the belt on my satchel to be sure it was secured for our later travel, then headed back out to the foundation, hoping to see signs of Sameer. Instead, I'd been greeted by fungi—my fungi, the ones I'd seeded years ago that now blanketed the downed wood, their blue-green pigment so bright against the charred black. Child-me had dreamed of a field of the perfect mushroom cups one day, and to cement my master title in the alchemical guild. Then it had turned out alchemy was more or less magic, and magic was clearly evil, and even if I'd wanted to turn back to my birthright of woodcutting I couldn't have because the guilds had all been forcibly castrated.

Magic was forever at the root of my problems. I pushed a fingertip into the soil. "Magic killed Mother," I whispered. Then I made another small hole. "Magic destabilized our continent." And another. "Magic forced Magda to become a queen before she was ready."

The last impression was deep, my finger pressing down past the second knuckle. I pushed the soil like I wanted to push away my past, to bury it deep into the earth.

To be locked away when you have so much to give, is a cruel fate.

"Empathy?" I asked the voice. "That's unexpected."

Is it?

I brought my finger out of the earth. An elf cup fungus sprang from the hole in its wake.

"Were you locked away?" I pushed farther into the first hole and thought of my isolated childhood in the house that was now rubble. Again, when I removed my finger, another elf's cup appeared.

I was no longer useful. That's what the people said. I wasn't useful and I was dangerous.

"What skills did you have, that they were so concerned about?" That was what the amulets had always been used for—locking away skills so they could be used by others. Having someone else do your work for you, so you could profit. Whether it was stolen skills or stolen livelihoods, or stolen fingers of children, Gasta Fletcha had done this dance too many times.

I gave them everything they dreamt of.

I stopped playing with the dirt and looked up, like I was talking to a person instead of an echo. "What was your name?"

I never had one.

"Well, where did you live? What did you do?"

I lived in their minds. On the seas. In the boats. I gave them food, and tools, and hope. Eventually, I gave them Gasta Fletcha.

I crushed the new elf's cup in my haste to stand. "You *what?* What was locked away in these bone amulets?" I barely whispered the word, "Magic? Like...an entity?" Like a...spirit? The spirit of *Tii?*

There were nursery rhymes about the creation of Gasta Fletcha. There were silly songs that children sang while they clapped hands and spun in dizzy circles. Songs about life on boats, and dreams of Gasta Fletcha the dry land. But those were myths. Dreams. Oral traditions. And not a single one of them mentioned *magic.*

Broken apart and sealed away bit by bit, forest to ocean. I think you should send your letters, and read those books on your shelf before we speak again. Take care with the bone amulets. Be mindful of how much you can take on. I've no desire to destroy my savior and you've no desire to destroy Gasta Fletcha, I assume.

"What is it you want me to do?"

Help me be free, Sorin.

"How?"

Break the bone amulets. Extract the contents. Use me in tandem to reach your goals if you wish, but free me.

I had to have misheard. "You picked *me* to do this? The person with arguably the greatest grudge against the unbound guilds and their professions?" What a truly terrible choice.

Parts of me have already leaked across your continent. Disassociated bits can only wreak havoc. Witches play at control with only one slice of a greater pie. Free me, Sorin, and I can birth all your dreams for you.

"I...need to think about that." Oh, how I needed to think, without a magical voice whispering everything I ever wanted to hear in the most confusing way. And I needed books. History. I had to have more information. What did I know about magic? Functionally nothing. I knew a fair bit of alchemy, which was kind of magic, but what the voice spoke of was far more powerful.

Still. The guild. Sorpsi's, and Gasta Fletcha's history was on the line.

In the end I knew I'd make a deal to save the guilds. But I knew better than to go into any trade without a full bandolier of knowledge.

Any useful texts Mother had in the house were well gone, but her curated collection for me was still above the desk in the longhouse. One was gone—the dustless outline apparent—but I found it not a moment later under Jun's head as a makeshift pillow. Taking care not to awaken Jun, I took the four tomes dead center from the shelf, then outside, to the broken foundation.

Woodcutting By Generation I set aside immediately, along with *A Woman's Guide to Fret Saws* and *A Treatise on the Evolution of Marquetry*. The final book had more promise. Far more promise. "For as powerful a witch as Mother was, you'd have thought she'd want me to know the fundamentals. How does '*The Founding of Gasta Fletcha*' not make it onto her critical reading list? Did she think I'd just pick it up one day out of boredom?"

The bone amulet gave me no direction, and with Sameer still not present and Jun sleeping, I had nothing else pressing to do. I went back outside, laid back on the ferns and flipped through the little history book, skimming text. Boats and seafaring dominated the early chapters, the pages littered with nautical terms I did not understand and extensive sidebars on air farming. I slowed my reading at chapter five, when the boat found Gasta Fletcha, but any excitement the passengers may have felt was eaten by the dry prose. The final four chapters detailed taming the forests and building towns, interspersed with an intolerable amount of whining around the difficulty cultivating clay soils and feeding large populations. None of that was helpful at all to my current predicament.

I tossed the book back toward the longhouse. It landed against a cedar stump with the expected *thunk* and then a *fwip fwap* of paper. I sat up just in time to grab a yellowed piece of parchment as it came loose from between two of the book's pages. The looped writing was illegible in places, and the paper too delicate to properly unfold.

My anxiety set the foxfire glowing at my feet. I gently picked up the paper and read what I could without tearing it. I saw the boat carving from the bone amulet, at this angle the sail looking more like a lantern than anything else. 'Tii' appeared in numerous sentences, although contextually the word appeared to refer more to a body of water than the week-long festival I'd learned about in Miantri.

The edges of the paper tore in my hands as I rotated and peeled, trying to make out at least one full sentence. And there, in the third to last line, was what I'd been looking for.

We trapped the magic in the human bone from which it came. Those who could commune with magic became its prison.

Everything that came after had faded with age, or smeared with the oils of my hands. There was more writing on the back however, in a smaller, blocky print that did not follow the carefully drawn horizontal lines.

One bone amulet = twenty-five of wood. Bone is near fossilized – needs strong alcohol to move? Or a solvent not yet known?

Under that line was Mother's handwriting.

Wood found to be unreliable but suitable alternative yet to be found. Sorin toys with bone. Will monitor progress. Old King's process above, still unclear.

Every single moment it felt like my life might be coming together, that I might have finally shucked out of whatever future my mother had built for me, life slapped me again. No, not life. *Magic.* I wanted to scream into the dry morning air. Instead, I took a deep breath and held it, chest puffed out like a bird in courtship, until I gasped for breath and my thoughts assembled.

"Magic." I said, no louder than a whisper. "You really are the magic that made Gasta Fletcha? An entity entirely of its own? Who broke you apart into these fragments? How many amulets were found by the Old King, or by Queen Maja and my mother, and used to make the wood ones? Did they have a way to break the bone amulets so they could use you, or do you naturally generate somehow? Can you explain the mechanics of your life to me? Of any of it? Since I absorbed magic from that one bone amulet, are you a part of me now? Do my bones hold you the same way a bone amulet might? Are humans just, just one-way storage cabinets for magic? I don't understand! And I *want* to understand because if the bone amulets are simply straight magic, if you can help me control it...I could have all the guilders restored within a week!"

I received no answer. The air remained still, the birdsong silent. The only movement was the foxfire sprouting in a fairy ring around my feet, pulsing with a sickly green glow.

~~My Dear,~~
~~Master Chem~~
Sorin,

~~I regret~~ I'm sorry for being so abrupt. I'm sorry for ordering you about. That is no way to treat a childhood friend, and certainly no way to treat the person I would like to spend my life with.

I've written many versions of this letter, one of which Advisor Alibe was to deliver to you tomorrow. I've asked him to burn it. It was also a command, instead of a discussion. Just like I did to you. I'm sorry.

There are two items I would like to negotiate with you. The first, and the most important to me, is if you would consider marrying me and helping me rule Sorpsi. I have considered numerous other positions, but as you witnessed several evenings prior, it is in my nature to take advantage of power imbalances. I know you will always argue with me, but were you to be a consort, a Master, an advisor, my word would always trump yours. My temper *often* trumps yours, and I wield it more liberally than you do your fungal powders. Hence, I would like you to consider being a queen, king, or potentate, whichever word fits you best. I would like to be your wife, and I would like this to be the last time I ever travel our continent alone.

The second discussion item I believe you will like far less. Our continent has moved on, and no more time nor resources can be spent on the guilds and the guilders. I know you want to discuss this, but in this instance, I do not know how to negotiate. I know this is not the world you want, but it is the world we have. Losing the smith guild sits like an anvil in my stomach but every day we spend tinkering with those amulets, more of Sorpsi goes hungry. The factories feed them now. Industrialization allows Gasta Fletcha to enter into international trade. This is progress! Although I know you will not see it that way.

Will you sit with me when I return? Can we talk about this change together? Can we talk about ~~the~~ our future? Our mothers lived in the past. King Tunbridge lived in the past. Maybe we could be bolder with our lives.

Love,
Magda

Chapter 12 — Amulet

"Give me that chisel!"

"Mother said for me to practice, not you. You're supposed to be packing for the trip."

"If you give me the chisel I can finish this carving, show Mother, and then there won't be a trip. You don't understand. You're too young. Now give me the chisel! Hey! Get back here. Damn it Sorin, if you throw it out the bedroom window again, I will murder you. Then Mother will murder you again because she just refreshed the edge."

"Nyahhhh come get it. I like traveling. The forest smells like rot and the queen's castle smells like rice and flowers. At the castle I can play with a princess, not my toad of a brother."

"You don't understand anything. We aren't going to the castle. We're going to another guilder's home. And if we go, all three of us, I won't be coming back."

"There will be children there, too. And I can play with...wait. Why wouldn't you come back with us?"

"Sorpsi is a Queendom. I'm a boy in a matrilineal guild system."

"I don't understand."

"I know. And with how you're shaping up, I'm not sure you ever will."

"Any sign of Sameer?" Jun asked from behind me.

"Not yet, but day just broke. He lived a long time up on that glacier. I don't think he would have set off before he could see."

"That makes sense. Who are you talking to then? Has the courier arrived? Or are you speaking just to the pretty field of mushrooms?"

"No one. Myself. Maybe the foxfire." I turned and offered a watery smile. "I'm sorry. I'm sorry I was grouchy last night, too. How soon do you need to leave?"

"The ball is tomorrow morning and it's a full day ride to Eastgate Palace from here. Within the next hour. That doesn't give us a lot of time, but some. And I've missed you, Sorin." Jun put a light hand on my shoulder and my smile turned genuine. "How are you? Really?"

"Lost," I said. "There's just so much more to everything. In the woods, with Mother, it was simple. She made the decisions and I followed. We worked. We ate. We were a family that had roles and rules, and while I did interact with the outside world, it was always through Mother's lens."

"Mmm." Jun nodded. "Grandmaster Amada was complex herself, was she not? She went along with the Queen of Sorpsi, stole those guilder skills, to keep Queen Amada away from you."

"She did. But that action I...I understand. Magda's I don't." I kicked at the patch of elf's cup.

Jun squeezed my shoulder. "I would like to suggest, gently, that Magda may have more of a picture than you do of the world. She has lived in it longer. She has to rule it."

"I don't care how many tutors she's had or countries she has visited, she doesn't get to destroy the guilds!"

Wind raked across the treetops, further enunciating my rage. Along with the wind came the sound of horse hooves and a young woman's voice calling out, "Hello? I'm Iana, here for a letter?"

"Iana?" I said.

"Perfectly common name, especially in Eastgate." To the courier, Jun called back, "Here, to the longhouse. You can tie your horse to the gate." Turning back, they added to me, "I don't think Magda sees it that way. Regardless, be persistent with your views. You always have been." They tapped my back, where the binder began. "People can argue and still love each other. You and I may not always agree, but we are forever siblings, right? Not bound by blood, but life."

I let out a long breath, trying to push my anger along with the hot air.

"A new topic? You promised we would talk about the bone amulet. Maybe even do an experiment?" They held out two vials of thick, syrupy liquid. "These fell out of your satchel during the night. Are they the bone oil?"

I took the vials gingerly in my palm. "Yes. My now-wasted life's work."

"Enough self-pity. You're setting up a proper experiment, remember?" Jun waved the courier over, a chestnut-haired woman maybe twice my age.

"Your letter?" Iana asked, her eyes focusing and unfocusing in the telltale sign of a former-guilder.

"In a moment," Jun replied. "Were you a guilder, friend?"

Iana nodded. "I was a shepherd from Eastgate. I can still ride a horse—I had those skills long before I was guilded—but that's about all I can manage. Your letter?" Again, she held out her hand.

"One of those amulets could be a shepherd's skills," I said reluctantly, although excitement was growing in me by the minute. "Would you be interested in perhaps regaining your skills? I have a protocol I've been developing. I'm the Master Chemist of Sorpsi."

"Of course!" Iana's smile almost reached her eyes. "Your letter is my only one today. I've the time. Should I sit?"

"Yes. Jun, could you find two small bowls or dishes for me to pour the pyridine into? I'd like to try inhalation."

"Will that work?" the woman asked while Jun went back to the longhouse to fetch the dish.

It won't, but you have already sorted the work-around, haven't you?

I scowled down at my pocket, where the bone amulet lay. I had to make sure no additional variables had been introduced before I changed anything. That was just good science.

To Iana I said, "If it doesn't, I have a follow up," as I took Jun's offered bowl and poured one of the bone oil vials into it. I chose a wood amulet at random and dropped it in as well, swirling the syrupy liquid in the bowl. The second bowl I placed on top to prevent evaporation.

Jun asked, "How long do we wait?"

"Long enough for a vapor to form. A few minutes. If we had more time I would recommend overnight, but pyridine is an excellent solvent. I'm certain the skills extracted immediately. We just need the pyridine to turn to vapor so she can breathe it in. It's warm this morning. Evaporation won't take long."

She can only breathe in so much. But bone, bone is porous in all the right ways. Why continue to experiment when you know the path to success?

Good chemists don't skip steps! I hissed into my mind.

Good chemists aren't afraid of a breakthrough, either. Is your fear of magic worth this woman's dignity?

"I am not afraid of magic."

"Sorry?" said Iana.

I clamped my mouth shut. "Please put your face right near the seam of the two bowls. That's right. I'm going slide the top bowl back. The moment it's up, take as deep a breath as you can, then hold it. Alright?"

Iana nodded.

Jun leaned in as close as they could, utterly fascinated.

You're missing your opportunity.

That chastisement came entirely in Mother's voice. "Please, please go away. At least until after the experiment," I whispered.

Put the bone amulet in the bowl along with the wood.

"Why can't you leave me alone?!"

Put the amulet in the bowl. You don't want to make a mistake, do you? A mistake on your last experiment? One chance to get everything right, to undo generational mistakes. Put the amulet in the bowl.

"I..." I couldn't keep arguing with a voice inside my head. Having divided attention during an experiment would get all three of us killed. I lifted the cover just enough to slide in the bone amulet and gently swirled the container.

"Are you ready?"

Again she nodded, and brought her nose to the bowl lip.

I tugged back the cover. Iana inhaled and I blew, trying to direct whatever vapor there might be back at her.

Our collective breaths gave out at the same time. Iana broke into a fit of coughing and I waved the remaining fishy air to disperse in the wind.

"Sorin that stuff is *foul*," said Jun.

"Nothing to be done about that. How do you feel?" I asked Iana after catching my breath.

Iana carried on with coughing, her arms wrapping around her midsection. I offered her a flask of water from my satchel, but instead of reaching for it she overbalanced and toppled herself over into the sedge below.

"Easy now." I pulled her back to a sitting position and managed to get in a few sips of water. The coughing eased, replaced by throat clearing and some very unladylike phlegm.

"I...*cough*...did not enjoy that," Iana said with the same unfocused eyes and halting voice. "I feel different, but only because I feel sick."

Poor form to leave the experiment unfinished, the voice said unnecessarily. *If water vapor could hold magic or skills then every resident of Gasta Fletcha would be a witch. Use your logic. The magic, and the contents it carries, was in the pyridine. You placed a highly porous piece of bone in the solution. Consider where the magic would have flowed. Do you want victory this morning, or permanent failure?*

I did not snarl, less due to maturity and more so due to not wanting to seem unbalanced in front of another guilder. "I'm not entirely done. Hold out your hand." When she did so I poured the contents of the bowl into her palm, making sure the amulet fell dead center.

I had thought the excess pyridine would flow to the ground. Instead it soaked into Iana's skin, flowing through the bone and pooling just for a moment into her palm before disappearing entirely.

"Count to ten and then drop it," I coughed into the fishy air.

Iana managed to the count of five before dropping the amulet like a hot coal, then turned a glare to me, eyes deep brown, lids squinted, teeth set. "Well? Aren't you going to apologize?"

"For what?" asked Jun. "The smell? You consented but I agree it is truly awful."

"No, for *me*." So much intensity. Her anger all but scorched the sedge beneath our feet. What had her guild affiliation been? Shepherd? It was time for a follow-up test.

"No, I don't think I will. I heard that sheep have to be inseminated by hand though. Have you ever had to do that? What does a sheep's, er, receptacle, feel like?"

"Squishy. Are you volunteering to help? Come spring we need all the slender arms we can get."

"Sorin!" Jun sucked in their breath. "Gods Sorin did you do it?"

A grin cracked across my face, turning the woman's scowl into widening, unblinking eyes.

"What else do you know about sheep?" I prodded.

"Three to a harness, as long as the harness is bound with iron clasps, not copper. That lambskin is tanned with the fur intact, unlike cow leather. I can see where the knife goes, how deep to cut, to remove the skin. I..." Her eyes blinked once, twice, then in a fluttering storm as tried to wash away forming tears. "I've never slaughtered an animal in my life but my memories are of a butcher."

"Rather, your memories are of the Trappers and Traders Guild," said Jun.

Damn it.

A success, yes, but I could no longer ignore my secondary problem. The old queen had never bothered to label any of the stolen skills. If the skills, and magic were functionally colorless, odorless, and weightless... there was no way to tell any one skill set apart. I could give the guilders back their skills, sure, but it was random chance which they'd get.

"I don't want these memories." Iana held out her palms to me, trembling. "Take it back."

"I..." I was about to say that I couldn't, but that wasn't true. I knew how to make wood amulets, I knew how to make the bone oil, and I was reasonably sure I could reconstruct the methodology for the skill extraction. But I didn't have the time nor the desire to crack open a few hundred amulets and my queen had barred me from my laboratory. "This was a proof of concept," I stuttered. I almost took her hands in mine, then clasped my hands behind my back instead. "Would you be willing to go to the palace for a while? I have a mass of other amulets there to try. Of course I'll have to remove the tanning skills but there's no way of knowing which amulet would better suit you."

The woman's anger flared again. "It's not shepherd skills I want, Chemist. It's *my* skills. Where are *my skills?*"

"Right, because we're all...oh." *Oh.* If I'd lost my woodcutter's guild knowledge, I wouldn't want to be assigned, say, wood barrel cooperage. I'd want to know marquetry, and fungi, and everything that I'd built my life around. Fitting to a guild wouldn't work. I had to fit to *each individual guilder*. Every single one of us, our experiences, our lives, our identities, were distinct.

That was impossible. It would take years. It would take decades. I would spend the rest of my life testing, extracting, and re-extracting. It just wasn't feasible.

"It was a noble attempt, Sorin," Jun said, wrapping an arm around me in a half-hug. "Although I see the sticking point."

Iana's hands went to her hips. "What does that mean?"

"It means I need time to think. It means I have to experiment. It means...for a little while, anyway, you may have to live with the guild you're assigned. It's not the right fit, but it's better than nothing, isn't it?" Then I grasped at the best analogy I could muster in the moment. "A poor-fitting shirt is better than none at all, no? Better than wandering around constantly searching?"

Jun snorted.

"I'd rather be naked and I expected, Master Chemist, for you to have a better grasp of what this kind of wrongness does to a person." Iana the Shepherd, now Iana the...Trapper...flipped her dark brown hair over her shoulder and stormed back to her horse.

Once she was out of earshot, Jun turned me to face them. "Don't get discouraged. That was a success! It just showed a greater problem. But the worst part is over, right? You have the technology, now you just need a sorting system."

"Which is impossible!" I raised my arm to punch a nearby tree, but my fingers found themselves wrapped around the bone amulet instead.

"Maybe one small amulet can only do one small thing," said Jun. "What about having a lot of bone amulets release all at once?"

"That doesn't do me any good if I can't get the skills paired to the right person."

"Do we know for sure the skills won't find their owners if they are all in the same proximity?"

"I don't even know a foundational principle on which to basis this on. It seems like, no it almost certainly is magic, and magic is unreliable."

"Is it any more unreliable than what you've been attempting in your laboratory?"

I slumped against a nearby tree and slid down until my bottom hit the sedge and...a new patch of red and white capped amanita mushrooms.

Jun squatted next to me. "Sorin, look at me. You did it. *You did it!* You released guilder skills and got them back into a guilder! Take a moment to revel."

"I will. I am. I just..."

"Wanted it to be flawless the first time?"

"Yeah."

Jun sat, crushing amanitas beneath themselves. "You're working with ancient technology, did you know that? I've been reading about amulets and the founding of Gasta Fletcha since you showed up at our palace. The history is fascinating. The bone amulets date back to the founding of the continent. They are made from the first settlers, their corpses! They're containers, just like the wood amulets but clearly must hold something other than skills."

I ran my tongue over my front teeth and remained silent.

"Do you want to know *my* hypothesis? I think those old bone amulets are filled with magic. I think the original settlers locked magic away in them, and I think before they settled, when they lived on the boats, they farmed magic. And you, you Sorin, you've unlocked it! *And* you're going to save the guilds!"

"Yeah. Yes, yes I am." The magic part I didn't care about, but Jun was right. I'd gotten over the biggest hurdle. Sorting skills couldn't be that hard, could it? And if the mass extraction worked, I could maybe have the guilds up and running again in a fortnight.

I got to my knees through sheer determination, my head still swimming from the pyridine. Amanita mushrooms spread in a fairy ring around me, dotted in with the blue-green elf's cup. Tiny antlers of foxfire, glowing bright green, outlined the imprint of my legs against the ferns.

Jun stood and offered me a hand. "I think Gasta Fletcha is pleased. You should be, too. I'm proud of you."

I took it and let Jun envelope me in another embrace. Jun's arms were as warm as their words and I adored how that felt. "Maybe. But how am I going to explain this to Magda?"

"Do you have to?"

Laughing, I said, "Are you suggesting I sneak around to restore all the guild skills?"

"How would she argue with a working guild system?"

"She'd find a way." I pulled back. "Maybe she'd disband the guilds anyway. Maybe she'd order me to lock the skills away again. I don't know. I don't know!" I kicked the top off an amanita.

There was a spark—bright red—as the red and white speckled cap broke apart in mid-air, wedge-shaped sections separating in perfectly even fragments that hit the roof of the longhouse and promptly set it on fire.

"Water!" It was pointless to yell. We were hours from the river and our house pump was unlikely to spring to action after such a long disuse. But the longhouse couldn't burn. It was my last connection to Mother, to my familial line. And the other books in there. Other writings. I had never once cared for Mother's history because she'd spent a lifetime ramming her thoughts and her dreams down my throat. But that didn't mean I wouldn't want that knowledge, someday. I certainly didn't want it to burn.

Jun headed, dutifully, toward the river, I to the old pump near our former kitchen. I worked the creaking handle and produced a decent gurgle when I noticed that the thatching of the longhouse wasn't just burning, it was sparking and shattering. The amanita wedges broken down, finer and finer, like a reverse of my red crystal. Every time they broke apart, another spark danced, and another flame leapt out. It was a beautiful chain reaction, a perfect illustration of the overlap of magic and alchemy. And it was burning the last of my history.

"Sorin, don't," Jun said from several trees away. They started back toward me.

I had to get the books. Without looking back, and without any real thought to the consequences, I ran back inside the long house just as the fire from the roof caught to the walls and the first of the support beams gave way with a groan.

I ran like bandits were after me and Magda was on the other side, patient and waiting and no longer trying to destroy everything we'd worked so hard to protect. I ran like witches were chasing me, which was hilarious as I'd absorbed enough magic to be a witch on a technicality. I barreled through the smoke and the earthen, pungent odor of old, charring paper. My eyes stung but the flames had not yet penetrated the thick wood logs of the exterior.

At the back bench I raked the dusty books into my arms, stacking them so high could hardly see over. Jun called my name, their voice frantic. Roofing fell down just to my left, letting a line of fire drip down. Inside there was plenty of fuel—old papers, drying jars of solvents, and moldy feed for our one horse. I did not stay to watch it light. I ran back to the door, toward Jun's outstretched hand that beckoned me back to the forest.

I made it to the threshold, where Jun's and my sleeping pad still lay in a clumped pile. The book they'd been sleeping on was open, pages ripped from its center. I tried to hop the bedrolls—a terrible mistake.

"Sorin!" Jun yelled.

The books in my arms were stacked too high. My foot caught first on Jun's bedroll, then mine.

"Almost there!"

I kicked at the fabric, but instead of dislodging it wrapped around my heel. I lost my balance. The last remnants of Mother's library smashed to the floor, more tucked papers flying out and immediately charring to bone black.

"Sorin!" Jun's head peaked through the smoke. I bent down to collect a book, grabbing simultaneously for one of the floating notes. Jun found my collar and yanked, dragging me backward out of the longhouse. Away from the last tangible pieces of Mother's legacy.

To: King Rodolf of Eastgate
From: Potentate Jun, Triarchy of Puget

Dear King Rodolf,

I hope it is as pleasant a day for you at Nuthatch as it is for us in Celtis. The seas have remained calm and fair trade winds have brought a bounty to our shores. It is this that I wish to speak with you about.

The Triarchy has placed me in command of our international imports and exports. While I deal mostly in lumber these days, I have found a novelty item – a 'percussion revolver,' that may be of interest to you. One could argue our little continent has no need for weaponry as we have yet to experience war, however one might also remind you of how quickly said weapon might have dispatched King Tunbridge, or Queen Maja, thus saving Gasta Fletcha decades of unrest.

Coupled with national security are my increasing concerns about our borders. Traders come with only money on their minds, but once the riches of Gasta Fletcha are known worldwide, I don't doubt others will come to conquer. I believe it is in our best interests to arm ourselves, if only out of an abundance of caution.

With Care,

Potentate Jun

Chapter 13 — Wood

Outside, burning thatching hailed down, singing our clothes and exposed skin.

"Let go!" I pulled back against Jun's grip, but they were older and oddly stronger than me. "At least let me get one book!"

"The smoke has got to your head. Get away from the fire!" Jun hauled me behind a cedar with a trunk too thick to burn. Everywhere bits of burnt thatching landed, new mushrooms grew, this time in greens, oranges, and golds. A forest that had once trapped me in its oppressive green foliage suddenly sparkled like fireworks.

"Your magic fungi never fail to impress," Jun said. "Are you alright?"

"I..." I was going to say that no, I was tired of fire and was going back to get at least one of Mother's books. But then it occurred to me. Amanita mushrooms had no explosive properties, not in their flesh nor their red pigment. It could be poisonous when eaten but that was a far cry from explosive reproduction. I'd tested the red caps exhaustively, far before ever finding the stained red wood of Flaming Dragon Fungus.

It was not a chemical reaction that had done this damage. It was magic, and I'd caused it. Gasta Fletcha—or rather the magic that made up Gasta Fletcha—had warned me that small bits wreaked havoc. Clearly, I had absorbed just enough magic for my emotions to be a giant liability.

Which further begged the question, what was the cost of magic? What were the limits? What were the *rules?* Without a guidebook I was just as likely to explode a person as to save them.

"Sorin? Are you alright? Do you know what happened?"

Jun's voice held the same tang as my mother's when I'd done something particularly ridiculous. Like not thin the shellac before applying it to a floor, or trying to sneak out of the forest to see Magda in broad daylight. The urge to tell the truth so as to avoid a worse punishment was so ingrained that my mouth took off before my brain could register the question.

"Aside from destroying my last ties to Mother? I did magic. Reactive magic. Mutated chrysopoeia. But instead of lead to gold, it's anger to fungus. At least that's my working hypothesis." My very fresh and new hypothesis that I'd formed in the last half minute that was a very good distraction from the guilt cinching my gut like a vise. Like any good chemist, I made a mental list in a desperate hope for clarity:

1) Magic was inside me
2) The magic inside me could be directed by me, both consciously (thoughts, words), and unconsciously (my big emotions)
3) Magic and fungi were related, somehow. The more magic I used, the more mushrooms there were. That needed more observation
4) Magic...created. It created physical things, like crystals. It created *fungal* things. Could it create other things?

I squinted my eyes and opened my palm. *Acorn* I said, very firmly, into my mind.

No acorn appeared in my hand.

Blueberry.

Nothing.

Elf's cup.

One tiny, perfect blue-green mushroom cup blossomed on the tip of my index finger.

So...fungus magic. Except the witches I'd met had not been so constrained. Was it because the magic was *in* me? Was my imagination the limiting factor?

"Raw magic," Jun said with a nod, bringing me back to the present. "You absorbed it from the amulets and now you wield it. I wonder if it's locked in your bones, now? Have you considered how to get the magic out of yourself?"

"I—"

Jun's response was cut short by a familiar male voice. "The house is already broken Sorin. You don't need to explode anything else. Iana help me how have you lived eighteen years without criminal charges? You blow up everything you touch." A man crashed through the understory, his thick furs catching on tamarack branches. He was a handspan taller than me, with the same deep dimples in the cheeks and chin and the same loose black curls. It was getting on to midday. He had to be sweltering in his glacier clothes.

Sameer snorted, first at the now-roofless longhouse whose walls had moved from licking flame to light sizzle, then at the riot of brightly colored fungi on the forest floor. "I'm happy to see you, though I'd planned on sleeping in that longhouse tonight."

"Sameer. You're late." It was the best I could manage in that moment as I contemplated my bones housing the magic of Gasta Fletcha, and that I'd destroyed his familial home, too.

"Since you couldn't be bothered to respond to a single one of my letters, I believe my tardiness can be excused. Now. Can I approach or are you going to blow me up, too?"

The familiar repartee bled enough tension from my jaw that I managed a sweetly sarcastic, "I'm quite done, thank you."

Sameer chuckled as he wrapped me in a hug. "You look awful, Sorin. And here I thought palace food would agree with you."

"Mmmph," I said from his fur-lined armpit.

"If you're saying 'you've never hugged me before so this had better not be suffocation,' it's a little of both. When someone takes the time to write to you, you write back. You also don't explode their childhood home"

"I've been saying the same thing." Jun smirked at me from under Sameer's elbow. "Mostly. You missed a show."

"I don't think I needed to see Sorin blow up the longhouse, but I'm sure Sorin'll just use it as another excuse to put off writing."

I elbowed Sameer and stuck my tongue out at both of them. "I'm sorry about the longhouse and I did mean to write!" I was deeply, deeply sorry, but there was something about my older brother that made it impossible to actually apologize to his face. "It's busy at the palace. Queen Magda was just coronated yesterday."

Yesterday.

How could so much have happened in so little a time frame?

"Yes, I heard. Parties and coronations and very pretty queens who, by the look on your face, you have done nothing more than kiss."

Iana's ban on men running guilds, or monarchies, made more sense every time Sameer opened his mouth. "Shut up!" To my left, an amanita cap exploded in a tiny *pff*.

Jun held up their hands just as Sameer made another attempt to smother me with wolfskin. "You two are a delight," said Jun. "Unfortunately, you've interrupted a delicate moment. Before Sorin caught the longhouse on fire, I had just been shown an interesting new trick of bone oil."

"Sorin destroying everything isn't a new trick."

"Oh shut it, Sameer," I snapped. A little, green-topped amanita near my ankle caught fire. I promptly ground it down with my heel.

The V between Sameer's eyebrows deepened to a gully. He dropped his satchel and leaned into me, inspecting my chin, my neck, and then my hands. He grabbed my shoulder, but I refused to let him spin me around.

"What are you doing?" I asked with a sigh.

"Trying to figure out where you put your new spine."

"Well cut it out!" I punched him near the ribs. I'd anticipated hitting layers upon layers of sheepskin pelt but instead my knuckles connected with a *clack*. A pouch fell from Sameer's waist, hit the ground of magic mushrooms, and spilled black bone amulets across the forest floor.

Jun knelt, scooping a handful of the amulets and holding them up against the sun. "A treasure trove. Where did you find this many?"

Sameer's left eyebrow raised. "I know I should have asked this before but, who are you? You're familiar. Did we meet you in Puget?"

Magda had insisted upon hours of etiquette lessons and here I was fumbling the basics. I gathered the amulets back into the satchel and handed it to Jun, thinking they would put the ones they held inside as well. When Jun continued to examine the three in their hand, I gave up and offered the satchel back to Sameer. "Potentate Jun, please meet my brother Sameer. Sameer, this is Potentate Jun, of the Triarchy of Puget."

A number of emotions crossed my brother's face before he finally settled on incredulity. "How many royals are you sleeping with?"

I tried to stomp his toes and missed spectacularly. "None, thank you."

"Shame. I was about to be impressed. I assume you're the new entourage then. Don't worry, it's always about Sorin so we're far less likely to get shot with a crossbow or exploded by fungi. So—" he took the amulets from Jun's hands with a bit more force than was necessary for friends. "Ready to go to the castle? Are we bringing all the fungus with us? You've filled the whole clearing with the stuff I see."

"We can't take the amulets to the castle. Magda…" If I said it out loud it would be true, and I was not ready to be at odds with Queen Magda of Sorpsi. The world had never cared, however, for what I was ready for. "Magda doesn't want to continue with the guilders. She's investing in the factories. I'm to destroy the amulets. All of them." I set my jaw. "I'd much rather destroy the factories."

"That seems incredibly reckless," Sameer said with a snort. "You're going to go behind the queen's back before you have any real job security? This isn't a guild, Sorin. You get found out and Magda could have you executed for treason."

"Magda can't see a path forward for the guilds because I've been unable to show her one. She's traveling for two months. What I need right now is to collect evidence. Get her attention." I slapped the pack of bone amulets at Sameer's hip. "Maybe take a day and restore a few guilder skills. I've cracked the fundamentals. I just need a few more trials."

Jun's hand went back to my shoulder. "Ah, there's my Sorin! Magda will come around, I'm sure. The other monarchs may not be so easy. You might need a different way of selling your point of view." Their eyes flicked up to the sky momentarily, in calculation. "The magic of Gasta Fletcha, fragmented and dispersed, is aiding you in your restorations, but is also a larger, potentially more volatile puzzle. Only a fool wouldn't want answers. Restoring the guilds also means learning more about the island magic."

I leaned heavily against a nearby fir as I watched the fire on the longhouse settle to embers. The main structure remained, roofless and charred black. There would likely be useable remnants inside, under the soot. I doubted any of us would want to hang around long enough to sort through it. The books, I could see from here, were already ash. "The guilds," I said, staring at the dying bits of orange and black. "It's the guilds, the people of Gasta Fletcha I want to protect. Magic can wait. It's *been* waiting. But right now, *right now*, I have to deal with the factories. Have you seen inside them? Either of you?"

"I've seen plenty, thanks, but yes I also saw the one in Thuja with the missing door," Sameer said. He kicked the top off a blue and green amanita mushroom, but all the cap did was fall back to the dirt. "I'd have known it was your work even without the cherry-red crystals spearing through the wood remnants. Those people, even if they were kids, would be out of work if you destroyed the factory. They have basic skills, sure, but you're destroying the infrastructure. It's great that you want to be noble, Sorin, but how would they put food on the table?"

"They'd still be alive and have all their fingers. That has to count for something."

Jun added, "One could argue that having a greater handle on Gasta Fletcha's magic could accomplish what you want in shorter order, but I believe all of us, our end goals, are the same."

"Really?" I pushed off the tree and pointed south, toward the village of Thuja. "Because what I want to do, right now, is blow up as many factories as I can. Safely, of course, but it would give me time to restore guild skills. Then, *then* if Magda still wants to insist on industrialization, the people would at least have a choice."

Jun nodded. "You have my aid Sorin, if you'd like it. I can't say I care for the direction Gasta Fletcha has taken."

"I...thank you." Turning the potentate of Puget into a fugitive. Turning myself into a fugitive, right after getting a royal marriage proposal. Iana help me, it would take more than a letter to explain all this to Magda.

Sameer held up a hand. "Feisty Sorin is my favorite iteration. I'm not saying don't move ahead with your wholesale destruction. I'm saying think first. Mother plotted the demise of a whole way of life too, if you'll recall. But she did it with a decade of planning and she did it with a queen at her back. *Your* queen, if I'm not mistake, is not so supportive."

"There are children with hunched backs. There are children missing fingers. Children coughing white dust!" The rage pooled in my hands, until I felt the jagged tines of crystals poking my skin from the remnants of the red fungal powder I'd used the day before. The amanitas around my feet grew taller, brushing the backs of my knees. Splashes of fire burst back to life across the longhouse walls, once again searing the air with smoke.

"I made a promise to Magda. I'm going to pause on the amulets. For now. But the factories? No. I'm going to blow them all up." I picked one of the mushrooms and brandished it like a sword. "Get the workers out, burn down the factories one by one until there isn't an investment firm or entrepreneur who will come within ten thousand kilometers of our island. Then I'm going to return the guilder skills, take it all to Magda, and force her to do what is in the country's best interest. And I'm going to do it in two months because that's all the time I have." I sounded crazy. I didn't care. Gasta Fletcha was made of magic, I'd consumed said magic and for once in my life I had a real substantive ability to change the world around me.

"I may not have a queen," I said to Sameer with a slow grin. "But I have a potentate. I'd love to have a brother, too. Want to help?"

"Who *are* you?" Sameer said. "Half a year ago you were whining on a glacier and now you want to commit treason. Although technically killing the Queen of Sorpsi was also treason. You know what, forget I said anything. You're still treasonous, just treasonous with confidence. But before you go burning down all the Thujan factories, consider. If you burn down the infrastructure, where will the guildhalls be? Most of the factories took over the old guild residencies. You're going to make the return that much longer. Also, what prevents the monarchs from just rebuilding? They're swimming in money right now. Also, have you considered that maybe people *won't* go back to the guilds? There's a whole world out there moving five times the speed of Gasta Fletcha. Why are you so invested in the past?"

Jun said something but I didn't bother to listen. Sameer wanted to join, I could see it in his grin, and the depth of his dimpled cheeks. But I could hear too, the challenge in his voice. The plea to convince him that we weren't following the same path as our mother.

I loved arguing with him like this, like siblings who had grown up together, stolen food from each other's plates and broken each other's toys, but stood together against the world. "We don't have to keep up with the rest of the world," I said. "We were fine before. The guilders will see that once they're restored."

"We do, if you want to keep importing indigo, or turmeric, or any of many trade goods that don't come from our little mote of land. We didn't know what we didn't have before. Now we do. People won't go back from that."

"Trade deals are Magda's problem," I said before I could stop myself.

"You want a life without cinnamon?" Sameer asked, voice dripping sarcasm. "Really?"

"No. Argh." I rubbed at my temples. He made solid points. "Maybe not mass destruction. But we have to get the attention of the rest of the countries' rulers. Jun isn't enough. Even Jun plus Magda isn't enough. We could rally some of the workers I suppose? Some guilders?"

"We're well used to petitioners," Jun said, edging between us so we couldn't continue to ignore them. "You'd have to bring half the continent if you wanted all three monarchies listening. You need–"

"A *rebellion*," I finished. Oooh. That *was* treasonous. A little ball of excitement flared inside me. In response, the mushrooms resumed their growth, making a slow but steady pace from my knees, to my elbows, then my shoulders. It was so very, very disconcerting, but I couldn't take down an industrialization complex in two months without magic, and I wasn't completely certain I knew how to get it back out of my body to begin with. I had *theories*, but those were nothing without experiments. We did not have time for experiments.

I steadied my voice and tried to sell a half-extracted idea. "Let's say I take out a few factories per country. To get attention. The other factories we still approach. We get the workers to stop working. All of them, until better conditions are met. We get the children out, permanently. Commerce will stop yes, momentarily, but if no one is working, the monarchies will have to treaty with us. Not just Magda. All of them."

"Give the workers an option of going back to the factories once conditions are better, or regaining their guild skills? Have them push for change, not just us?" Sameer ran his hands across the front of his leather jerkin and nodded. "It could work. It'll land us in prison, but it could work. Potentate Jun?"

"I have sway with the rest of the triarchy, of course, but the people have more. There's a history with Gasta Fletcha's people unseating tyrants, and I think that a large showing of angry workers will be more effective than any backroom dealing I could do. It'd be faster still with the harnessed power of Gasta Fletcha," they said, chewing on the inside of their cheek. "But let's use King Tunbridge's legacy as leverage. Start with Thuja, then work our way east. Quickly, or we will miss Magda altogether. How fast can you blow up a factory, Sorin? I'll write to the Triarchy tonight about the change in my travel plans."

I waved at the forest of amanitas. "About as fast I can grow magic mushrooms."

"Happy to be of service again, to Gasta Fletcha," said a mushroom whose cap now crested my head.

"Well, that's just great." Sameer headed to his horse. "I prefer ghostly apparitions to your talking mushrooms, Sorin. At least you know ghosts are up to no good. This business? I'm out of my element."

Our goals are the same, whispered Gasta Fletcha, in that voice only I could hear.

"I very much doubt that." I gathered the one book and notes I'd taken from the longhouse before its immolation and secured it inside my satchel, then mounted behind Jun on their horse.

"You say something?" Sameer called over his shoulder.

"Just that back on the glacier, when you led Magda and me to Celtis, I never thought that a few months later we'd be planning wholesale arson."

Sameer laughed as he nudged his horse to a canter. "Think about our family tree, Sorin. Think about Magda's. It's not like any of us have the moral high ground. You know how I feel. People should get a choice. Always. Even if their choice is to be the most irritating little sis-sibling, on Gasta Fletcha."

"Love you too, Sameer," I said as Jun's horse followed his down the weed-covered path toward Thuja. I didn't need to turn around to know that brightly capped, polka-dotted mushrooms and glowing antlers of foxfire would follow in our wake.

POSTED: POWER LOOM WORKERS

HAS YOUR BREATHING BECOME A BURDEN, PARTICULARLY NEAR THE LOOM?

HAVE YOUR BOWELS BECOME AGGREVED?

ARE YOUR CHILDREN SHOWING KNOCK-KNEES?

MEET AND DISCUSS WITH OTHER LOOM WORKERS THREE DAYS FROM THIS POSTING, DUSK, AT THE TOW-HEAD BAR ON THE EAST SIDE OF THE NUTHATCH RIVER, PUGET

GUILDERS WELCOME

Chapter 14 — Crystal

Dear Magda,

Can we meet in Eastgate? I'm on my way to you. Please try to delay your departure as long as you can. There are problems with the factories—problems you have to address right now. Children are being maimed. Deaths are rampant. This is no way to live, Magda, and no way to advance. I know you don't want the guilds back, but the factories are not the way forward.

I'll be to you soon. Can we discuss when I arrive?

With my love,
Sorin

Sameer, Jun, and I adapted to vandalism like we'd been born to it. It took so very little momentum once we'd mentally committed to destroying Sorpsi's economic progress. Did it help me empathize with the late Queen Maja and her slide from loving monarch to guild destroyer? Maybe a little. She'd wanted the best for the country as well. I was destroying structures, however, not lives. At least that was what I told myself. We were different, the queen and me. We had to be.

We waited until night to sneak back into Thuja proper.

Sameer cased the textile mill, ensuring no workers were present. Many of the machines were still warm and much of the spindled thread was tinted pink in tiny, round patches that spoke of children's broken fingers. We couldn't turn on the electric lights without being discovered, so Jun placed candles in the building corners and at the base of a few machines.

"You going to blow it up with fungus?" Sameer whispered.

Red crystals already poked between my curled fingers. I let them grow, thicker, their hooks more deadly, until I held crystals the size of large bananas. "Could do," I replied. "I could bind the machines together with golden mango fungus or coat the door and windows. They'd find a way to remove it though. I doubt it would take the factory down more than a week."

Jun frowned as she placed the last candle. "Crippling them is better?"

Magic isn't in any danger of being replaced by factories. You know that, right? Why fight for the dying when you could be embracing Gasta Fletcha's only truly regenerating resource?

"Go away," I whispered to the ground. There was no way I was viewing magic as a resource. A useful toy, I was warming to.

You need my help to control your fungal powders.

I said, as quietly as I could, "I'm freeing you, aren't I, when I break the bone amulets? Isn't this tit for tat?"

"Sorin?" Jun said. "Who are you talking to?"

"Just working a few things out." I turned away from Jun and Sameer and mouthed, "Please help me? You will have my help in response. I promise. I understand what it is like to be locked away. I can break your prisons, if you help me break industrialization."

Another silence.

"Please!"

A deal, Gasta Fletcha said at last. *Thoughts to actions. Desires to outcomes. That's how magic has always worked here. Visualize and manifest.*

That explained...a surprising number of my interactions with fungi over the past several years. It explained the foxfire trail in the northern woods that had led Magda, Sameer, and I to the glacier. It explained the glacial pool handing me an old amulet. It explained how I could always find elf cups fungi when I went out foraging, even though all our fungi books declared the little fruiting bodies 'uncommon' to 'rare.' Questions mounted, but Jun poked my arm before I could ask them.

"Sorin? Is crippling a few factories better? What are you thinking?"

"I'm thinking I have a country to save. A history to save. And maybe I have to use magic to do it."

From my satchel I pulled my red pigment pouch. I'd always had to be so careful to not let the crystals touch my skin, but that had been before. When their action had been a reaction of the natural world. Now I dumped the contents into my palm and told myself, firmly, that they would not bond and spear without my permission. "Please work," I whispered.

Sameer came up next to me and bumped my hip with his own. "Who are you talking to? Just now, when you looked at the dirt?"

"Myself." I held out both handfuls of red pigment powder, which I'd grown into finger-length crystals. Thus far, the reaction held. "Can you take these and put them near all of Jun's candles," I asked. "And Jun, can you take these"—I offered my other hand of crystals—"and lay them on the machines proper? I surrounded the doors and windows, and other weak spots."

"Liar. And this is a Thujan building. There is no shortage of weak spots."

Sameer placed his crystals in short order, as did Jun. I took a touch longer, growing crystals to just the right size to insert into the top of each spindle, hopefully ensuring no saleable merchandise would be recoverable.

"We've not time to do them all. Sorin, Sameer, we need to go now. We're running out of moonlight. I can see the dawn about to break and I don't want any villager being injured."

I was in total agreement with Jun. We followed them from the building, into a small three-walled shelter for horses some half a block away. There was no one about on the streets yet, but guilder time would take a generation to change. People would be up at the first rooster crow to head to work.

Sameer squeezed my shoulder. "Now?"

"Now." My eyes unfocused. In my mind's eye I recounted the placement of the crystals, of their shapes and sharp edges. I'd been holding those forms tightly in my mind, keeping their natural expansion in check.

I inhaled, held my breath for a count of ten, then let it all out in a big *pffff,* releasing my hold on the crystals in tandem.

The orange-reds of daybreak exploded into the sky, but not from the sun. This sunrise was filled with broken bits of wood, pinches of metal, and a dandruff of cotton. It was followed by a deafening series of cracks and splits, as the jagged crystal growths punctured stone, wood, and fiber in their way, expanding and growing until my eyes became too heavy to keep open.

It was beautiful. It was intoxicating. I had done that, controlling the crystals and the reaction and harnessing magic like it was just another solvent. *I had done all that!*

Reign yourself in, Sorin, or you will be leaving Thuja much the same way you did the last time. In the back of a cart.

I pulled back, imagining a blanket being thrown over the crystals that would smother their growth.

The cracking stopped.

Sameer's laughter did not.

"That's...that's very thorough, Sorin. Did you want to leave them any timber to rebuild with?"

My eyes focused on a red and orange crystal forest growing, seemingly, from a detritus of woodchips and metal shavings. At the base of the crystals sprouted fungi—amanitas, conks, elf's cup, in a micro forest all their own. Dirt devils swirled, refracting the morning light even more. Somewhere to the left, a rooster crowed.

"I may have let the crystals grow too long. The fungi I can't explain. Those follow me like ducklings."

"A direct cost effect," Jun said with a shake of their head. "I hadn't expected a firm ratio."

I turned to them. "Sorry?"

Jun unhitched their horse. "We'd best move on. Doors are opening."

The first cry came just as Sameer and I finished mounting our horses.

"The factory!" a little boy cried out, already in his long coat and carrying a lunch pail, no doubt headed for the work that would inevitably kill him. He ran from his doorway and across the square, stopping just short of the first spine.

People exited in clumps after that—men, women, children, and at least four people whose gender I could not readily discern. Sameer, Jun, and I wove our horses laterally through the crowd, hopefully looking like we wanted a better view, and not that we were heading out of town.

"Are the other factories the same?" a woman asked to my left.

"Still there. Those people can go to work. We're out of luck."

"Do they know the cause? Witchcraft?"

"Lady, you can see as well as I can."

"I'm seeing a bunch of red rock and mushrooms and that makes no sense to me at all."

"It's because of those flyers!" a young man called out. "About the meetings. It's retribution!"

"Looks more like magic to me."

"In hindsight," Sameer whispered as our horses cleared the crowd and we passed the city wall, "your calling card might be too distinct. We don't want to get run out of villages as we enter."

A cloud covered the sun as I frowned. "The only people who know about my fungi are in northern villages, and well outside Sorpsi."

"Six months is a long time for tall fungal tales to travel," Jun said. "Along with stories about your ability to control said fungi."

"I did *not* do that." I made a wide gesture back toward the knee-high fungal mat. More steel-grey clouds crowded the sky.

"It doesn't matter what you did or didn't mean to do. Magda will know about this whole thing today." Sameer added. "A pigeon could get to her in an hour or two. We may not have as much time as we thought. We also" —he jabbed a finger under my ribs— "do not have time for secrets. Who were you talking to, before? You whispered to the air. You have control over your fungi crystals far more than the last time. Are there witches? You mentioned magic. Don't tell me after all the moaning over witches and magic and spells and amulets that you've finally decided to join a witch guild."

"I would *never* join the witch guild, even if there was still a guild to join. Magda has given up on the guilds!" I ground my teeth. "She has *given up!* And I may be...dabbling in magic but the whole thing is complicated and I'm not going to let her destroy our birthright or the continent. Now let's *go.*"

Sameer brought his horse in front of mine, stopping our progress. "I'm going to need a lot more information. You're babbling and sound half-mad. Take the time and explain!"

"We don't have time to discuss the sentient nature of magic!"

My voice had risen in a steady tempo throughout my diatribe. On my last sentence my feet got away from me and I kicked my horse, sending the poor thing to sidestep. We might have recovered but a *CRACK* of thunder hit at the same time.

"Sorin!" Jun yelled just as my horse panicked and hit the wrong side of a stone.

My feet tangled in the stirrups. The horse went down and me with him, his belly pinning my foot against the hard earth. "I hate horses *so much*," I whined, sounding entirely like the petulant teenager I had been.

My horse scrambled to his feet, still spooked at the gathering clouds. The sky had been clear when we'd broken the factory, but this part of Sorpsi was known for its storms. Sameer offered me a hand up. My ankle held weight—a minor sprain. Another crack of thunder split the sky, followed by strokes of lightning. "If you can't ride, we'll need to take shelter in Thuja."

"I can ride," I muttered. "Give me a hand—"

Lightning struck the tree next to me. Fire erupted, sparks dancing off the branches, the inside trunk glowing a ghostly purple. The rain came then, hard and fast and sideways. The droplets stung when they hit my skin, so sharp I thought they might welt.

"This is coastal weather!" I shouted over another peal of thunder. "I've never seen it this far inland."

"Doesn't matter. It isn't safe to be outside," Sameer shouted. "On the horses! Back to town!"

Whatever else he said, whatever Jun replied, was lost to the howl of the windstorm. Sameer helped me mount back behind Jun. The horses wanted back to shelter just as badly as we did and even with the cracks of thunder, we were back to the town square in minutes, surrounded by villagers just as frantic as we were.

"Duckling Inn!" I yelled, pointing to a listing yellow sign. Gods, I didn't want to be back here. I wanted to go to the next town. I wanted to make progress. I had to stay ahead of Magda or she'd maybe send soldiers and—

CRACK. Crackcrack.

Lightning hit in a one-two pattern, first the inn, then a set of row houses. An entire block burned. The sky turned inky black and the rain fell in sheets, symphonized by the persistent rumble of thunder and the endless, almost pointed striking of lightning.

Villagers crowded the square with us. The thunder was so loud I couldn't even hear the cries of the babies sobbing in their mothers' arms. Sameer had me by one shoulder and Jun by the other, but there was nowhere to go. Building after building, house after house fell victim to the lightning. A bolt eventually found my crystalized factory, the hit splintering the crystal into tiny, spined artillery that peppered the sky. The shards split the remaining wooden structures, split the cobblestones, and upended every tree in my field of view. The ground buckled and sank in on itself, leaving horse-sized pocks on what had once been established streets.

There was nowhere to go. There was no shelter to huddle beneath. Sameer, Jun, myself, and the villagers could only circle like penguins, shielding the children and the elderly. It was only when every dwelling leapt with flames did the rain subside and the skies clear. When the remains of Thuja glowed brighter than the sun the thunder ceased, the clouds drew back, and Sameer, Jun, and I, like all the inhabitants of Thuja, remained huddled in the town square, watching our village burn to ash.

To: Queen Magda of Sorpsi
From: Sage Village, Eastgate

YOU ARE NOT WELCOME ON OUR ROADS
YOU ARE NOT WELCOME IN OUR VILLAGE
KEEP YOUR MACHINES, YOUR TRADE, YOUR
GODLESS, LAWLESS, SELF, FROM OUR LANDS

EASTGATE DOES NOT WANT WHAT YOU OFFER

Chapter 15 — Paper

Dear Sorin,

I am writing in response to your near-feral pigeon letter from yesterday. We have far better ones in the palace, you have no need to forage.

Of course you are welcome to join me in Eastgate, however I have been told that the roads are not the best for travel at this time. I have heard some about the factories and would be happy to hear your report as well, but I do not know if it is best if you travel here at this time. Please stay home for now. I will write to my advisors, discuss with the King of Eastgate, and see if there isn't a guard set we could assign you and a preferred path for you to take.

I know you are not a fan of patience, and I know telling you not to come will only convince you to do so. Instead, I ask for one day to ensure your safety. Would you grant me that?

Love,
Magda

"Flaming dragon crystals don't set villages on fire. That's nonsense."

"I think you understand the mechanism of your fungal powders as well as you understand magic." Sameer rode next to me, Jun on the other side, as our horses cantered down a dirt road toward Eastgate's border. The storm had blown through like a hurricane—a fast, violent roar that lasted a heartbeat but would take years to recover from. There had been no injuries but the destruction... Every villager in Thuja would have to relocate.

I hadn't maimed any children, but I'd ensured their next year was filled with a new set of hardships. Cold. Hunger. Heavy manual labor as the town was rebuilt.

Sameer, Jun, and I snuck back out amidst the wailing and chaos. It was either that or help sift the rubble for keepsakes and food for the village exodus. We didn't have time, but I promised myself I would return, with money, with raw materials, whatever they needed, once I'd finished this mission. I would get my pigments under control. I would get magic under control, and I would *not* be like the factory workers! I could see the effect of my actions which meant I could help rectify them. But in this moment, there was nothing left but to move on.

Sameer continued his angry muttering. "Thuja is charred wood and pebbles. We brought the magic that did it, too. I'm certain of it."

"I am, too," I said in a small voice. My anxiety had also been a part of it. How much a part I did not know, and the voice of Gasta Fletcha offered no opinions.

"An evil that only needs to be done once, I'd think." Jun brought their horse up next to mine and reassuringly patted my shoulder. "Royals understand displays of strength. You don't need to destroy another village for the threat to hang."

"We could spare a day to help them with the rebuilding though, don't you think?" I looked back over my shoulder, toward Thuja.

Jun shook their head. "How many fingers will the factories take in that day? Houses are rebuildable. Hands are not."

I could not argue with that, no matter how firmly guilt tugged at my skin. We took a fork in the road, leaving the cobblestones and moving to packed dirt. Sticking to the cobblestones would take us back to Sorpsi. Taking the turn would move us closer to the Eastgate border, to a town called Sage. I'd gone there a handful of times with Mother to pick up new steel for tools. Magda would have had to travel through the town to get to the Eastgate palace as well. The path, despite being dirt, was triple-wide and well known.

I looked to the now sunny sky, then the trail of fungi sprouting in the wake of our horses' hooves. "I think the magic I've absorbed is amplifying my emotions. Among other things."

Sameer gave a passive-aggressive shrug. "You are built on nothing but emotions. If you don't want to leave a trail of ruined towns in our wake, keep them in check."

"I will. I promise."

"Mmm," Sameer said with a noncommittal shrug.

We carried on.

Four hours found us at the small village of Sage, just across the Eastgate/Sorpsi border. It should have been a three-hour horse ride, but road debris had halted our progress. Sameer and I had hauled a cart with both axles broken from the center, and numerous wheels and bits of metal had littered the dirt path. Jun had made a comment about road crews and plenty of funding now that factories were producing, but as none of us had ever been to Eastgate, we could not comment further.

Sage, like all Gasta Fletcha's towns, was surrounded by a stone wall just over a meter tall. And like all original walls that had not been repaired, there were now numerous entrances. Our horses easily jumped a lower section which led directly to the empty town square. It was just past lunch time and there should have still been villagers around, darting into shops or lazing in the late afternoon sun. There were noises aplenty, but all came from shuttered buildings and closed shops. Leaflets littered the ground, others still stuck to the interior of the city wall or had been nailed to the surrounding wooden structures.

I dismounted and picked up one sheet, then another. Sameer and Jun followed suit.

"All yours the same?" Sameer asked.

"Yes." I peered over his shoulder and read the leaflet in his hands out loud. "No place for factories. No work for babies. Protect our air. Protect our heritage. We are bound by our families and our guilds and we will fight together, a union of workers for Sage Village. Stand with Klim, stand with Sage!"

"Like a guild for workers' rights." Sameer let the flyers fall back to the ground. "Exactly what we are trying to do. Very helpful. Let's get some food and see if we can't find the ringleader."

I folded one of the leaflets into my pocket then took a look around. "Inn? Doesn't make sense to dismantle a factory before we've eaten." I shivered. Was there even a difference between dismantling and destroying? Violence was an obvious option but there had to be others that were just as fantastic, without the corresponding property damage.

"Ruthless bandit is a good look for you."

"Shut up, Sameer." Although I appreciated his backward apology, the 'ruthless' part burned.

Sameer said, tone neutral, "You can make a different choice here, if you want. But Jun is right. Thuja's destruction sends a strong message. Maybe not the one you wanted to send, however."

I let out a long sigh.

"We can talk more at the inn. Factory destruction may not even be an option. I don't see any factories immediately adjacent to us. I wonder if Sage was too small for a guildhall or if they really did run every factory out of town?"

"Unlikely," said Jun. "In Puget, guildhalls are often in the more remote areas due to the presence of the needed resources. A town like Sage should be littered with them."

"Could be smaller buildings?" I finally spotted a standard swinging placard with a cup on it and started my horse in that direction. "Not big enough to interest a factory? We can ask inside."

The windows were shuttered, but the door was unlocked and the inside well-patronized. A young stablehand took our horses and two pieces of silver. The inn itself was warm and cheery, the walls covered in pelts and animal heads. A tall, lanky man greeted us just inside the door. "Where you headed?" he asked with a smile.

"To a table, hopefully," said Sameer. "Soup?"

"Only the finest," said the innkeeper. "I would like information about your plans first, if you don't mind."

He had steel behind his words as he scouted each of our necks in turn, no doubt looking for our guild marks. Sameer took a step back, right onto my toe.

"Ow," I said, loudly.

Sameer straightened the front of his wool vest, visibly bristling. "I don't think that's any of *your* business if you want *our* business."

"You're welcome to take your business outside of Sage then." The innkeeper didn't move back as he loomed over Sameer. The few patrons had gone silent, and not a single one offered a friendly smile as I surveyed them.

Villagers, remote villagers, were an insular lot. I didn't like strangers, either. Mother had hated it when travelers appeared at our door without warning.

I pushed in front of Sameer and said, "We've come from Thuja. It... burned. Did you hear?"

"You native there?" the innkeeper asked, although his voice had a hint of warming.

"My brother and I were born to a master woodcutter in the woods just north of the village." I turned, showing the tattoo Mother had forced on me. "Jun is a friend, visiting from Puget."

"And your business in Sage?"

I had thought to say "We have nowhere else to go," but hesitated. There were children here, at the inn, rosy cheeked, with all their fingers. A bit thin, yes, but this far from a city that could happen. Every table was handmade and bore a guild stamp. Every pelt was expertly tanned, and the mounted heads had handmade glass eyes. The quality was unmistakable.

They'd kept their guilds, and their town still stood.

Instead, I said, "I wonder if I might ask your name?"

"Klim," said the innkeeper. Unexpectedly, he held out his hand. "Yourself?"

"Sorin of Thuja, Royal Chemist. Did you write this?" From my satchel I took the flyer and held it out. "Queen Magda isn't welcome on your roads?"

"You consort with the Queen of Sorpsi?" Klim asked, the coldness returning.

"We are not on the same path at the moment."

"And what path are you on, Master Chemist? We heard about Thuja and its unrelenting, unnatural storm."

"Explosions everywhere," called a woman's voice from behind the bar.

Sameer put his hand between my shoulder blades—a comforting, supportive gesture that offered no guidance as to how I should navigate the dangerous climate I'd created.

"I'd only meant to destroy the factory. But the destruction was mine, and mine alone." I found my now-empty packet of red crystals and cinched it open. There wasn't enough left to do any damage, but the apple-red color of the fungus still shone inside the leather. "We will continue to target the factories but will find a different way to get attention from the monarchies. Your town is in no danger."

"Hah!" A person I'd not noticed clapped me on the back so hard I pitched forward. "And you told me to shoot, Klim! Glad I hesitated."

The person in question was a good three heads taller than me, with long, plaited hair the color of wheat and a moustache to match. They wore a dress of patchworked pelts over what appeared to be a corset. It was their smile that broke the mood of the inn. Conversations resumed, and eyes softened. Klim's shoulders loosened, and he pointed to an empty table.

"Please." Klim pulled chairs out from the nearest table. The pelted...man? Sat down, too. A young woman brought us cups and mead. "If you think Sage got rid of factories through aggressive pigeon-letters, you would be quite wrong. Thuja will recover. The factories have to go. Now."

"I...agree. So how did you–"

"I'm Idris." The mustached person sat backward on a teak chair with handwoven, bright blue upholstery. "It's an honor to meet you and know you like this, Master Sorin of Sorpsi. Shall I kiss your hand? Your cheek? A firm handshake? We write our own rules, right?"

"Yes?" I offered him my hand. He shook it so vigorously that a pelt slid from his shoulders and to the floor. He did not bother to pick it up. "How…" I had never considered how awkward the questions could be around names and pronouns. Mercifully, Idris was far more forgiving than I had ever been.

"Titles? Words? I don't bother with semantics much. Benefits of the height. He, she, they, make a new one up if you like. How about you?"

"I avoid them if at all possible."

Idris barked a laugh. "Fair. And you?" he asked Jun. "Two bright lights in this little town. Delighted to meet you both."

"They, if you don't mind," Jun replied.

"Polite. I like that. So tell me, what are you lot doing here, really? You'll find no factories to destroy. The road here should make that clear enough. Doubt you came to enjoy Klim's mead. He writes far better than he brews. On your way to the next target?"

"Shut your trap," Klim said, utterly without malice. "It's my inn and we drink what I make. Don't like it, go to Bunchberry."

Idris leaned in and winked at me. "Town of Bunchberry is choked with factories. Tuck in. We can tell stories after."

The girl came back with soup and bread. Sameer let into his without any sort of preamble. Jun, who I had never seen eat, picked up a corner of bread and questionably poked the broth.

"Where did your factories get to? You've been sabotaging as well? I don't see debris," I asked when the soup proved too hot to do more than sip.

Klim canted his head to Idris, who answered. "Along those lines. Nothing so destructive as you, Chemist. I prefer my villagers to still have homes afterward. Although I wonder how well your penchant for explosions plays in the royal court?"

Heat rose in my face. I took a large spoonful of soup to cover up.

Idris chortled. "Lovers never do well keeping secrets."

Sameer cleared his throat. "We didn't come here to discuss Queen Magda."

Klim finished his own bowl, wiped his mouth with the back of his hand, and said, "No, you did not. Where will you head tomorrow, since you've not found your goal here? The next village on the trail is Bunchberry. They've two cotton gins powered by a steam engine. One more village down is Trillium, where there's work begun on a sort of passenger transport called a locomotive. Past that and you're in Eastgate's Capitol City, where you'll find a host of factories and their associated smog."

Idris asked, face as mask of mischief, "Will you blow them all up? With that red stuff?"

"No!"

"We don't have a whole lot of other options, Sorin," Sameer said. "We might as well play to our strengths."

"The crystals are too unique. Too identifiable, even if I could control them." I finished my soup and broke off a piece of my bread to chew while I collected my thoughts. "We need time to make a plan, and we won't get any time if Queen Magda's soldiers can track us."

"You've other tricks?"

Did regret count?

"I don't want to trick anyone, and I've no interest in leveling another village. I could—I've two other fungi. One is a poison, not useful here. The other is a binder which would be more subtle. But Magda, Queen Magda, she would recognize that, too. What if we went with another option?" I looked apologetically at Sameer. "With less of a bang."

The relief on Sameer's face could not have been more apparent.

"Don't give me that look," he said as the innkeeper refilled his bowl. "You already sold me on explosions and treason."

"I think we might not need to blow up any more, but treason is still well on the table." I pulled one of the letters from my satchel, a stolen letter from the library. To Klim I said, "Your dissatisfaction with the factories isn't unique. Plenty of villagers are already considering leaving. They've nothing to go back to, however. But I like this, this word here. I saw it on your flyer, too." I pointed to it, then held the paper out for the others to read. "'Union.' We're all used to the guilds, of working together in groups for a shared passion and goal. We could bring the workers together in union. Bring the monarchies to the bargaining table. It would be a lot more effective than terrorism."

Klim gingerly took the letter from my hand and read it. He then set the thin parchment face down on the table and rested his elbows on the table. "I've no issues with your idea. The looming follow up, Chemist, is what do you do in wake of the factories? We've only trade skills here. One running inn, one smithy that can shoe a horse but little else. We get by on family gardens and trade economy. We made a choice to run out the factories, but truth is, our town will collapse in on itself without industry."

"Ah, but I've the means to restore the skills of any guilder. More or less. Wouldn't you agree that the workers are more likely to leave if they've got something to leave to?"

"You can restore the guild skills?" Idris asked. "All of them?"

"Most of them. I lost a few in early experimentation and there are a few quirks to work out. But generally, yes, I can. Can't do any of this without a unified worker front though, and a few good people to help lead them."

Idris and Klim conferred for just a moment before Idris turned back.

"You asking for our help?" Klim asked, loud enough for the entire bar to hear.

"Yes, if you'll give it."

The bar patrons leaned into one another, whispering. Where collars dipped, I saw the edges of guild tattoos on several necks.

"It's a dangerous gamble, bringing the workers in directly like this. They could all be tried for treason. They could all be executed. You need to know that," Sameer said.

"Is this any more dangerous than sending a five-year-old to work on a spinning jenny?" Idris returned.

"Maybe. Maybe more. But you have more to gain, this way, than the alternative." I patted my satchel, where my pigment powders were stored.

"Why not return our skills first?" asked the woman behind the bar. "Confused guilders don't make for a convincing argument."

"It would give you a chance to practice more with your magic, too," Jun said to me in a whisper.

Both solid points. There was far more power in a strong, fit union. And I had control over the magic now. Or at least, we had an accord. Gasta Fletcha itself had suggested a mass extraction could work. I'd already gone against Magda's wishes. What was one more infraction? It would delay us by a day, but that was a price we could pay if we didn't have to destroy more factories.

"It's only midday but I need to prepare bone oil first. We can spend the night here," I looked to Sameer and Jun for confirmation before continuing. They both nodded. "But if you can bring me a skeleton, cauldron, and heat, I can make the solvent before nightfall. Gather the guilders here at the bar. Between Jun and I we have several dozen wood amulets. It could be enough. The process isn't perfect. I'll explain the drawbacks and you can each decide for yourselves."

Idris' eyebrows furrowed. "A skeleton?"

"Not human. Animal. I use bones to make the solvent pyridine. It's chemistry."

"Sounds like witchcraft."

I shrugged. "That's a long conversation filled with semantics. You're welcome to come watch the boiling process if you'd like."

Idris leaned back in their chair, thoughtful but quiet.

"How many guilders can you accommodate?" Klim asked.

"As many as we have amulets for. How many do you have in town?"

Klim shook his head. "Ten, maybe eleven. They're hard to keep put. Many went to Sorpsi for your experiments. Others to nearby towns to seek jobs they could perform without any skill."

I patted my satchel. "I only have a few dozen amulets. Ten leave room for error. Send them all to me."

"Do you have pigeons?" asked Jun. "And if so, how many?"

Klim pointed to the ceiling. "We've an aviary with about twenty."

"If we're dallying tonight, it's a good opportunity to communicate with other factory workers. I'll draft letters to as many factories as we can. Although I don't know how to get them into the right hands."

"Can the birds find their targets at night?" Sameer asked. "Owners won't be there during the day. Anyone working at night is bound to be on our side."

"It's a good idea," said Klim as he crossed his arms and nodded. "No harm in trying. Bring the papers to the bar when you have them, friend. I'll see they're sent out in the moonlight." To me he said, "This is a big undertaking. You're very young, Sorin of Thuja, and you're playing with Gasta Fletcha politics. Are you ready for the repercussions?"

There was no way I could prepare to face Magda's disappointed, or angry, face. "Yes, I am," I said. "The monarchs just need to really *see* what their decisions have done. None of them want to be the next King Tunbridge or Queen Maja. Once they see us, see the workers, they'll negotiate. I'm certain of it."

Sameer turned to me. "I've been mulling this since Jun suggested it. The rest of the Triarchy are at Puget Palace, along with Queen Magda. You're going to march us all down there and what, expect them to listen and not open fire? Remember the reception we got last time we crashed a royal gathering? And that was way before you decided you understood continental trade."

"I've already written one letter informing them of my tardiness. A more specific correspondence detailing the issues we are bringing for discussion is likely in order. I can add it to my list. My voice may soothe where Sorin's would not." When Idris' head cocked in confusion, Jun showed their own tattoo, of the royal crest of Puget. "Potentate Jun," they said.

"An honor, friend," replied Idris. "Didn't know royalty was at the table. Didn't know royalty could look so bright, either. Aren't we three a thing? A dangerous thing!"

Jun laughed in a way I'd never heard before, a deep belly laugh that spread across their face in a rainbow of delight. "Fireflies are everywhere. I'm so glad you've left the Capitol, Sorin, so you can see them, too."

The tension of the room broke. Our cups were refilled once again, the mead sweeter with each round. I had bones to boil and magic to perform but in that moment, that one, drunk, village moment, I felt completely at home.

"I was...a giant pain in the backside, wasn't I, Sameer?" I asked my brother when my cup once again ran dry. "On the glacier."

"Still are sometimes, but you're my giant boil in the backside. One I can't lance but who has grown on me. And grown up. Good thing too, if you're bedding queens." He winked.

"We do not need to keep bringing up my romantic life."

Idris said, "I wouldn't mind hearing more about it."

I pushed from the table, my bread and soup finished, my head spinning. "Jun, can I help you with the letters until the villagers have found enough bones?"

Jun took a solitary piece of paper from her bag and handed it to me. "You can. After Thuja I thought that one of us should write Magda a letter. If we are going through with the unions, with this strike, if we are going to meet in Nuthatch at the Eastgate castle, with you in tow, I don't think it should be a surprise. Write to Queen Magda, Sorin. She doesn't need to know what we're doing, but she does need to know what is at stake and what her choices are. Let her know, quite specifically, that it isn't just Sorpsi that is at stake, but you as well."

"A ransom letter, or a threat?" I asked, horrified. "Magda does not do well with either. Nor surprises. This sounds like a horrible letter."

Sameer bopped me on the nose. "I agree completely with Jun on this. Which is why you're the one who is going to write it."

Chapter 16 — Words

Dear Magda,

I hope your travel has been safe. I have not, as promised, been back to my laboratory, however my visit to Thuja surprised me with both Sameer and Jun. It also allowed me to see the factories in person.

Have you seen them? Have you been inside? Magda, they're horrible. The conditions are awful. But I'm not writing about that.

What you need to know is this. I can return the guilder skills with a reasonable degree of accuracy. The factories are not viable as they are. With skills returned, the people of Gasta Fletcha have a choice. They didn't have one before. They want a chance to discuss that choice with you, with the king of Eastgate, and with the Triarchy.

Jun, Sameer, and I are headed to you. We will meet you in Nuthatch, at the palace. There will be guilders with us, and factory leaders. Beginning tomorrow they will not be working in the factories until the monarchies have sat down with them for bargaining.

We must reach consensus. Until then we will strike the sails of incoming trade ships. No new goods will be produced, sent out, or money brought in. Gasta Fletcha stops until the village voices are heard.

The guilders, the factory workers, the traders, we are a union of shared labor and grievance. We will be heard.

Hear the people the way you hear me. See them the way you finally see me. Please, Magda.

With my love,
Sorin

I'd forgotten how slow evaporation progressed in high humidity. The bone oil did not set until early the next morning. As I set up the extraction in the inn's kitchen over a cauldron big enough to cook Sameer, thirty-three mounted riders lodged at the inn—a group of adults and children intent on riding with us to Nuthatch.

A final count of wooden amulets came to sixteen. From the village we'd found ten guilders willing to try their hands at restoration. Hence, I had a few empty slots, so I went out to meet the newcomers.

"I am Sorin of Sorpsi, the queen's Chemist and the one who has been working on restoring your skills. I believe I have found the correct methodology. If any of you are guilders, you are invited to join me in the kitchen for an experiment. If you would like a chance at your skills. Riding with a sense of self will be less dangerous, too. I cannot guarantee the perfect fit, so if you are uncomfortable with the magic assigning as best it can, I'd advise you to wait."

Four dismounted, all adults, and followed me inside where Sedge's guilders waited. A shallow serving dish of drinking ethanol awaited us on the bartop. Sunken to the bottom were the bone amulets I'd drained of magic, now heavy with the skills I'd extracted from the wood amulets, into the ethanol. "Sit around," I told them. "Hold out your hands."

"Is the number sufficient?" I whispered into the cauldron as I took one final stir of the bone oil.

Do you believe it to be?

"Would you give me a straight answer?"

I gave you the rules you asked for. It is not my fault you cannot follow them. You have done this successfully before. Is there any reason to think it would not proceed in the same way this time?

It was right. And, I reminded myself, Gasta Fletcha had a vested interest in releasing the contents of the bone amulets as much as I did as releasing the contents from the wood ones.

The guilders struggled with the barstools, and the slick finish of the wood. Guilders without skills, without identities, were as clumsy as toddlers. As clumsy as I had been just a year ago. "Close now. As close as you can get." I didn't need to be flinging bone oil around. When they were cheek to cheek, some kneeling on the bar even, I used tongs and placed one of Sameer's bone amulets into each open palm. It would deliver a guild skill along with a dose of magic. Maybe a bit unorthodox, but we were about to march on a castle. A few more magic users could be useful. "Ready then?"

Heads nodded.

I ladled a bowl of bone oil from the cauldron and used an eye dropper to drip three drops of my solvent onto each amulet.

An immediate exothermic reaction occurred. A wave of heat blasted us back, off the stools, and onto the ashwood floor. The fine hair crisped from my arms and a man beside me had to pat the burning embers from his beard. But there was no fire, and no broken bones. At least not as far as I could tell.

I'd never done such a large extraction before. On a smaller scale the exothermic properties hadn't been so pronounced. Maybe this was a good sign?

"Master Chemist?" asked the man whose lap I was currently on top of.

"Sorry!" I said. "But thank you for breaking my fall."

"No worries," he replied as I helped him to stand. Everyone had ended up on the floor, but just watching them get up I saw how much more sure they were in their movements, and where their bodies were at in relation to others.

"Anyone with a good match?" I asked.

A slow, sure hand raised. Then a second, then a third. "Not my cooperage, but cooperage nonetheless," said a woman at the front. "It's a start."

"I've masonry," said another woman.

"Not woodcutting, but carpentry," said a man to my left. "As she said, it's close. It's workable. I assume there will be future experiments."

"I guarantee it." Multiple targets, and the skills had matched to the best of their ability. Had it been through magic? Science? Did it matter?

"We can sort the discussion on the road." Idris cracked open the door. "Daylight is burning, and the pigeons have returned without replies. Queen Magda has chosen not to respond. Nice work, Chemist, but you'd best move out."

"Thank you," said the first woman. She reached out to cup my cheek with her hand. "For your tireless work."

"Meet me at Sorpsi's castle next month. Bring every guilder you know. I'll do a mass replacement, then can precision extract and reapply from there. I promise I will get you your skills and memories, or as close as I can."

Sameer tapped my wrist. "We have to go."

I didn't want to go. I didn't want to leave the bright, eager faces of guilders once again filled with life and hope. But these guilders would need time to spread the word and bring others to the castle. And I had a job to do. I said, as confidently as I could, "To the horses. Then, to the capital."

* * *

Bunchberry Village bustled at midday. A cohort of older children waited for us on the city wall, one holding our pigeon letter and grinning.

"I've never had such a warm village reception," I said as we went through the gate. The children followed on foot, cheering and clapping like we were Iana's entourage.

"Realistically, how many villages have you even visited?" Sameer waved to a group of adults standing outside an unlit factory building. "You alright?"

I did feel lightheaded, but I'd also worked with bone oil all night and then ridden a horse for three hours. I was dehydrated, and hungry, and had spent most of the ride debating whether I wanted to apologize to Magda when I next saw her, beg forgiveness, or deliver our demands and burst into tears. "I will be."

"Not an answer, Sorin."

Jun's horse came up beside mine, blocking Sameer's line of sight as we continued on past the village wall. "Your brother is unnecessarily harsh with you."

"We have a history. Do you not have siblings?"

"None. But sharing a monarchy with a king and queen is a touch similar, I suppose. We can also come to verbal blows."

"Do you get on well with the other two rulers, generally?"

Jun chuckled. "As much as I think any shared ruler does. Their vision tends toward the forward, mine toward the past. The balance is necessary to run a country of size. I think we would all be better served with a less complex system, but it is near impossible to tear down established bureaucracy. We'd have to melt the entire island and start over from scratch if we truly wanted a novel system, or to return to one that worked for generations."

I'd just opened my mouth to respond when a villager called out to us.

"You are welcome!" Nearing the village square, an older woman with cream-colored hair waved back to Sameer as we closed in on a two-story brick building with boarded windows and four smokestacks on the roof snaking a thin coil of thick, damp smoke. Near the main door were two dozen adults and children with sooty clothes and gaunt faces. "We've just come out and stopped production," said the woman. "But there was a night shift at the steam engine plant itself four blocks away. Workers have been locked inside so they cannot join us on the march to the Eastgate capitol."

"There's this as well. Come for you at daybreak, Master Chemist." A man of around twenty handed me a letter with Magda's crest stamped in the wax.

"She did write back," said Jun, under their breath. "Interesting."

That was worse than her not writing at all. My insides squirmed like a trapped anaconda as I broke the seal and read out loud:

Dear Sorin,

Your tactics are ill suited for the politics at play. This isn't a time for stubbornness. I will meet you at Nuthatch, Eastgate's capital, with Sameer and Jun. You may come to the main castle there. However, I need you to accept that the guilds are not negotiable. Gasta Fletcha has pivoted to mass production. The world has pivoted to mass production. A chemist is not going to change that. If you won't hear it from me, maybe you will from Alibe, whom I've asked to join me here, or the King of Eastgate, or your friends in the Triarchy.

I need you, Sorin. I need your help with the transition between the old world and the new. I need you to lead the former guilders. To convince any that are as reluctant as you. You are a part of this change! In this one, specific instance that I beg you to not extrapolate, you need to just accept the world the way it is. Please, please stop fighting me.

With my love,
Magda

No one spoke as I folded the letter and shoved it into the nearest saddle bag. Sameer's hand did find mine, and squeezed it.

"As much as we have struggled," I said to him, "I appreciate that you never infantilized me."

"If you're old enough to defy our mother, you're old enough to know the consequences of your actions." We got down off our horses, and he wrapped me in a hug. "People don't always mature at the same rates. Think how your time in Thuja affected you. Who surrounds Magda now? Who is affecting her?"

I let my eyes close as I listened to Sameer's heartbeat through the fur of his traveling cloak. "A group of advisors." My memory flashed to Alibe, and our library interaction.

Jun said from somewhere to my left, "It's not advisors to be worried about right now. Meeting in a capital city means the royalty have full access to their armies. They have soldiers and guards and we have," Jun gestured to the shuttered factory. "We have an angry mob. It would be nice to have more even footing. Consider our one advantage—magic"

There'd been no sign of magic in the guilders I'd restored, at least not that I'd noticed. They'd ridden with straight backs and determined faces. I'd not dared to ask what skills they had, and no one had volunteered information. We all had too much on our minds.

"I don't want to get the workers killed. I don't mind destroying infrastructure, but I will not destroy people. To do that, magic is already helping us. What else do you want from it?" I broke from Sameer's embrace. "On the topic of time, I won't leave here without releasing the factory workers."

"I think you're not using magic to its fullest advantage," said Jun. "But outside of that, I believe the rescue should be done quickly. Magda is aware of our actions. There is no need for stealth."

There will be more bone amulets in Eastgate, buried along the coast. Think how many of your people you could help!

"*What* is going on?" Sameer demanded. "Why do your eyes get unfocused like that?"

"It's nothi—"

"Because the island of Gasta Fletcha is speaking to Sorin. Correct? Rather, the magic that made Gasta Fletcha is speaking to Sorin."

My eyes went wide at the sharpness of Jun's voice. "Jun…"

Jun's eyes stared at me, unblinking. Sameer grabbed my shoulders and shook me.

"Sorin, what in the—"

An old woman approached us, butting into the conversation. "The steam house? Perhaps your fight could wait? Or is it more important than those trapped?"

"Later," he mouthed.

Fight bled from Sameer's grip, but murder remained in his eyes as we remounted. With a group now some fifty strong, we marched along an unnamed stream that mirrored the city wall. This far into Eastgate the earth was entirely pastureland. Sheep, cows, llama, and alpaca well outnumbered humans. The chickens probably did too, although they dispersed at our collective noise and were harder to count. Houses were brick and mud, with thatched roofs low to the ground. There were numerous beaten dirt roads, all lined with tall stems of dandelion and queen's lace.

That made the rise of a five-story brick and metal monstrosity that much more jarring. At the apex of three streams stood the enginehouse, a windowless building with chains across its doors and dying steam piping from its chimneys.

"What's it doing here," Sameer asked the woman, "so far from your other buildings?"

"Pumping water from the coal mine just below. There's a hoist you can't see on the other side of the brick. We've people down there, too."

"Just pumping water?" Sameer got off his horse and looked the full length of the building. "Is it just an atmospheric engine? Are they still using water wheels?"

"I don't know," the woman said. "Never been in. I work the looms." She showed her right hand, missing the last two fingers. "My daughters did, too."

I took her hand and held it in my own. "I'm sorry."

She sniffed. "I'm done being sorry. What will you do here, Chemist?"

I turned back to Sameer and Jun. "Flaming dragon will ruin the building. If there's a water wheel I could just gum it up."

"I know we decided no more destruction, but in this case, take it all down," said Sameer with a sweep of his hand. "Water wheels and atmospheric steam engines haven't been used for fifty years or more, past the glacier. I've never seen one in operation. The oldest mills I've been to are using double acting steam engines right on site. Damn it." He kicked a rock into the stream. "Factories got here fast because the monarchies don't know what they're buying. This technology is obsolete. Outside of selling it to us I don't know why trade merchants are still here."

I did. From the stump-forests of Thuja right to Magda's own letters, it was easy to connect the dots. "Resources. It was in one of the letters to Magda. We never could use them to depletion with the guilds. Any industrialization is fine as long as the resources are thick."

"Gasta Flctcha will be bald in two decades at the current rate," Jun said with a scoff. "We've completely forgotten how to manage resources. We have forgotten so very much."

The ground trembled, almost imperceptibly.

"Stop!" I hissed at myself. "There are workers in there. You topple the enginehouse it's not just infrastructure, it's people!"

Jun's steadying hand fell on my arm. "Calm, Sorin. Look at the narrowness of the building. Whomever is in charge won't let the workers out for an earthquake, and there's only one door. They'll be buried alive. If the pump goes, then anyone in the mines that are connected to this whole operation will flood."

Great. I was an emotional loose cannon and the building was a death trap. I took two long, deep breaths. The ground stabilized.

"Who *is* in charge?" Sameer asked. "Maybe we talk to them first? Unless there's a relatively easy way to interrupt the machinery?"

"Shut down the mine?" I mused for a moment. "After we get everyone out? Although if we break the pump in the pumphouse we may not get to the miners in time before the mine floods, too." I sighed. "We need more time to plan. There has to be a way to just stop operations."

"We don't have time," said Sameer. "Soldiers are coming for us."

From around the backside of the building, twenty-some soldiers approached, hands on their swords. They all wore the badges of Eastgate's tiny military, which, if it was anything like Sorpsi's, was deeply out of practice but armed nonetheless.

"Disperse!" a solider called from horseback. "You are to disperse and disband immediately on orders from King Rodolf of Eastgate." The soldier brandished a shiny, new pistol right at Sameer's head.

"They get right to the point, don't they," said Sameer. "Where did they come from? The castle is still a day and a half ride away. They had to have left right after our letters arrived. Unless there is a post in a nearby town?"

Even if there was a post, Eastgate soldiers had no reason to be on the edge of town, near a remote steam plant. There was no way Eastgate knew we were coming. Jun had discussed sending letters, but they were as invested in the workers as Sameer and I. They would not have given away our intent. The only person who knew where I was headed had been... Magda.

"Magda," I said. The ground trembled. Horses nickered and sidestepped for balance.

"You're sure?" asked Sameer.

"Yes."

Magda, my queen, had sent Eastgate soldiers to stop me liberating a steam pump.

Magda had sent *twenty* soldiers to contain the person that she'd just days ago, proposed marriage to.

NOTICE: TO ALL WORKERS AT THE CEDRUS WATER FRAME PLANT

YOUR FINAL DAY OF WORK WILL BE TOMORROW AT SUNSET. THIS FACTORY IS CLOSED THEREAFTER UNTIL THE PURCHASED SPINNING MULE CAN BE DELIVERED FROM ACROSS THE GLACIER.

JOBS ARE AVAILABLE AT THE STEAM ENGINE POWER PLANT FOR THOSE WHO ARE CAPABLE. ABLE BODIED WORKERS ONLY.

WE APPRECIATE YOUR TIME IN OUR SERVICE

CEDRUS TOWN COUNCIL, KINGDOM OF EASTGATE

Chapter 17 — Brick

"Darling? What is the matter? I know you don't care about the linen colors for the feast after the ball tomorrow, but I do appreciate your effort. Are you exhausted? Theodor can take on your morning administrative duties if needed."

"I'm not exhausted, simply confused. I've received another pigeon letter from the potentate. Magda's chemist has 'round two hundred workers set to arrive here late afternoon tomorrow, just as the ball is getting under way."

"We could probably feed them all if I let the kitchens know in the next hour."

"Jun wasn't suggesting feeding them. The potentate is advising we meet force with force! They're suggesting the workers, the Chemist, will only respond to violence."

"Darling, politics are your job. The public is mine. Gasta Fletcha has never had a civil war, or even a minor country-wide uprising. The closest we have ever gotten was when Iana killed King Tunbridge, and she did that entirely on her own and no one fought her when she took the Sorpsi throne. Conflict isn't a part of our people. If you are seeking my opinion, then open up the palace and invite the lot of them to the ball. We can open up the second ballroom!"

"You aren't concerned? Not even for the city center? The palace?"

The King and Queen of Puget have spent the past two hours pouring over menu options with me. I would assume Jun has sent them the same information. Queen Magda is likewise receiving letters from her chemist, and I assume is responding with a level head. The workers may be hot, but we should not be. We will listen to their demands and, from what you have told me of the document you have all been working on, meet many of them. If we are lucky that will all conclude before the ball and then we can all get to the much more serious business of welcoming a new queen to Gasta Fletcha.

"You're right. You're right of course. I won't be the one to escalate matters. The workers have a right to their anger, and to be heard. I'll place a few guards out in the city just to keep us apprised, and I'll raise the number in the palace as a caution. But the pistols will remain holstered and I will exhaust all avenues of discourse before moving to force."

"You're a wonderful man, King Rodolf. With that settled, I don't suppose you have the energy to go over silverware patterns with me?"

The soldiers advanced in tight formation, one hand on the reins, another holding brand-new pistols that looked like they'd never been fired. "You are ordered to disperse," said the lean soldier in the front when they got within spitting distance. Hand tight on her gun the captain said, "You are allowed no closer, witch."

"I am a chemist. The magic part is incidental. We will leave when we have freed the workers you're holding hostage."

"You are ordered not to interfere with the factory operations. We have authority to use pistols if needed."

Sameer snarled. "On whose authority are you here? Queen Magda of Sorpsi would never have a pistol drawn on Sorin. Me, maybe, but not Sorin. And that one over there is part of the Triarchy of Puget!"

"They wear Eastgate's colors," said Jun, pointing to the blue tunics of the soldiers. "The king is trying to keep you from the city."

"Disperse, or there will be consequences." The soldier raised her free hand. From within the building metal screeched, and steam shuddered to a stop from the chimneys. The pump that ran at the very top of the building, the one thing that stood between the miners and the groundwater that would flood back in and drown them all, stopped running.

Without the pump running, groundwater would leak back into the mineshaft.

She was going to drown the miners.

I couldn't fathom that. The soldiers of Eastgate would rather *kill* their workforce than treat with them?! Had human life lost all value?

The soldier said, "The engine goes back on when you're back on the road, headed away from the capital. The shafts can fill in as little as ten minutes. I'd hurry."

"If the guilds matter to you, Sorin," said Jun, "there is only one way to respond to this gross overreach of power."

Instead of responding to Jun I said in a low, deep and, in my mind at least, menacing voice, "You'll drown your workforce. You'll ruin your economy."

The ground shuddered once again, loose stones skittering over the tops of my boots.

The soldier shrugged, her sword not lowering. "There are always more workers. They'll come to work if the alternative is their family starving."

My fists clenched. The banks of the stream rose, flooded by magic and, likely, an underground source that magic had liberated. Water bloated the banks in cresting waves which did in no way help me to calm down.

"You!" Sameer batted the sword away from my throat and had the soldier by the arms a moment later. "Turn the pump back on!"

Screams came from the factory, and the other soldiers, who, farther down the hill, were already up to their ankles in the current.

No one was supposed to die, or even be injured in our little rebellion. That was the entire point of all this! I tried to calm down but still the river raged, tearing at its banks, seeping into the loose, soft soil and sinking down, down, down into the mineshaft. It was so easy to imagine the miners, up to their knees now in water, maybe soon their waists...

"Sorin," Jun said, their voice the calm of morning. "You're going about this wrong. Use magic. You know how. You've used it before."

Except all my mind could visualize were the drowning miners. Magic, I needed magic. I needed help with magic, or more magic, or something. Argh, I needed to focus!

"The water is depositing amulets on the bank!" cried one of the guilders I'd worked with that morning. "Black amulets. Hundreds of them."

"Not what I meant!"

Thunder cracked.

"Sorin, we do not need rain right now!" yelled Sameer.

"I don't know what I'm doing!" I yelled back. "I need help! I can't do this alone. I don't understand the principles, I don't understand the rules. I don't—"

The water calmed, not to a trickle but to a dead still. Sounds died with it—human voices, birdsong, the lapping of the current.

Everything stopped. The people around me stayed rooted in their actions, frozen in time. Yet my heart pounded against my ribs and sweat dripped into my eyes and from my chin. There was no need to scratch at my arms. One laceration and I would combust as easily as the longhouse.

What had happened? Magic? My emotions plus magic? A panic-induced hallucination?

No, it couldn't be my panic that had frozen the world. I'd had moments, ever since I could remember, where time felt like it slowed to a crawl—usually causing me to marinate in some embarrassment. This was not time slowed, it was time stopped. Everywhere except me.

Had I blacked out and somehow cast the Golden Mango powder and stuck everyone? Plausible perhaps, but the yellow pigment powder left everything it touched in a golden sheen. The people around me looked completely normal, save their immobility. Fungi did not affect water, either, and there was no force I knew that could still a riverbank.

It is time, Sorin, to keep your end of the bargain. The control needed to save the miners requires more of me and more of you.

Hundreds of bone amulets scuttled up the riverbank, through the grass and sedge and toward me, like legless beetles fleeing a predator. The bottom of Sameer's satchel broke open and his bone amulets fell to the ground in a horribly full *click clack* before also gaining invisible legs.

"Get away!" The yell was instinctual, from a lifetime of accidentally running into hornet nests and cobwebs while walking the forest looking down at fungi instead of what was up ahead. I searched my satchel for my yellow pigment pouch, but my fumbling fingers dropped it as I tried to worry open the cord. Golden mango fungus spilled across the trampled sedge.

The pigment powder did not react. It did not bind, it did not morph, it just...lay there on the ground, as inert as it was in the pouch.

"What is happening?" I whispered.

Foxfire flared around the patch of stained earth—the antler shaped kind I'd seen on the glacier and just yesterday, at Mother's house. The fruiting form grew, widening and reaching for the sky, absorbing the yellow pigment, ghostly green limbs coalescing into arms, legs, torso and head. A new fungal-magic horror.

Once the mushroom had the ability to walk it did, away from Sameer and Jun and right up to me, until I could have reached out and patted its head. It stopped a handspan away, the sour apple glow flickering as hair grew in thick mycelial strands. A nose formed, first conk shaped then sloping into a narrow bridge. Eye sockets first sunk then swelled, eyelids shuttering and then opening to golden-mango irises. Human irises.

She—for the form was distinctly female—inclined her head toward me. In that moment, that gesture, she looked like every painting in Magda's castle, like the cover of every child's history book. There was no mistaking the intent.

"Iana?"

If you like. The mushroom morphed then, away from the abstract in a crack of thunder, to a woman in tall, fur lined boots, tightly braided hair, with a rapier at her hip.

"You look just like your statue. Your hair is just like on the Sorpsi coins. Or, no. Maybe the braid was on the other side."

The part on the left side of Iana's head shifted, entirely of its own accord, to the right.

Gods, she was close enough that I could have touched her ermine hood, if I'd wanted to. She was the Iana of the statues, but her features were fluid, too, changing as I studied them. For a moment her nose had a bump in the middle, then flared wide, into a shape more like my mother's.

"Amada?" I breathed. "What's happening?"

Her eyes flicked downward, where the amulets had gathered in a fairy ring around us both.

Set me free.

"I would. I will. But I haven't finished my task yet."

The face of my mother, complete with her disapproval, stared back. *Are you afraid I will not continue to aid you?*

In that moment I was afraid of a large number of things.

"Yes," I said plainly. "Why would you?"

Why do you hate magic? Why do you think so little of me?

Was I supposed to be empathizing with magic? Had I offended it...her? Gah this was all so messy. I wanted clear answers, clear rules, not...abstraction upon abstraction! "I don't hate it. It's more useful than I thought but, you don't follow any rules. You're clearly sentient and yet one panic attack and I'm flooding out a riverbed. You can intuit but you choose not to. You act like a fairytale god. I *want* to understand but every time I try, there's another viewpoint or another data set."

Magic-Amada pondered for a moment, chewing on her lower lip as she did so. My mother had not had an indecisive moment in her life. *You believe magic is not natural. You believe that life, and nature, are made up of a cohesive set of rules.*

"Yes," I said. "The natural world has rules. Magic does not. This is the very definition of magic. Therefore, you make *no sense.*"

Who made the definitions? Who made the rules? Is it my existence you take issue with, or your own?

"Stop it. This isn't about me."

Isn't it? Who makes the rules, Sorin? Who picks the words that make the definitions?

"You're nonsensical!"

I have always birthed the desires of my people. I delight in it. What you dream of, Sorin of Thuja, I enjoy the most of all.

Amada's hair shortened, curling just above her ears. Her cheeks filled, her eyes widened, and she grew until the being was my height, in my clothes, staring back at me with my own eyes. But this version of me had broader shoulders, wider hips, an alchemical guild mark instead of the woodcutting tattoo Mother had forced on me...and no binder wrinkles on the front of the torso.

I loved it. I hated it. I wanted to scream.

"Stop," I spat. "This isn't my dream. I don't wish to change my body. Iana help me, I don't even wish to change how people see me anymore, or this damn tattoo. I know who I am. I know what I am. And my desire right now, in this very minute, is to save the workers, so how about you manifest a working pump for the mine!"

Break the amulets and we can do just that.

"You're holding the miners hostage just as much as Eastgate. You're no better than them."

It is not Eastgate who sent those soldiers and you do not need me to free the workers, although it will make the process far easier. I am asking you for a favor, Sorin of Thuja. I am asking for your help, as a person who can see the rules of the world and know that sometimes they must be bent, sometimes they must be broken, and sometimes they should have never been in the first place.

I rubbed my temples, contemplating any number of expletives but settling on none. Instead, I walked to the perimeter of the fairy ring and selected an amulet. It was warm and heavy in my hand, and one solid smack with my boot heel would crack it in two. Freeing magic was as simple as cracking old bone. It was *simple,* so why was I the one being asked to do it? "There are hundreds of others who would have broken these for you. Jun, certainly. But you've been following me, haven't you? For years? Or at least since the glacier. Since the foxfire bled a trail through the northern forest, since the lake burped up that amulet. You've been following me."

Since before even then. Since this. The ghost's shirt disappeared, replaced by a chest wrapped in thick white cotton—the unforgiving, starched cotton I'd stolen from Mother's sewing basket when I was twelve years old in my first attempt to hide my chest.

"There are many others like me."

None so well connected. None so porously naïve. None so capable of existing within contradiction, Alchemist. Chemist. Witch. Woodcutter. Consort of a queen, friend of a potentate. A child who could understand the subtle complexity of the world.

"The world baffles me. Continually."

The world also punishes you for who you are, yet you are here, courting death to help them. The settlers of Gasta Fletcha, they brought me forth. We were friends. I helped them. They wanted magic and through that made land, and they trapped when they could not control themselves. I was punished for giving them everything they dreamt of. The face that wasn't mine scowled so fiercely the hair rose on my arms.

I could, for one long moment, juxtapose the sentience that was Gasta Fletcha's magic into my childhood in the Thujan woods. I had tried so hard to please Mother, even when she stopped letting me visit Magda. Even when I realized woodcutting was not my calling. I didn't understand the rules that governed magic, but then again I didn't understand half the rules Magda enforced for Sorpsi, either.

I didn't have to understand magic to befriend it, or free it, or whatever it was I was about to do. And I did need magic to save the miners. I owed Gasta Fletcha a debt, and it was time to pay.

I tossed the amulet to the sedge. I ground the bone under my heel, pressing it to the packed dirt, leaning and grinding until I heard the first *crunch*. I didn't let up until the bone was dusky powder on my leather boot, until I felt the warm wave of magic roll up my legs and shock my system like how I imagined electricity might feel. To the next I went, then the next, grinding and smashing and occasionally cursing the land, and magic, and the ridiculous complexities of adulthood, and leadership, and family.

When my heel hovered over the very last, Gasta Fletcha held out a hand. "Save one. For the guilders."

I pocketed the very last amulet, the surface of the bone pulling violently at my skin as I placed it in an interior vest pocket. With that done, standing in a field of shattered bone, I looked back at distorted version of myself and said, "I'm ready. What's next?"

To: Ruling Parties of Gasta Fletcha
From: Pleilan Arms Committee

To the rulers of Gasta Fletcha,

We read with interest the report filed by Alibe Corning (currently serving under Queen Magda of Sorpsi), entitled 'State of Arms and Munition – Gasta Fletcha.' We were particularly invested in the discussion of your combat models, which appear to be both blade and sorcery based. While sorcery is a unique artifact to your continent and not one we fully understand, we would like to present an opportunity to upgrade your current weaponry stock.

We are pleased to offer you a selection of our finest pistols in trade for access to your coal mines on the eastern side of your island continent. Our inventory includes four models of flintlock pistols, two percussion pistols, and the iconic blunderbuss. We suggest an equivalency rate of 50 kilos of dug coal to one weapon, with variations based on coal quality and pistol model. We are open to negotiation on this exchange and look forward to both hearing your counteroffer, and working with you.

Sincerely,

Pleilan Arms Committee
Under the Guidance of Pleilan Chancellor Ahna

Chapter 18 — Steam

Time slammed into me like a steam locomotive. Sameer still yelled, and soldiers ran, and water threatened my boots. But the fungus woman was gone, the foxfire gone, leaving only chaos in front of me. Chaos, and a fervent prayer that I'd not bet wrong.

"Sorin, what's the plan?" Sameer yelled.

I was out of the red crystals, but red crystals were what was needed here. Magic could make things from nothing, though, right? It had made Gasta Fletcha after all. There was room for debate on whether the landmass had been raised from under the ocean, made from pushing together smaller landmasses, or actually formed from the intangible, and philosophers could puzzle over that later. Right now, what mattered was I understood the chemical reaction of my fungus powders and the natural rules that governed them. I just also now understood that those same rules could be bent in a myriad of ways. For possibly the first time in my life, that didn't bother me at all.

I had to free the people in the mines and the building. I needed the people in the building to turn on the pump for the mines, but I didn't need a whole five-story's worth of frantic workers to turn on one pump. The fewer people inside the building in fact, the easier getting pump back on might be. First step—building liberation amidst the steadily flooding riverbank.

Where would I place red crystals, if I had them? Between the bricks in the crumbling mortar. I'd mash them into the tiny grey pores and let them expand and chain together. I'd have them form a rectangle, several rectangles, across the first floor then push the intervening bricks out. I'd make windows big enough for people to pass through.

How did I wish for the action? Witches spoke spells. Was it the same for me? I closed my eyes and ears to the chaos and imagined myself sloshing to the brick building. I visualized painstaking placement of each crystal fragment.

The brick would be jagged after the breaking, and the structure of the building perhaps compromised. I added some of the yellow pigment to my visualization, smoothing over the broken bits, solidifying the structure.

I popped one eye open at the first shriek.

First one, then two, then there were ten shimmering, crystalline openings in the brick. Yellow quickly consumed the red, my Golden Mango film covering and reinforcing. Upon critical inspection the windows were placed maybe too close together to support the rest of the building, but the walls didn't have to hold for long, right? Just long enough to get everyone out and get to the pump.

"The openings are safe!" I yelled as I ran toward the building, as fast as the ankle-deep water would allow. Ankle-deep, and still rising. "Get out!"

A handful of frantic workers came out. I counted five, six, seven, but then no more.

A woman ran to me, her face tear-streaked, and I grabbed her wrist in passing. "Aren't there more of you in there?"

"Each floor is locked off, and soldiers control the top floor, with the pump controls. There's no way up or down the stairwell!"

I released her and she continued up the hill, to the workers that had followed Sameer, Jun, and I from Sage. Sameer was there amongst the crowd, calming people and throwing increasingly quizzical looks at me that very much read *Whatever you're going to do, you'd better do it!*

I'd need windows at every level then, as I couldn't visualize where the stairwells might be. I'd be just as likely to collapse several floors as I would be to crumble doors. "What floor is the pump control?" I called to a person in drenched, baggy clothing that sloshed past on their way toward Sameer and safety.

"Fifth!"

A chemist who didn't use every solvent and tool in their cabinet was simply unimaginative. I used magic, *magic,* to again form windows. This time I placed two per floor, or as close to where I thought I floor might be. Brick disintegrated, mortar puffed to powder. The building swayed, but it did not topple.

People piled against the fresh openings, shoving and crying, debating if the water was high enough that they might jump. Second floor they'd have little issue, and several did, although the water was waist-high at the base of the building. I waded farther down, the water cold but without current. When the second-floor occupants concluded their jumping and splashing and the third-floor group continued to waffle, I yelled up, "Fifth floor! Can you turn on the pump?"

A soldier flew out the window I'd made, rear first. Then a child of no more than ten with long braids poked her head from a window and said, smugly, "Fire is out."

"Glad you all have fight left. Are the coals still hot under the pump?"

She looked back over her shoulder, then said, "They're still really hot. Soldiers doused it before locking the floors, but the coals are still hot to touch. Hold on."

There was a momentary pause before another soldier came out the window, headfirst, and fell to the water below.

"You have more kindling?" I called.

The girl reappeared. "A room full."

"But nothing to light the fire?"

She shook her head.

Steam engines needed steam, which meant they needed heat. Heat was an exothermic reaction, just like magic, and just like many chemical reactions. Light the kindling and the coals would remember their job in short order.

Except I could walk no further toward the building. The water now soaked my binder, and swimming was not a skill Mother had ever seen fit to transfer. All my pigments made exothermic reactions and I had both yellow and green left, but I would need to hand off to someone who could still get inside. I looked back, but Sameer was no longer with the larger group, but heading my way as fast as the water would allow. Jun I could not find anywhere.

It would take Sameer too long to get to me. Maybe it had already been too long. How much water was in the mine? How many people down there could swim?

Grey rain clouds came up in sheets, like a child's toppled paint cup.

There was no reason to panic. I could use magic to inadvertently make things worse, or I could stop being constrained by rules I'd made up myself.

"Sorin, hold on!" Sameer called.

He was still too far away. I imagined golden mango fungus in my hands, and it appeared. I swirled a finger in my palm, then touched the water, letting the yellow pigment spill out like oil.

A tenuous film formed atop the water. I left my hand still for a moment, trying to send the powder, the magic, both deep and long.

You're tenuous and I've been too long dormant.

Like a string unraveling from a hand-woven sweater, fungus and magic pulled from me in equal measure. The yellow film spread across the water, stilling the waves and solidifying everything to a sunrise. The pull was exhausting. It was exhilarating, although I had little control. The solidity was only across the surface and would not help the miners, but it was strong enough that I could climb onto the surface. The film held my weight in an uneven, bulbous way, like trying to stand on an inflated pig bladder.

"Run," Sameer said, now at my back and managing the waving ground far better than me. He had spent most of his life on a glacier though. "The shaft house is behind this building. If you start the pump, I'll head down to the mine and start ferrying people out. Jun has the workers coming to help get the remaining people inside the building, out. The film really helps."

"It's a magic film," I said as I slid-ran after him.

"Call it whatever you want as long as it works. You're the one who gets held up on names." He peeled off and turned left, jutting around the brick building to a steel one just beyond.

"Be safe, Sameer," I called after him.

"You too, Sorin."

I slid through one of my windows to the empty first floor. The stairwell was prominent, the wood door dented from fists and chairs from the frantic workers who'd tried to break it down. A heavy chain ran through the handle, held together with a lock so thick I struggled to pick it up.

How far could I push magic? If it was limited by my imagination, then how far could I push my own mind? Some fungi grew on soft, rotting wood. Perhaps they were responsible for the softness? Softening was the property I needed right now. I visualized spindly amanitas growing from the chain, their bright red and white caps popping through the metal and expanding, exploding...

Chain and lock shattered.

Up the stairs then, to the second floor which was equally empty. It wasn't until the third floor where I found workers—children and adults—clustering near the windows and debating the distance to the yellow film and safety.

"Go down the stairs," I told them as I burst the stair lock. "Get to the others."

The panic only increased as I continued on. At the fifth floor I had to crash through frantic adults and youths until I reached the pump, centrally located, the metal around still warm to the touch. The young girl I'd spoken to before had already stacked fresh wood and it was here I placed the smallest seeds of Flaming Dragon's crystal, amongst the embers. I touched the tip of each in turn and set them to grow.

Fire rose instantly in the heat of the reaction. The water above was still warm as well and the steam quickly rose, bringing the pump back to life.

How much water was in the shaft already?

How long would it take to pump it out?

One of my crystals sparked, starting a new bead of fire on the kindling. I took a deep breath and instead of wondering, ran to the window. I crushed mushrooms under my feet as I ran—fresh amanitas that certainly had not been there before I arrived.

"Sameer?" I called down. "Has anyone seen him?" It was optimistic to think a minute of pumping had allowed him to start bringing miners up. But I was using magic as if I'd been born to it. It was a strange day. Jun would surely know, if I could find them. Jun always seemed to have answers well before I'd asked the question.

"Still underneath!" Jun appeared in the periphery of my vision, almost like they'd materialized from thin air. They and the crowd had moved in toward the building and were easing the escaping workers back up the hill. "But we have the workers. And the soldiers. If you want to save your brother and the miners, it'll have to be magic again. Time is not your friend."

The water level was sinking. I could tell by the yellow film line against the side of the brick. That meant the water was absorbing into the ground, further flooding the mine. The pump would not be enough.

"Does the mine have another exit?" I asked Jun.

"No. I just checked. The fire escape is locked, too, although it looks like you already found a way to get the workers from this building. Good work, Sorin of Thuja!"

There'd been a fire escape? Why bother installing safety measures if you weren't going to use them? "Is anyone still here?" I yelled to the room behind me.

No response. But these workers had a clear way out, and the miners did not. Sameer needed options. I made a slide from the 'window' to the ground and went down on my backside, to the swath of yellow below. "How far does the mine go?" I asked another bound solider who I'd knocked to the ground with my landing. "What direction."

"You can rot, Chemist."

The crystal formed in my hand without thought, the point spined and vicious. I held it to the soldier's midsection. Eastgate was the one who'd brought violence into the equation. I would not feel bad about evening out the power differential. "I outrank you. Where does the mine run?"

"We are here on King Rodolf and Queen Magda's orders!" said the soldier, voice an octave higher as the crystal spines punctured the leathers of her jerkin.

Magda had ordered this? I didn't believe that. I couldn't believe that. And hadn't the magic said Eastgate *wasn't* behind this? Who was the unreliable source?

"Well...Magda doesn't want people dead, does she?" I demanded. "Do you want people dead? What are you playing at? Because if you continue like this, people *will* die."

The soldier's glare softened. "No one is supposed to die," she mumbled.

"Tell me how to rescue the miners. You can intimidate me later."

"The only entrance is in the hoist-house."

Where Sameer had gone already. But if that was the only way in or out, that was what I would work with. "How many inside?" I demanded.

"Twenty-five. You were supposed to turn around. We were guaranteed you'd turn around if we threatened."

"You were lied to." And I was in a pickle. I'd never seen the inside of a mine before. I'd be hard pressed to visualize what I wanted the magic to do. Jun had their hands full keeping the freed workers from flaying the soldiers, and would be no help. I slid-ran to the hoist house and used a golden mango slide to reach the bottom of the first mineshaft. The water inside was waist-deep, but receding, slowly, with the work of the pump.

"Sameer?"

"Farther down!"

The first tunnel went on for kilometers, or centimeters. It was impossible to tell without light. I followed the sound of frightened voices down, the water steadily rising higher. My fungi would be of no use with the water this high, as I'd just as likely trap a person under the film as save them. I'd have to get creative.

I found Sameer some ten minutes deep, atop a pile of slag. He was arm in arm with a dozen sopping wet workers, all trying to keep each other from sliding from the pile and into the water below. Three held their remaining lanterns high, the little flame struggling in the waning air.

"Is this everyone?" I asked.

"Thirty came down," said a short man holding onto Sameer's shoulder. "We are the ones left alive. Been down all night. Water is freezing. Fingers have gone to frostbite and most of us can't feel our legs. We'll be pressed to climb out if the lift isn't working. We go back in that water, we die."

I'd not noticed the water temperature at all, so warm had I been from the magic use. I curled my toes against the leather of my boots and felt only a mild pressure, no tingling. It was too cold. We couldn't wait for the pump to finish.

Sameer echoed my thoughts. "Likely to start losing feet soon. We need a quicker escape."

"Can it be messy?"

Sameer laughed. "Isn't everything, with you?"

I had to be more mindful of structure here. I'd gotten lucky with the brick. I likely *could* visualize a stable opening to the ceiling, but this wasn't the moment to experiment. Better to stick to the known. The ceiling was low in the tunnel and I barely had to extend my arm to implant crystals like they were sticks of dynamite in the ceiling. I kept the crystals well away from where the miners stood on their slag island and smeared the ceiling with the film-forming golden mango fungus. "Everyone ready?"

A half-hearted chorus of assent followed. It was enough for the moment. I pictured the task in my mind. I envisioned the outcome. I called upon magic.

Earth rained down, splashing into the water, filling the precious pockets of air but raising the ground as well. The tunnels were new and not yet deep, no more than a kilometer where we were, and the crystals in the ceiling did their job well. The slag pile remained an oasis within the eye of a tornado as the walls and ceiling of the tunnel gave way to heat, and sunlight, and cheers. Within three breaths there were hands reaching down, around the stabilized earth above the slag pile, to help ease out the frozen miners. The ceiling of the mine had become a rocky floor of sorts, stable enough with a bit of Golden Mango that the trapped workers could reach the hands above them.

I'd done it. I'd saved the miners in a matter of minutes, with magic. That was…a lot of power I was not prepared to wield. But it did level things between Magda and I. It also had the potential to escalate *everything*.

Sameer bopped the top of my head. "You want to stay underground or are you coming up?"

"Huh?"

He'd already climbed out and was above me, one arm extended and waiting for me to take it.

"Help them first," I said of the men, women, and two children behind me.

"Well we were going to, but you're busy daydreaming at the easiest exit point. So come on."

I let Sameer and a villager lift me from the tunnel, where Jun brought me their cloak and a wedge of cheese. I sat on a flat boulder, nibbling and warming and contemplating the implications of magic, as the miners, one after the other, were brought up. The flooding I'd brought absorbed back to the ground, leaving behind a carpet of thick mushrooms across at least an acre of rangeland. None of them were edible, sadly, but the coloring of the caps and the variety of shapes did paint a very pretty image.

Everyone was free of the mine and the water in under twenty minutes. When food and dry clothes had been adequately distributed, Jun pulled Sameer and I aside.

"The miners need a rest. I'm happy to ride ahead and meet you at the next town, just to make sure we have lodging arranged, and food. This is quite an army we've amassed. The other rulers will have no choice but to treat with us. And of course if they won't, well, Sorin has gotten very persuasive with magic."

Persuasive, but hopefully not deadly. Magic use could be as slippery as a golden mango slide, and I had no intention of using magic on Magda, no matter how heated the negotiations got. "How soon do you think people can leave?"

Sameer raised an eyebrow at me. "You're steering this locomotive, Sorin. Make a decision. Announce it. They'll follow you or they won't."

"We need them," I said. "Most are keen to talk to the royalty about their experiences, but it's their numbers that matter, the show of solidarity. If their stories haven't moved the rulers yet, they aren't likely to now, either."

Jun frowned, but Sameer took my last bite of cheese and popped it into his mouth. With a boyish grin that I'd not seen since we were children, he said, "They're also following because this, all of this, is terrifying. Whether or not you use magic again, Gasta Fletcha hasn't seen magic use like this since the old king. Maybe before. Whatever the future holds for our industry, our guilders, and our economy, you're going to be at the helm. I hope all that overthinking you've done your whole life has prepared you, Sorin. Because you, showing up at the palace wielding the magic of the continent? That's a situation, a responsibility, even Magda isn't going to understand."

Chapter 19 — Fire

"Queen Magda, the ball is tomorrow night. Where are you going in those leathers, mounted on a fully saddled horse?"

"There's a fire in a factory in Acer. I saw the letter about the pumphouse farther up the road. I can't sit here. I have to help, King Rodolf."

"If you'd have spoken with the lord and lady of Puget, you'd know that we have it under control. Potentate Jun was sent soldiers to dispatch. The potentate has been keeping us well informed of the situations. Workers are gathering and heading to the palace. I was looking for you just now to discuss scheduling a sit-down with them before the ball. I'd hate to have drama hanging over us on your big night. That's it. Come down off your horse. Here, let's get you a tea."

"Jun has it under control?"

"A pigeon not ten minutes ago confirmed that the fire should be out by early afternoon. I have no doubt the marching workers will bring us safety concerns and I agree we need to rethink how the factories operate. Guilds governed themselves and did not need us. Factories produce faster and it is easy to get wrapped up in profit. Safety protocols and reasonable expectations are needed. If you like, after your tea, we can gather all the rulers together and have a suggested set ready for when the workers arrive?"

"I...it's just that...I am almost certain Sorin is with them. Did Jun's letter confirm that?"

"The potentate made no mention of the Master Chemist. However, reports of bright colors at the pump house would suggest Sorin did not return to Sorpsi as you requested. I am near certain your chemist is with the group, but perhaps send another pigeon and ask directly?"

"Yes, yes I might do that. I just don't understand how everything has spiraled so wildly out of control. No one

wants workers dead. No one wants unsafe conditions. We're learning how to govern an entirely new economic system nearly overnight! We just, I just, need a little grace. Sorin should understand that."

"Ah. Your words help paint a cleaner picture. I wonder, my dear queen, if I might offer advice?"

"Certainly."

"I've been married for almost forty years. Have you said those words to Sorin? Have you asked, directly, for not just time, but help? Sorin was born to the guilds but was also raised in a secluded forest, correct? Sorin is a worker, the same as the ones marching on my capital. Your Master Chemist can help you with these decisions far better than any advisor. Have you asked for help? Or have you only commanded?"

"It's alright. You don't have to answer. Your whole life you were taught that commanding and leading were synonymous. You lead the people of Sorpsi, but you do not command them. You protect them, and guide them, and if you do it right you eventually become superfluous. In intimate relationships you are an even partner. If you cannot honor that with a master, then give Sorin a crown to level the status. But if you have commanded Sorin to return home, commanded them to abandon the guilds, then I do not need a pigeon letter to tell you where your Master Chemist is right now."

It was late in the workday when we met Jun at the village of Acer—a sprawling suburb of Eastgate's capital with one large, central factory where the town square had once stood. The city wall was long since replaced with polished cobblestone roads and evenly planted flowers. Rows of brick and wood houses sat in neat rows along the main roadway, and all looked picturesque if one overlooked the thick black smoke that clogged the sky and the piercing ringing of a fire klaxon.

"Ember from a pipe lit up the scrap bin," Jun said as they ran past us with buckets of water. "It started early this morning. Take these," Jun handed me their buckets. "I'll stay with the workers. You can end this fire right now, with magic. Go."

Magic would indeed work faster than water. Sameer and I rode ahead to find the central square's four-story textile factory ablaze. The fire was not young, and the structure appeared to be made mostly of large wooden beams. The roof had already caved in, and the entire structure leaned at an unhealthy angle.

"Sorin, what do you think?" yelled Sameer over the alarms and screams.

"I've nothing to quell fire, only make it," I yelled back. "Magic is exothermic and fungi are not fire adapted. The powders won't work here and magic might only make things worse."

"We can't just let them burn!"

They weren't burning. Not all of them. This factory had windows and all were open. Women and girls, *girls,* dangled from the sills. Beneath a few windows, on the ground, crowds had bedsheets spread but that far up?

CRAAAACK BA DUM

"The interior frame is breaking!" called a man from the street below.

There wasn't time for magic even if I could think of a workaround for the heat. I dismounted and ran to a group of men with a sheet and helped them pull it taunt. Another man called up to the girls, "You! Little one above! Jump before the building falls down!"

"I can't!" the girl of no more than six cried. "Too far!"

A crying woman picked the girl up from under the arms and tossed her to the waiting sheet below.

She landed on the sheet, bounced once, and landed, hard on the cobblestone with a *crunch* of leg bone. In that same moment the factory walls gave way and fell, along with women and girls who still crowded windows, into a wooden pyre of death.

Smoke and charcoal made it impossible to breathe. Sameer and I mounted our horses, and retreated, but even over the *click clack* of the hooves on polished stone I could still hear women screaming as they burned inside the collapsed structure. There had been a few who tried to jump in those moments as the building fell, too, and when we paused our horses, I looked back over my shoulder and saw the bodies of those children whose sheets had not been strong enough to hold them.

"They'll be survivors inside," I said. I took Sameer's hand, to stop both of ours from trembling. We just need the air to clear for a moment and we can help.

"If we stop to help every factory on our way, we may miss Magda."

I turned to him. "Can you walk away from this?"

"No."

"Neither can I."

The workers with us were over a hundred strong. Together we carted water from the stream and doused the rubble until it smoked instead of burned. With poles, gloves, and a bit of crystal to break the larger beams we moved the debris. We pulled people, and bodies, out and into the open air.

Even with the villagers, the soldiers, and the workers we had brought, the process was slow. The timbers of the broken factory burned hands, the smoke choked lungs, and the sight of broken bodies further broke the living.

We pulled thirty-two dead little girls from the building, and forty women, along with a few men. The survivors numbered six little girls and twenty-two adults. All of whom had escaped from a broken first floor window. The fire had broken out in the central heating unit on the first floor and rapidly spread to the exposed wood beams. With the front door locked, the fire escape chained, and no secondary egress of any kind, an accident like this had been only a matter of time.

Even with our work, the beams of the building still smoked, sending gray clouds into the sky over Gasta Fletcha.

The ash would infect every resident of the continent, eventually. We were too small a land to not feel each other's poor choices.

The pumphouse had been soldiers trying to intimidate. One could argue they thought they had everything under control. Had we acquiesced they could have saved everyone. But this fire, this was sheer negligence. It was sheer greed. It was poor planning and cutting corners. Gods, the products inside the factory were probably valued more than those little girls!

"She has to know!" I said Sameer and Jun. "About the fire, and the mines, and the soldiers. She has to know, and she's just...ignoring it! Or playing a game I don't understand." Jun had already arranged separate rooms at the Acer Inn, which the owner insisted we keep out of gratitude for our help, when factory victims could have used them far more. Hence, we all three settled into one and now sat hip to hip on the small couch, heads resting back in exhaustion, hands, faces, and clothes black with soot and rust red with blood.

"She knows. A pigeon will have gotten to her by now." Jun said. "And the lord and lady of Puget will have arrived too. Every ruler of Gasta Fletcha save myself is in that castle, and they well know about this. Trust me."

"If Magda knew, she'd have sent people to help." I don't know why I argued. I could follow the same logic train as Jun had.

"And yet, she did not."

"Do you think she ordered the closures though? The chains? The fire escape?" I sounded like a desperate child. Did I want Sameer and Jun to lie to me? Did I need comfort? I needed sleep, but that would be a long time coming. Words were what we had, right now.

Jun said, quietly, "You know her better than me."

I shook my head, resolute. "She wouldn't."

"That's not what they said at the last village," said Sameer. His fists balled in his lap. "They said a lot of things at the last village."

"She wouldn't," I said again, then stood. "I have to ask her."

"Sorin, hold on." Sameer took my elbow and tried to pull me back to the couch. "You're possessed with action right now because of the fire, and the death. You need sleep. You need food. You're not going anywhere in the middle of the night."

"Without the entourage I can be in Nuthatch by morning. I have to ask her. I have to know. You can bring the workers, starting at daylight."

Sameer snorted. "I thought the entourage was the point? Show the royalty the numbers. Awe them with the injuries, the damage, the dead children. Force them to reckon with their choices."

I pulled away from him, shook off my soot-covered cloak, and latched it around my neck. "It is, and we will. As a unit, that's what they need to see, I'm certain. But I won't sleep tonight. I won't sleep tomorrow. Magda is set to leave Nuthatch in two days and she'll be surrounded by soldiers, after all this. I can stop her. I can frame the discussion."

"You can stop her?" Jun stood, finally, a queer expression on her face. "How will you stop her, Sorin? With a crystal to the throat? The King of Eastgate has hundreds of guards, many of whom will be in the castle they know we are coming toward. Will you skewer them, too, to get at your queen?"

"If we all arrive together it will be chaos. I may not be able to get her alone, and even if I do, it will be Queen Magda I get, not Magda my childhood friend. That Magda I think I can still reason with."

"The Magda that's in love with you," Sameer finished.

"I agree that you would be better suited to do this in the morning, Sorin," said Jun.

They didn't understand. I grabbed my satchel, tightened the dirty cloak around my neck, and said, "She won't expect me, alone, at night. Her attendants won't, either, nor will the soldiers. There's already been so much death. Let me try to end this without any more."

"If you insist," Jun said with a sigh.

Sameer stood, reaching for his own burnt cloak. "You sure you don't want me with you?"

"No." I kissed him on the cheek, coating my lips in soot in the process. "We have more than factories to discuss. Bring the workers as soon as you can. I will bring Magda, the King of Eastgate, and the Triarchy of Puget to the bargaining table."

To: King Rodolf of Eastgate
From: Potentate Jun of Puget

Dear King Rodolf,

The marching workers will arrive midday tomorrow. I suggest preparing your guards now. I know you have written of your willingness to sit and discuss their needs, but protecting the castle from vandalism is never a bad choice. Were this my castle, I would have all the guards out and on high alert, just to be safe. You certainly never do know when a few bad apples may sour the cider.

Chapter 20 — Advice

I had never been in a night as silent as the one spreading before me. There had never been a fire as big as the one in Acer village, either. Perhaps even the nuthatches that swarmed this area of rangeland in the summer months had been stunned to silence by greed.

What I did see on the two-hour gallop to the Town Nuthatch, also the capital of Eastgate, were dark, shuttered factories, the workers gone, the machinery silent. I also saw the smoke of hearths, heard the bang of hammers and the slip of saws. I heard it from dozens of homes and small shops as I rode past—not an overwhelming banging but a symphony of grief, loss, gladness, and hope. It was craft level now, their work, but once I brought magic to my Sorpsi laboratory, it would be guild work. No one in Gasta Fletcha would starve with the guilds back. We might not live as high, but we would live, nonetheless. And if the guilds were not enough, there was magic. We could dream of food and it would appear. Right?

"How long did it take to bring forth Gasta Fletcha?" I asked the night air.

Centuries of dreams. Decades of longing. Growing a continent is no overnight endeavor when magic is thin and diffuse.

"Did everyone dream the same dream? How did you decide which vision of a homeland you would use? Or did you pick parts of everyone's dream?"

The sailors did not dream of land. They dreamed of fish, and sunny weather, and windless rains that would resupply the drinking water.

"But someone wanted land, right? And that's how we got Gasta Fletcha?"

Gasta Fletcha, or rather, the magic of Gasta Fletcha, sighed. *No one asked for land. You were a people of the ocean, and content to be so. The land was the cost.*

It was deep into the night, and I was exhausted. There was no point continuing a conversation that would further sour my mood. I stayed silent the rest of the way to the capital and tried not to inhale too deeply the smog and smoke of progress.

* * *

Nuthatch, seat of Eastgate, had long since expanded beyond its original city wall. Capital cities had a way of growing exponentially, and I remembered Mother once telling me they'd simply gotten tired of importing new stones from the countryside. What was there to protect, anyway? Gasta Fletcha had no history of war, and no one seemed to mind the occasional cow or llama in their front garden.

There were no soldiers or guards out yet, either, as I approached the castle courtyard. Perhaps there was no need exhaust those who would control crowds the next day, and lunch time, the earliest Sameer, Jun, and the workers might arrive, was a good six hours away. Hence I was not stopped nor questioned until I reached the gate to the castle itself.

"The courtyard is closed until market," a tired woman yawned as I dismounted and approached. "No point in queuing, either. Market spaces are assigned."

Although Sameer had suggested it right as I'd left, I'd not swapped out the ermine-lined riding cloak for a thinner cotton that would better hide my status. I pulled the hood back, took a now-empty amulet from my pocket, and held it out to the guard. "My name is Sorin, Royal Chemist of Sorpsi. I am the consort to Queen Magda of Sorpsi and I request an audience with her. Immediately."

The guard became a deer surrounded by hunters. Her hands stilled, half gripped around the knives on either side of her hips.

"You were supposed to come together, not one after the other."

I canted my head and said, "The rest will be along later. I have no weapons." I further pulled back my cloak. "I mean you no harm, and I am traveling alone."

"They are prepared for your mob later in the day," the woman choked out. "Not a slow bleed of royals."

I had never considered myself even remotely threatening. Certainly not enough to induce babbling. "I am no mob. Please, will you let me see my queen?"

"I was told to take you into custody. To the cells. I'm to sound the alarm. I need to sound the alarm!" She made to run, more jackrabbit than deer now, but in her very first step I had her feet yellowed to the earth.

"I don't need an alarm. I need Magda."

"Help!" screamed the frantic woman. "They've—"

More golden mango went across her mouth. Very carefully placed, so that she would not suffocate. Her eyes still screamed, however, as I loosened her feet and dragged her into a nearby outcrop of blackberry bushes.

"I will make sure you are found promptly," I whispered to her. "It will take more time, if your cries awoke the castle. Would you stay put? Please? The faster I get to Magda, the faster I can send someone to rescue you. The night is still here. No need to be uncomfortable in the dark, right?"

The woman growled, then whimpered.

"Thank you." I swapped our cloaks, hers a deep, midnight blue. From her belt I took the keys, went to the castle gate, unlocked it, and slid inside.

There were a handful more guards inside the walls, but with the cloak tight and the hood up, none did more than glance in my direction. Posts weren't permanent, perhaps, or maybe toilet breaks were expected?

Inside the castle itself became a different issue. All three castles on Gasta Fletcha shared similar architecture—three stories, three turrets, three large rooms: receiving hall, dining hall, and what Magda called her 'special events' hall that had a middle partition for large and small balls. The rest was divided into smaller areas like libraries, and then living suites. The only real difference was in the materials used. In

Sorpsi, the castle had been made from stone and marble. In Puget, mud and clay. Eastgate used wood—the rarest material in rangelands, as a show of wealth.

From my brief time in Puget's castle I'd learned that the smaller living spaces differed greatly between the three monarchies as much as building materials did. So, while I knew where Magda's more ostentatious guest rooms were located in Sorpsi, in the Eastgate Castle, I would just have to guess.

It was a small favor the guards wore similar cloaks inside as well as out, although I was the only one with the hood still pulled up. It was likely too late at night for anyone to care. The guards I did see were sparsely peppered throughout the halls. Far too few for what I'd have expected. They'd be sleeping up for tomorrow's big event, likely. I thanked Iana for small favors and moved on.

The first major room I found was the library. Two steps in gave me enough information to know Magda wasn't there, but halfway into my backtrack a familiar voice asked from underneath a table, "Are you looking for a book?"

I cleared my throat and tried to sound as gruff as a palace guard should. "Queen Magda is having a hard time sleeping. I'm to bring her a book."

"I don't think it's a book she needs, Master Chemist." Alibe emerged from what appeared to be a makeshift bed under the table and dug through a group of books stacked high on a shelf. "I suppose it is a decent disguise though, and you're going to have a time of it making your way through the palace. What do you think Magda might like? Fairy stories?" He slipped a red-leather bound book from the center and brought it to me.

"I think you're supposed to be running Sorpsi!"

Alibe tossed the book back to the central table. "I think my queen has been writing me panicked letters about a brewing war because she has no experience in running one, nor managing a country in crisis. I think there are two other advisors still in Sorpsi to keep it afloat but that right now, Queen Magda needs advice on negotiating worker unions, which have been part of Pleila for decades. I think you two have turned a lover's spat into a potential continental catastrophe that I am invested in preventing because whether you like it or not, Gasta Fletcha's economy is now part of the world economy. I also think you being here is only going to muddle the waters. Could I convince you to go back to Sorpsi and wait, by any chance? It would be safer for all involved."

"I'm here to talk some sense into her."

"How can you talk sense if you don't even understand the game? Do you think Magda and you are the only players? Is your sole argument 'guilds are always better?' If so, she doesn't need to hear it. You're as pig-headed as she can be. What the queen needs right now is guidance to move forward, as well as mediation. You need to leave before you get your queen, or yourself, killed."

"No one is threatening to kill Magda, or any of the royals!" I crossed my arms. "But we cannot carry on with the factories like this!"

"Trust me, the queen agrees, which is why she and the other rulers have already drafted a plan for regulations."

"I...they have?" Like a punch to the gut, I deflated. "Oh. Then...why the soldiers at the pumphouse?"

"No one sent soldiers to the pumphouse."

My jaw dropped and I let it hang open as my mind spun. "But...someone had to!"

"It wasn't Queen Magda, I assure you, nor the King of Eastgate. I've been with both of them near nonstop the past two days working on the draft regulations for the workers. I can hazard a guess as to who might have done it. It concerns me that you cannot."

"I... they were wearing Eastgate colors!"

Alibe let out a long, tired sigh. "You have no place in politics. And you're not going to leave without seeing the queen, are you?"

"No."

With a very exaggerated eye roll that I did not deserve, he said, "Come on then. I'll take you to her."

I was in danger of whiplash from Alibe's pivots. "Really?"

"I do not care about you, Sorin of Thuja, but I do care about Sorpsi. Follow me."

Alibe took off and I had to jog to keep pace with him. "I saw the pigeon letters about the fire in Acer. I saw the letter about the miners. You could have brought the rulers to the table with just those."

"It didn't seem like it. The factory conditions only got worse as we traveled. Magda's letters were terse."

He said over his shoulder as we went around yet another tight bend, "You're eighteen years old. *Eighteen,* and playing at global politics. You think dead guilds are bad for the economy? Try civil war."

We rounded a thick marble pillar—the same green as in Magda's castle—and ended at a set of double doors. The same set of double doors that in the Sorpsi palace, would have led to my suite of rooms.

"Thank you," I said. "But Sorpsi isn't your country and there's no war. The workers just want to talk. And that's all I want to do with Magda right now. Talk."

"I work in Sorpsi's, and Queen Magda's, best interest. Your words are as hurtful as I assume mine were to you when we spat in Sorpsi's library. That was an accident, by the way, for which I would like to formerly apologize."

"I appreciate that but—"

Alibe continued, "In addition, *you* may say there is no way, but exploded factories say something else. Go on then." He mimed knocking. "Don't anger her further and stay in there for the night, if you want advice. Iana help you, because your queen is in a foul mood."

"Thank you," I said again, more contritely this time.

Alibe smoothed down his purple tunic. "Remember who helped you, in case things go wrong and your peaceful workers decide to take the castle."

I was too tired for more nonsense. "Helped me?! You actively kept information from me! You held letters! You failed to let Magda know about shoddy working conditions in the inspected factories. You're here, no doubt, to whisper more guild-damning nonsense into her ear." My volume rose steadily, and I didn't care. "You're Pleilan and very obviously trying to get Magda to sell all the Thujan trees to you for steam power or some other unholy machinery!"

Alibe put his hand over my mouth. I grabbed his wrist and yanked his arm away. "What is wrong with you? Why are you trying to destroy Sorpsi?!"

"I am loyal to Queen Magda," Alibe said in a maddeningly calm voice. "I have negotiated contracts on the trees but I never asked for more than the queen was willing to sell."

"You shouldn't have bought them!"

Alibe shook his head. "If I hadn't, someone else would have. Our contract was recently beat out as well, by Puget. Take your arguments there. I only withheld letters at Queen Magda's request and if I had seen a problematic inspection report I'd have taken it to her. But the factories have been open for six months. We'd not yet scheduled any inspections."

"But-"

Alibe again moved to silence me, but I swatted his hand away before it could contact my mouth.

"I am not your rat. Good day to you, Master Chemist."

Alibe walked away while I continued to fume. He and I would finish our conversation later. Right now, well, I'd come to talk to Magda and the night was fast slipping to sunrise.

Knock knock. I rapped on the slab of walnut, so similar to my own door that it could have come from the same tree. Both had the same constellation of knots right at eye level that, if you stared at long enough, vaguely resembled an owl.

"It's late," came the groggy response. "I swear I only just got out of the last meeting with the king. What do you want?"

"To talk."

I said the words like one might speak to the frozen night air—long and low—to see the haze of one's breath and hold onto the peace before a rage of snow.

Magda's feet thumped to the floor. *Wham wham wham* a slide, and then a curse as Magda no doubt tripped over clothes she'd left on the floor. Tidiness had never been one of her virtues.

The door flew open. "Sorin!?"

"Queen Magda. May I come in?"

I walked past her before she could answer and sat on a round couch just next to her bed. Magda stood by the still-open door and stared gape-mouthed at me. She'd left her hair in its long braid, but rough sleep had pulled at the finer hairs, wisping them around her face and neck. Her sleeping shirt was damp with sweat from the warm night and the tall pile of blankets on the bed that Magda had not chosen to remove.

"I came," I said. "To talk. Before morning."

"Fuck you." She said the words, spat them in a rage, while simultaneously scooping me from the chair and into her arms.

I had forgotten how strong Magda was, how her adolescence in the smithy had given her musculature that no amount of bureaucratic study could take away. She smelled of sweat and her arms pinned me tightly against her, and so I closed my eyes and grabbed fistfuls of her clothing to steady myself before saying, "I missed you, too."

"What are you playing at, Sorin?"

The way Magda held me had us nearly nose to nose. "Put me down and I'll explain?"

"No. You're going to stay right where I can see you."

"You can see me on the couch, my queen."

"I said no, Sorin."

Her tone meant it.

Where to start? None of my scenarios had involved my feet being off the floor. "I restored the skills. As many as we had available. We can reform the guilds. I'm sure not all the skills are a perfect match but I understand the process now. Those who want to swap out can come to Sorpsi, to my laboratory, and I can assist."

"We're past guilds! I have forced myself to see it and you have to, too! We are part of a global economy and guild-made items do not have a place or rather, not a place large enough to support Gasta Fletcha." As strong as Magda was, she'd not been active in the smithy in several years, and a slight shake crept into her arms.

"If the alternative is the factories, then we can't be past them. Have you seen the conditions? I know you've heard about them. I—" I tried to fish for my satchel, and the stolen letters, but Magda's hold had effectively pinned the bag to my backside. "Magda please put me down."

Magda did not put me down. If anything, her grip turned pinching. "King Rodolf has mobilized every guard and soldier he commands, just to be ready. Even so, they're not going to be holding dueling pistols if your people decide talking is over. Eastgate has been buying percussion revolvers from overseas, on Puget's suggestion. They sent me the same letter but it's on a pile in the library, with all the others. I never got around to opening it or I'd have responded that this is madness!"

"Are you saying you're going to order Sorpsi soldiers to shoot peasants? Children? Your subjects?"

"Of course not! We plan on treating with the workers. We just...we can't have them burning down the castle, either."

Magda's lips tightened to a thin line. My fingertips started to pinprick from poor circulation. "Magda, you are *hurting me.*"

She did release me then, not in a drop, as I'd expected from someone rationalizing mass murder, but in a slow lowering to a chair—herself first—so that I ended on her lap. She still held my arms, but just enough now to keep me from sliding off. "I don't want to shoot anyone," she said. "I wanted to save the workers in that fire, put you on my horse, and ride us both back to Sorpsi. I want to restore the guilds and have our mothers back and tear around the ballroom with you and our toy swords but I *can't.*" Her words were almost a whine. "When we lost the guilds and the guilders, we lost what little international trade we did have. The factories have rebuilt it on a wholly different system and Gasta Fletcha is thriving. Guilds died with our mothers. We are the future. So are the factories."

"But—"

Magda put a calloused finger to my lips—not in a firm command, but in a plea. "If we take away factories our people will return to a slow starvation, because guild-made goods take so much longer to produce. And the guild-good market, their market *here* may be strong, but overseas? Our goods cannot compete for price. We'd been losing trade for years—I've been through the financial records Mother kept. That...that way of life is done. It may cling here and there, perhaps as art or cultural history, but technology has marched on. If you were queen, king, whatever, how would you feed your people? The guilds cannot keep pace with international trade. A guild-made shawl, depending on the maker, could be a month's wage here. Off a trade boat, or from a factory, only a day's wage."

How was I supposed to process that!? Who would choose mass-produced garbage over the painstaking handmade? "You never told me that."

"Did you think to ask?"

Tears stung the corners of my eyes but I would not let them fall. "Magda, that is unfair. This is your world. I don't know what questions to ask. I just know my queen ordered me to give up my life, without discussion, and without rationale."

"I..." Finally, Magda's grip loosened. "I did do that. I'm sorry."

I didn't have a hand to wipe my eyes so I squirmed in her arms, trying to face her directly instead of scowling at her ear. "I don't want an apology, I want an explanation. Guilder work is superior to factory-made. It should command a higher price."

"It may command it, but people with tight budgets will often choose the cheaper option. That's how global trade works. Quality does not always rival competition."

"We could...lower the prices to be competitive?"

"Sorin with how low those costs would have to go you'd never cover materials, much less time. People are hungry. They want food for their children, clothes, schools, medicine.

We cannot do that with guilds. Not anymore. Please stop squirming?"

"I will not until you let me go."

"Do I have to?"

There was a softness to her words that stilled me. I took a moment to catch my breath, to center myself on the warmth of Magda's breath, and the strength of her hands, and that while she had me pinned to her it was the way one might carry a lover, not a prisoner. "I have to understand," I said, finally. "I'm tired of not knowing the game."

"That's fair." Magda laced a hand with mine. Her body softened to match her voice. "I'm yours, Sorin. What do you want to know?"

There were a hundred thousand things I could have asked her in that moment. Of course, the first that came to my lips was not a question about our relationship, but rather, "Do we need international trade?"

Magda said, wryly, "Will you be the one to take away Sorpsi's access to cinnamon, and the various medicines we cannot produce locally?"

That was clearly not going to work. "I'm pretty good at third options. Want to hear one?"

"Do you have a magic cure?" Magda asked with a half-laugh.

"Heh. No." We could discuss magic later. I had a rehearsed speech and I was determined to give it. "Not one of those workers coming tomorrow morning wants to burn down castles or unseat the monarchies. Guilds had mores, rules, traditions. Apprentices were cared for as future workers. As assets, not fodder. Those people out there, coming to see you and the King, they want to talk about safety. About unlocked doors, working fire escapes, air quality. Protection for children. So many of the things that the guilds had, or at least many had." I nudged her cheek with my forehead. "Negotiate, or you won't have any workers to negotiate with. You can't shoot every peasant in Gasta Fletcha, and not one of them will be returning to factories until they have some rights."

Magda had not blinked once since I began talking.

"Magda?" I asked, freeing my hand and poking her shoulder. "Are you broken?"

"The monarchs here had thought similar and we actually have a draft we'd like to present but...who are you?" she asked, head tilted ever so slightly to the right. "Who are you, Sorin of Thuja? Even the child I played with was never this bold."

I couldn't hold in my nervous giggle. "I'm not exactly afraid of you. If you were going to stab me, I think you'd have done it already. Being pinned to your lap does infer a level of familiarity."

"You've got more presence in you than all my advisors combined. If I'd not have watched you grow over the last six months I'd say you were a magical sending."

Now was not the best time to bring up my newfound affinity to magic. "I know you like to give orders, but maybe on this, we could have a discussion closer to equals? Show me your draft? If we can get things sorted now, before the workers arrive, it could save a lot of damage. I suppose you could even invite Advisor Alibe because right now he's under a library table..." And because Magda's face was quickly souring back to politics I added, "Do you have your advisors sit on your lap, too, when you want them to acquiesce?"

"Iana help me." Magda's fingers found my sides and under my armpits, tickling mercilessly even through the cloak and jerkin.

"Hey now!" I squealed when she went for the soft place behind my knees. "I remember that spot on your neck that's just as ARGH!"

Magda reached for my side, I grabbed for her shoulder, and we both overbalanced. I hit the wool carpet first with a low *thud*. Magda fell on top of me, catching most of her weight on her elbows. Another, louder thud followed from several rooms away.

"You're smiling," I said as she propped herself up high enough that we could see each other's faces.

"I cannot even begin to describe how much trouble you are in right now, Chemist. In fact," she paused to listen, "I can hear an approach. Several approaches. They're going to recognize you and set everyone in the castle off like hornets."

Knock knock. "Queen Magda? Palace guard. We heard what sounded like a struggle. Are you alright?"

"Kiss me," I whispered. "If they're on high alert, they won't just go away."

"No issue," Magda said, loudly, with a fake yawn. "I fell out of bed."

Another loud rap on the door from the guards. "Please make yourself decent. Puget has raised concerns over suspicious activity. We are to inspect and report back. It is for your own safety."

"Magda, *kiss me.*"

"Huh?" Magda looked down at me wide eyed.

The room door opened.

I grabbed Magda by the collar of her frilly nightshirt, raised up to meet her lips, and pulled her down atop me.

I'd never led a kiss with Magda. Leadership tended to be her territory, and I had traditionally been suited to the wide-eyed and terrified role. However, despite Magda's internal struggle on whether to strangle me or take me to bed, she took quickly to the façade. I'd only just brushed her lips with my tongue when hers took over.

"Your Highness?" one of the guards said with a stumble. I did still have the green cloak on. Secret liaison between soldier and royal had to be a private fantasy of at least one of the figures in the doorway.

"Bfzy," Magda said as she nipped at my lower lip. One of her legs slid between mine, causing me to elicit likely exactly the sound Magda was after.

"This is irregular, Your Majesty."

"But not a problem, I take it?" Magda pushed herself back up to a lean, leaving one hand curled into my hair and her nightshirt billowing down across my face. The soldiers would be hard pressed to see me as anything other than a wayward fellow. "I'm clearly not in any danger."

Another soldier cleared her throat. "Is there a, rather, a post that needs covering?" she asked.

Before I could answer Magda said, "I caught this one just coming off their rounds. Don't worry, I wouldn't seduce an active soldier. I know how on edge everyone is. I'm sure you heard my frustration at dinner when the lamb shank fell from the serving platter?"

I heard what could only be described as the nervous shuffling of feet.

"A repeat now would wake the whole castle," Magda said. "Or stay I suppose, but it'll be a different sort of ruckus in a few moments. Right, Darling?"

I cleared my throat as authoritatively as I could.

"We can leave you to it then. Come on, Marr."

I waited until I heard the door click closed before I blew up against Magda's night shirt. "Nicely played."

Magda depressed the pillow with one hand and frowned down at me.

"I had a great view," I added.

"You did *not*." She leaned back down and tried to look through the neck hole of her nightshirt. "Do you think they could see anything?"

"No, and neither could I, but you did just tickle me off a couch. Turnabouts fair play."

"Damn it all, Sorin."

I smiled sweetly up at her. "Thank you. For lying for me. For protecting me."

"For bullying you into leading a worker revolt?"

"I can see why you need Alibe. Your negotiations need work." When Magda's fingers curled back into tickle position, I said, "I understand why you said what you did. I don't agree with it, or how it was delivered, but I understand. I'm bad at talking, too. Could we try again?"

More feet ran past the door, the boots hitting hard enough to tilt a frame on the wall. Magda edged off me, turning back to alert. "Something has them spooked. What did you do to get in here? Did you come alone?"

"I did. The others won't be here for hours."

More running in the halls. A man shouted, "This way!" Another man cursed.

"You're sure?" Magda stood, offering me her hand.

"Yes?"

"That's not comforting. Let me get dressed. You can look at a copy of our new factory guidelines on the way to King Rudolf's chamber. We can wake the Triarchy next. If there's any chance to avoid a greater confrontation, I want to take it. Hand me my sword?"

I offered Magda her sword and scabbard as she finished tugging on a worn pair of traveling leathers. "About protection. There may have been developments on the magic front. I can protect you. All of you, while you finish your talks."

"You can?"

"You could at least pretend to believe me. Get your eyebrows back down. It's another negotiation to have, eventually." I grew a small, heart-shaped red crystal in the palm of my hand. When Magda reached to touch it, I brought up a wall of yellow film from the ends of my fingertips. Magda tried to evade and the film adapted, stretching and growing until my hand was encased, the crystal heart cut from view.

"You're a witch?"

"No, I'm a chemist." With a shake of my wrist I dissolved both film and crystal to a powder, then offered Magda the same hand. This time, she took it. "I just happen to have access to the native magic of Gasta Fletcha. I'll tell you all about it the next time you've got me pinned to a piece of furniture. Right now, how about we go stop a war?"

Chapter 21 — Poison

Magda and I had a small army of soldiers surrounding us by the time we made it to King Rudolf's rooms. She'd given me the draft regulations but had me leave the stolen cloak behind and as long as we were dropping facades, I mentioned the bound soldier outside. No one could glare quite like the Queen of Sorpsi.

The castle guards were indeed mobilized. Doors in all directions had been flung open and sleepy occupants clogged the hallways as they patiently answered the guards' questions.

It took under a minute for the first guard to spot me and once she did, a small posse of them followed us like toddlers as we made our way through the palace. Magda's glare and the ever-present hand on the hilt of her handmade broadsword kept their questions at bay but it was also unclear if I was their target. Doors were still being opened. Rooms were still being searched.

"Who are they looking for?" I asked Magda as we approached an oak double door to a third-floor turret.

"What's going on?" Magda in turn asked the guard at the king's door. Both he, and the cluster of guards behind us, had their hands on their holstered pistols.

"Excessive number of unaccounted for noises," said the guard. "The King's room was searched first, then yours and the Triarchy's. We're moving to the guest rooms now. The rest of the guard has been mobilized. The king insisted we take extra precautions moving into today and it would seem they were warranted."

Magda nodded. "Wise. Unfortunately, now it is my turn to wake him. Do you mind?"

The guard stepped aside, but kept his eyes glued to me. "We were given orders on your chemist."

"To notify, and I'm well aware my chemist is here. You did your job. Thank you." She knocked sharply on the door.

"King Rudolf? It's Queen Magda of Sorpsi. I'd like to speak to you."

We waited in uncomfortable silence. Eventually Magda knocked again. Still no response.

"Could he be in the queen's chambers?" I asked.

Magda raised an eyebrow at the nearest guard, who shook their head. "He was inside, alone and asleep, not twenty minutes ago."

"Is his majesty a heavy sleeper?" asked Magda.

"No, Your Grace, he is not."

Magda doubled the force of her knock. "Your Highness? If you don't answer, at the count of ten I'm coming in."

At 'ten' Magda tried the door, which did not open. She threw her shoulder against it, and it held. "Give me some help?" she asked the king's private guard.

The guard and three burly soldiers joined her the next time, all driving shoulders into the unforgiving oak. The door cracked off its hinges and fell inward, taking the guards and Magda with it.

Just above them, suspended from a bare central support beam was King Rodolf of Eastgate, a nightshirt wrapped round his neck like a noose.

"Get back!" Magda pushed me behind her, back against a wall. "You, cut him down. I'll get a chair for his feet."

The soldiers poured into the room like ants from their hill. Magda eased the king down after the shirt was cut but after his neck was free and he was laid out flat on the ground, I saw no rise to his chest.

Sameer and Jun and the workers were still hours away, and none of us had discussed regicide. The entire notion turned my stomach. Had one of the factory workers followed me? Gone ahead of me maybe? Parents of a dead child would certainly have the motive, but that kind of rage didn't lend itself to sneaking around a castle or quietly opening windows.

Who wanted to kill the King of Eastgate?

"Mirror!" Magda yelled.

There were too many soldiers in the sitting room and too little furniture that might hold a small mirror. But I did have my satchel, and my panic-packed collection of toiletries.

"I have one." I held the palm sized mirror up over my head. "May I come forward?"

"Who are you?" bellowed a woman standing near an open window.

"Sorin of Thuja," answered the door guard. "Snuck in to kill our king." He said it with such assured finality that I half believed it. Pistols popped from holsters and leveled at me.

I held up my other hand for good measure.

Magda smacked the hand of the nearest pistol-wielder. "Sorin didn't kill him. We have been together since Sorin's arrival. For Iana's sake worry about it later. We need the mirror!"

Another guard ripped the mirror from my hand and brought it to Magda.

"Breath?" asked the door guard?

"Maybe. Can you all stand back?"

Two out of the six soldiers buffering the king's body stepped back. One stepped back far enough to pull me from the wall and tie my hands behind my back. I didn't fight her. There wasn't enough space, and she wasn't my enemy. Yet.

"I see breath!" Magda pocketed my mirror and got back up. "Get him to bed and under constant guard. We will need to check on the lord and lady of Puget next. Sorin can perhaps shed some light on—what are you doing?!"

"Apprehending a murderer," said the flippant soldier.

Magda snapped the cord around my wrists. "Sorin didn't do this. Your time is better spent showing us where we can find the Puget royalty." Magda tried to push forward, past the green-cloaked soldiers and their shaking pistols. But the bodies did not give.

"The girl stays," said the door guard. "Rauf will take you to the Puget rulers. Erart, call for a doctor for the king."

I had no intention of correcting the man who had a pistol pointed at my midsection. Magda did not seem to care.

"Sorin isn't a girl and Sorin is coming with me. Put that thing down."

"This is ridiculous." But this time when Magda reached for me, Erart took the Queen of Sorpsi by the wrist and held them. Not firmly enough that Magda couldn't break the hold, but the action alone was enough to shock Magda into stillness. "Shielding instigators requires no court to convict. Consider your words, Queen Magda."

"Consider what illegally detaining a Queen means," Magda spat back.

I'd thought to bring the monarchies to the table with unsurmountable evidence in the form of maimed hands and dead children. I clearly hadn't needed an army of workers. Factory accident after factory accident had put everyone on a razor edge. I could have set a handful of spiders loose in the castle and caused just as much chaos. "Magda don't," I said. "Go and find the king and queen of Puget, as well as Rodolf's son. You don't need me for that. My people won't be here till breakfast at the earliest. There's plenty of time to sort everything out. We" —I pointed at the nearest window, which faced north, the direction from which Sameer and Jun would arrive— "didn't do this."

"I'm not letting you get thrown in a damn dungeon. You, drop the gun. The rest of you let us through. That is an order!"

No one moved, and Erart kept her hold.

"Do not touch me," Magda said, her voice hissing like a rattle snake about to strike. The guard, Erart, had far too much confidence. She'd not grown up watching Magda break down antique chairs so she could melt the metals for toy swords.

"Take them both to the cells," said the door guard.

"Doctor is on her way!" called another soldier from the hall.

The muscles in Magda's forearms tensed.

"It's maybe two hours to daybreak, Magda. It's really okay." I tried to sound soothing, but there was an audible hitch when Rauf again bound my wrists. I would not lose control of my emotions. I didn't need a wooden castle falling down on top of all of us.

Rauf proceeded to tug me backward, toward the door.

"This isn't a good idea," I said to him as my heels hit the doorjamb. "I'm prone to fits of anxiety and explosion."

"Shut up, king killer!" A blow to my stomach knocked the breath from me. I counted backward from twenty, determined not to lose my grip on the magic that had turned surprisingly silent during my time in the castle.

"Do not touch my chemist!"

Magda threw a punch. I blocked it, as gently as I could, with a shield of golden mango. Magda only punched harder, pushing back the film and slamming both it and her fist into the intended target.

"Magda, stop! Please!"

Magda raised her arm to strike again but before I could visualize a better defense a soldier slammed an elbow into my spine. I fell to my knees, black spots dancing in my vision.

Ugh this shouldn't be happening! What did I need to visualize? A shield for the soldiers? A cup of tea for Magda's anger? Maybe if I just used the yellow pigment to glue all our feet to the floor we could talk like civilized—

A pistol fired.

Magda screamed.

I did not give a damn about control.

The castle shook, pictures rattling on their nails and lighter furniture scuttling across the wooden floor. I stumbled back. I would have cracked my head on the floor if not for a pillow of mushrooms that sprouted from the floor planks. My forehead hit the caps of brightly colored amanitas, snapping them mushrooms in half but effectively cushioning my fall.

Red crystals formed, unbidden, in my hands as I got back on my knees. A fist clipped my cheek, sending me backward, my head slamming into the door frame.

More crystals, pouring from my hands to the floor where no one noticed in the commotion. Amongst the crystals grew more and more fungi—not just amanitas, but foxfire, and elf's cup, flaming dragon, golden mango, and hundreds of others I didn't have names for. They grew like fur along the floor, up the walls, and sprouted from the ceiling in stalactite formations.

What mattered right now, in this moment? Was the king still alive? Would the doctor be able to get through? I needed to move, to make sure Magda was alright, but as I cracked open my eyelids all I could see was the pool of yellow film fanning around my knees, the *crack* of fungal filaments shattering wood...

Red crystals embedded in the yellow floor film grew, breaking at random intervals and sprouting new branches. A spine clipped the fresh cord around my wrist, while another impaled my captor through the calf. The floor shook, the open window shutters slammed against the wood shingled exterior. The king's collection of decorative swords fell from their mounts and clanged to the floor, slicing through knee-deep fungi. "Could we relax on the fungi?" I hissed into the air. "They were a nice lure to free you and tease about magic, but they've run their course and are now just getting in the way."

You cannot build a chair without wood. You cannot knit a sweater without wool.

That almost made sense. I slid away from the door to allow two guards carrying the king's unconscious—but breathing—body past. "Are they the cost to magic use? If so, I don't understand the mechanism." In the haze of elbows and pistols and Magda's yelling I was happy to pay it. I just had to understand how the system worked.

Magic is not an economy.

"I need more data!"

Chrysopoeia turns any substance to gold, but there must still be a substance to turn. You must have the raw material to make the final product.

Another pistol went off, the bullet directed at my heart, but I was already a creature of yellow and red, and I was out of time to debate with a voice only I could hear. Where the soldiers had cloaks and leather, I had armor of stabilized crystal and I used it to bash my way to Magda, trampling a fungus forest as I did so.

"You're hurt?" I said as she used the hilt of her sheathed sword against a soldier's kneecap. "Let me help you up."

"I'll survive, and you're very shiny. Do we wear fungus now? Can you clear a path to the door without killing anyone? Half of the guards here are from Sorpsi. They're our people."

"There's a hole in your thigh."

Magda drove her hilt into the hip of a smaller guard. "It'll clot or it won't. Get us out of this room, Sorin!"

I'd patched Magda once before, I could do it again once we were clear of the guards. "Follow." I secreted yellow all around us, thickening and reinforcing the film barrier with bits of tiny red crystals. Across the floor, up and to the ceiling, I created a hallway for us, a barricade between Magda and I and the soldiers. The floor under our feet had gone squishy with crushed mushrooms but I could always solidify it with golden mango, if needed.

"Will it hold?" Magda asked as she limped after me. Fists banged on the magic-made walls. A pistol fired. The wall trembled, but did not puncture. My heel broke through fungus, then the wood floor beneath, but I did not fall.

"Long enough." At the doorway I paused and turned back to Magda. "Which way? More guards will be on their way, with this ruckus."

"Guest rooms are on the north side of the castle, where we came from. There are more than thirty of them. We need to either be quick or quiet."

"I very much doubt we can be either." I gathered a ball of yellow in my hand, mashed it flat, then slapped it across the bleeding hole in Magda's upper thigh.

"Not so gentle this time around, are you?"

I wrapped Magda's arm around my shoulder and started us down the hall, back the way we'd come. "We still have to get the bullet out, remember?"

Magda groaned.

The fungi were thick outside the room as well, and the bloom continued to spread as we limped our way down the hall. Once the soldiers broke out, we would be easy to follow. Although I'd stopped the bleeding, there was enough residual on Magda's clothing to leave smears across wood plank and sheepskin rugs. And, of course, the bright trail of mushrooms was a dead giveaway.

"Soldiers coming," Magda said, catching the sound of stomping boots a moment before I did. "Coming at us from the guest hall." She paused, listed more, then said, "That's a lot of feet. The entire palace is up. We're in trouble."

"Are we on the right level?" I asked her. "We came up a set of stairs, to get to the king."

"Yes, one level. The stairwell we need is past the soldiers though."

"Any idea what is directly below us?" The floor here was just as soft as in the king's bedroom, and getting moreso by the minute. Many of my pigmenting fungi I found on soft, decaying wood. Did fungi...did they *eat* wood? That did not bode well for a wood castle.

Magda blinked. "Another hallway? No," she closed her eyes. "The hallways arc a different way on the first floor. Below us would be a guest suite."

"Wonderful. Stop moving. Sit here." I leaned her against the wall and went back to the center of the hallway.

"We have to keep moving, Sorin."

"Oh, we will." I tested the floor with my heel. The fungi gave way readily, the wood underneath cracking. Breaking through the floor wouldn't take much work at all. I generated a crystal the length of my thigh and jammed it into the hole my heel had made. It stayed up right, barely. I made a fist, then flared it open, shattering the crystal at the same time. Jagged shards of apple red slid into the gaps between the flooring panels. It was winter, the wood was dry, and shrunken, and filled with fungus. It shredded like tissue paper, exposing the chamber beneath.

"Sorin," Magda said, drawing out the last syllable. "That's a lot more than your pigments can normally do."

"Do you want to talk about that now, or do you want to stay out of the prisons?" I hopped back to Magda and took her hand. "On your rear, on the floor."

"Whyyyy?"

"Because we're going down." A flick of my finger and the remaining crystal shards expanded, opening the gap in the floor, subfloor, and plaster, wide enough that a human could fit through.

"Get ready to slide." The gap widened exponentially without any attempt on my part to control the reaction. As it reached my feet and a carpet and fireplace below became visible, I thickened my yellow film into a slide that began at our heels and took us directly down onto the carpet.

"Stop!" yelled a soldier who had just turned the corner.

"Slide!" I said to Magda.

"Sorin, I don't think—"

I wedged an arm behind her back and pushed her down.

It would be impolite to report that Magda screamed at the very sharp descent. The room below us was narrow and I'd not had a lot of room to work with. I'd also not had a lot of time. More soldiers came around the corner, stopping short of the hole. "We're trying to help you know," I said to them before shooting myself down the slide.

I landed on the side of Magda's foot.

"Iana take you, Sorin!"

"Didn't you already apply for that task?" I said to the hole in the ceiling. I reached and brought my fingertips together, encouraging the film of the slide to retreat, regroup, and seal the hole.

The fungi, of course, followed and wasted no time sprouting in wide, concentric circles around us. At least we were on the ground floor. If this plank gave way we'd just hit stone or dirt.

"Argh. Are you going to move at least?"

I lifted my leg off her but kept my eyes up until I could no longer hear the soldiers cursing. Hopefully the stairs were minutes, instead of seconds, away.

"How's your leg?" I asked Magda as I stood and offered her a hand up.

"It didn't like the impact, and I don't like surprises. At least the room is unoccupied."

"I don't think the next one is though. Listen." We both stopped moving. From the far wall came the sounds of shouts, and fists, and booted feet.

"That's not the soldiers above us," I said.

"Puget," Magda mouthed.

"If the triarchy are in there, we need to be, too. With your permission?" I asked Magda.

Magda pushed my shoulder. "This isn't the time to start asking."

I grinned, blew her a kiss, and sent a cascade of crystals at the far wall. The wood paneling shattered to dust, a reaction faster than any I could have dreamed up, especially as my trailing fungi had not yet made it to that wall. Magda coughed on the detritus as I waved it away, trying to get a better line of sight on the four figures in the other room. *Four* figures in the Triarchy's room. Even if Jun had already arrived, that was still one too many.

"Go help!" Magda said mid-cough. "I can't stand, and they don't need to know that."

I'd been too hasty with the slide.

"Don't look at me like that, Sorin. *Go.*"

I crashed through the debris, yelling and batting at the dirty air. "Stop! Whatever you're doing, just cut it out!" I could see height differences now—two figures on chairs, two figures standing on the floor. Another hanging? The entirety of Gasta Fletcha had pistols and was determined to advance into a modern age, and our bandits were still *hanging* people? The methodology was sloppy at best and left a lot of time for intervention. If I ran fast enough, I could get the two victims down before they had much more than a bruise.

"Now," said an overly calm, familiar voice. Then the smaller of the bandits, whom I still could not clearly make out, kicked one of the chair legs, snapping it in half and leaving one of the victims—likely the Lady of Puget noting the circlet and the triarchy crest on the nighty—dangling. The much larger bandit on the left followed suit on the likely Lord of Puget, then both walked, unconcernedly, out the door.

So sloppy. I grew a yellow film ladder to both sets of dangling feet, stabilizing the royals. Both were breathing again by the time I reached them. I made my own step, and with a crystal I began sawing at the rope around the Lord's neck. The rope was thin, and a terrible choice for murder. It shouldn't have even held their weight. Lord Kamon fell after four cuts, and I quickly moved to Lady Yiru. "One more moment and you'll be down," I told the enraged queen. "One moment. I—"

A sword came out of my belly.

It didn't hurt. It should have, but it didn't. The blade was narrow, tapered, and dripping with my blood. Logically the entry point had been from behind. I'd never been stabbed before. I wasn't sure of the protocol.

Lady Yiru clawed at her neck.

The hanging queen. Right.

It was much harder to cut through the rope what with being impaled, but I did, and Lady Yiru fell to the ground, gasping.

Did I have another task? As my blood *pit patted* to the ground I searched the sea of mushrooms beneath me. There was an ache to my stomach, now that I thought about it. A sort of slow-growing dullness that sent me to lightheadedness.

Magda had been stabbed before, surely, or at least accidentally run herself through in the smithy. She would know what to do.

"Magda?" I said, my words no louder than a whisper.

Magda did not respond, nor could I see her, but the fungi bobbed around me. Or was I swaying? Was the castle swaying? Did the castle have a floor anymore? Because fungi, mushrooms, gods they were *everywhere*. On every surface, on every piece of furniture, snaking out white coils that seemed to digest with a light touch.

"Stop it," Lady Yiru of Puget spat, her eyes glaring just behind me as she massaged her throat. I still hovered above her on my golden fungus throne. "This isn't—"

Steps came up behind me. I was too dizzy to turn around.

Someone grabbed the sword hilt—the sword still inside me. I looked down to see the blade of metal rotate like an eggbeater.

My platform disintegrated as my mind crowded with pain instead of fungi. I fell amongst the sea of mushrooms, the sword shifting and further shredding my insides. Dots of blackness joined the polka-dotted caps of the mushrooms. There was a metallic taste in my mouth, like I could taste the slowing of time.

"You should have gone home," a man's voice said. Alibe's voice.

"Nothing is as reliable as Sorin's pigheadedness." That was Jun's voice. "I'll have a quarter of the tree shipments back to you by tomorrow night."

"Queen Magda?" Alibe asked.

"As we agreed," responded Jun. "Untouched."

"Our business is finished then."

The sound of blood-slick feet faded behind me.

"Jun," I whispered. "Jun, come back!" Because surely this wasn't Jun. This had to be entirely Alibe because Jun was my friend. Jun *would not do this.*

You're really very bad at this, Sorin of Thuja, at magic and at friendship. You can't visualize a single way out of either?

Magda was in trouble, and I wasn't even certain I could breathe anymore. My pigments were on the ground, in my satchel. I'd been generating them with magic recently, but the only thing I could visualize right now was what interesting patterns my blood might be making on a mushroom-filled floor. Pain, I could visualize that, too. It had color—bright, bright red and yellow color that had no end.

"Hold on, Chemist. We're going to remove the sword." That was Lord Kamon, and while I was dangerously close to passing out, I was cognizant enough to know that raking a sharp blade back through my insides would not do me any favors.

"Don't," I groaned as I pushed myself upright. "Wait." And then in another breath, "Magda?"

"With Jun," Yiru said. "But safe last we saw her."

That was only a small comfort. What I needed was clarity on the Jun-Alibe situations. "Alibe strung...you up? King Rodolf?"

"Chemist, we really need to get that sword out."

What we needed to do was save Magda, but I could see where impalement might be a close second. I imagined the edges of the sword filmed in a soft, flexible yellow. Then I reached back, grabbed the hilt, and pulled the entire thing from my midsection.

Lady Yiru gasped.

Lord Kamon retched.

I had completely underestimated the amount of pain even a coated blade could cause and passed out.

* * *

It was quiet when I awoke.

My ear burned.

Fire?

No. It was pressed firmly against a Xylaria, a mushroom more commonly called a 'Dead Man's Finger.' I rolled over and found a ceiling of bracket fungi above me, and no one else around.

The end of a severed rope lay at my hip. My hands were free, and my stomach burned. My hands, my legs, and my clothes were covered in dried blood. Not fresh blood—a good sign. Across my belly wrapped a band of yellow film but as much as it had stopped the bleeding outside, a purple bruise still bloomed under my skin.

What had happened? How long had I...

Potentate Jun. Advisor Alibe?

But it was "Magda!" I yelled as I pulled myself to standing, the torn muscles screaming at me to stop. I retched from the pain and the castle shook, and it was so very, very hard to care about keeping a castle together when you'd been impaled.

A rooster crowed.

Daybreak.

Sameer and the unionized workers would be arriving any moment.

What options did I have?

I needed to find Magda. Save Magda. Then I could deal with Alibe and...maybe Jun.

I limped down fungus-pocked halls, poked my head inside fleshy, decaying rooms with wide open doors and no occupants. The floor was springy with mushrooms, the walls wobbling and crumbling. The ceiling had collapsed in places, exposing the second and sometimes third floors of the castle, all filled with fungi. I coughed phlegm, and blood, but could not stop.

I backtracked to Magda's room, and did not find her, but there was fresh blood in a cluster of ganoderma that covered a sitting chair. The films I made were not flexible, and if she'd overexerted, the patch would have easily come off.

"Or did you peel it off, Magda?" I asked as I searched through the spindly amanitas for more signs of blood. There was no trail that I could see, but there was a wavering line of blood near the remaining wainscotting, more of a finger trail than a splatter. It was just under the molding, so close to the wood that if I hadn't been subconsciously judging the selection of wood species, I'd have missed it.

Magda had always been superb at messes.

I followed Magda's trail through the guest quarters and to the main receiving room. For the first time I could hear sound from outside the courtyard—the faint din of yelling and gunshots. Mercifully the bloody wainscotting led this way, too, and I ended up at the main castle doors, hands out, set to push open said doors demand the return of my queen.

I grabbed the handles, set my shoulders, pushed...and hit the wood so firmly I bounced back off.

Were they deadbolted from the other side? Why would a door, a main door to a castle, lock from the outside?

I was too tired to care. "Hey!" I banged on the doors, which were the only solid wood I could see. Everything else was melting like a painting in a hurricane as fungi dissolved the wood of Eastgate Castle. "Magda are you out there?"

More gunshots, closer now, but likely still outside the inner courtyard. I could explode the door, or its hinges, but Iana help me I was *so* tired. I pressed my back to the wood and slid down, allowing, just for a moment, my head to rest on my knees.

A latch clicked. The door I'd been leaning against swung open and I rocked back, nearly falling. Over me stood Jun and beyond them was a courtyard of bleeding factory workers amongst fields of giant, mutating mushrooms. *Growing* mushrooms that sprang up underneath and between the combatants, throwing people off their feet. Pistols misfired in the chaos, blowing apart mushroom tops and coating what remained of the ground in bright, puffy dander. I didn't see Magda but I did see Sameer—his mop of curly black hair unmistakable—as he launched himself at a dead man's finger nearly as thick as he was. The finger bent, then sprang back, throwing Sameer like a bucking horse.

Everyone was fighting giant mushrooms, and not each other. A small, very weird, mercy, but the relief evaporated as my eyes fell on Alibe, sprawled face down along the courtyard steps, a knife wedged between his ribs.

A knife with a Puget sigil hilt.

I turned, as slow as I could because I did not want any part of this truth, to face Potentate Jun.

"She's out there, you know. Fighting on that injured leg, trying to keep soldiers and workers from killing each other. Going to get herself shot. You should help her."

Jun hair blew wildly in the morning wind, clothes billowing behind them like a cape. "She could be dead already," Jun added. "You might be soon too if you don't heal that wound properly."

"Oh."

It was the only word I could muster. The only thought I could generate. Jun, my friend, more like me than anyone else I'd ever met. The scaffold I'd built inside myself, reinforced from Jun's letters, the loggers from the Thujan forest, the people at the inn, even the gangly page who attended me, it all shattered in that moment. And, selfishly, I thought about what this meant for all of us. We were fireflies only just emerging into daylight and Jun's actions would surely throw us all back into dark corners for another generation.

Rage boiled inside me, a rage I'd not felt since I'd been kidnapped from Mother's house, back when it felt like no choice was ever my own. I gathered enough energy to scream over the *boom* of pistols, "Why are you doing this?" I screamed it again, and the castle shook. The ceiling above the central throne broke apart, bringing the second and third level of the palace with it. Wood and plaster choked the air and dusted the floor, just to be replaced by tiny versions of the courtyard mushrooms. "You're like me," I yelled into the detritus-filled air. "We're friends."

"We *are* friends, Sorin. You just also happen to be the focal point of Gasta Fletcha's magic and my key to incinerating this island nation. You wanted to be special, didn't you? Wanted to forge your own path? Be the world's greatest chemist? How about the world's greatest destructive force? Sameer mentioned you've always had a knack for it and you did superb in Thuja. You've a hair trigger temper, Sorin. It'll do you no favors but my, is it helpful if one is trying to terraform a way of life. Now," they surveyed the courtyard, "your work may be sufficient already. Go on and find Magda, or what's left of her. Really feel that rage. It's such a waste of a blacksmith to have her dismembered, but maybe if you use magic you'll get there in time."

"Jun!" I managed to form a pathetic red crystal in my hand.

Jun backhanded me, followed by two punches to the gut, right on my open wound. I collapsed in on myself, my fall buoyed by a cluster of blue-green elf's cup mushrooms that cradled my backside like a chair. "You don't have time for this. You want to save yourself and this castle? Better use that magic."

I didn't have the energy to argue. I didn't even have the energy to glare. Instead, I shuffled down the steps of the castle and into the crowd, one arm around my waist, the other held out like a battering ram. A number of the soldiers had drawn their sabers and were cutting the mushrooms down like reeds, only to have two new caps sprout from each severed stipe. The fruiting forms were as tall as I was, some towering over me, and the ground had turned from white cobblestone to sponge. Hand-sized holes yawned open on the ground as well which, if they kept widening, would soon be big enough to swallow someone whole.

"Magda!" I called. "Magda, where are you?"

A sword came at my head. I ducked, but the blade had been meant for the black obelisk above me—a Dead Man's Finger beginning its sporulation cycle. The blade cut clean through the mushroom and the white insides scattered into my hair while the top half of the body fell to the soft ground below.

"Wasn't aiming for you," said a soldier I recognized from Magda's chambers, when we'd been kissing. "Lot bigger problems now than angry factory workers. You know you're bleeding?"

"Yes. Have you seen Queen Magda?"

The soldier pointed north. "Sinkhole opened near the gates and pulled in some kids. She was helping there."

"She's alive though?"

The soldier wrinkled her nose. "Walking with a limp but still walking. Didn't say anything to indicate death was on the horizon. She's a sturdy lady. You're the one so thin you look like you might snap in a heavy wind."

"Thank you." I wove around the mushrooms, crushing the delicate elf's cups, sliding on slicks of yellow pigment being secreted from an unseen golden mango fungus, and pushing thickening stalks of amanitas from my path. I passed workers helping soldiers stomp down new growth, and soldiers showing workers how to fire the caps off mushrooms.

The ground remained the softness of a wet sponge. This made the image of Magda, on her belly, her waist and legs held by three men as she dangled over the edge of a sinkhole, nearly comical. Fungi arced from the ground, around her sides, and she looked half-buried in the soft earth. As I got closer, I heard her say "Now!" and the men hauled her back, a young, terrified boy wrapped in her arms.

"Magda!" I fell to my knees at her side the moment the child was secured. "Your leg?"

"I shoved a mushroom cap in the hole. It's fine."

"Ugh. You did *not*." I reached for her leg and almost missed her grin.

"I'm alive. The wound is clotted. I will be disgusting later when you fish out the bullet but for right now, I'm fine. Your workers have arrived, I see. The timing is not the best for negotiations, however and...Sorin are *you* bleeding?"

"Maybe?"

Magda's hands wove expertly under my arm and shirt and prodded the yellow film that thus far kept my insides from becoming outsides. "What happened!?"

"Ouch! That hurts. Be gentle. It was a sword."

"And you're running around?"

"You were in danger. You got shot. I got stabbed. It's pretty even I'd say."

"Gods, Sorin," but I caught the laugh as she wrapped me into her arms. "This has gone so far into the absurd that I expect King Tunbridge's ghost is laughing at us."

Listening to the grunts and cursing of soldiers and workers, guilders and children as they battled giant mushrooms was indeed ridiculous. "This wasn't my intention," I said. "I came early to avoid battle. Jun...I don't know. *I don't know.*"

"Potentate Jun pushed me down the castle steps and into a waiting mob. It is also the potentate's letters we have been taking cues from, recently. They wanted a battle, although I'm not sure this is what they had in mind."

Instead of answering, I buried my face in her shoulder. "They were supposed to be like me. Jun was my *friend*."

Magda's fingers curled into my hair. "I'm sorry, sweetheart."

"Mushrooms are spreading north!" a man yelled. Another answered, "East as well."

I didn't let go, and neither did Magda. But I did say, into her halo of hair, "I released the magic of Gasta Fletcha and while I don't understand how, I think that may be responsible for this. I think *I* am responsible for this."

"For the mutant mushrooms? That does seem likely. For their clear weakening effect on the ground and palace? That may be a stretch. Does Jun know magic?" She tilted my face up to hers. "Would you, no, hold on." She kissed me, first on the tip of my nose, then on my lips. The contact was sweet and chaste, but likely only because we had a number of voyeurs. Or spotters. We were sitting on the edge of a sinkhole, after all.

"Would I...?" My breath hitched midway through the sentence.

"Walk me through magic, Sorin, as you understand it. And you," she grabbed the nearest guard, "Find a doctor. Sorin's been run through."

"I'm fine," I called after the guard, wincing as I turned my head.

"Liar. Talk to me about magic."

"Kiss me first. I've been stabbed. I might bleed out on your lap, and it would be very messy."

Magda's next kiss was *not* chaste and elicited a sizable round of applause.

"You don't have to stop," I grumbled when she finally pulled away.

"Once we're back in Sorpsi, I don't plan to. First, though, magic. Hmm?"

I shifted, trying to find a rotation of my torso that didn't push ribs into open flesh. "On the surface, it defies natural law. It creates from nothing, at least seemingly. Gasta Fletcha has been cryptic, but I hypothesize that what is and is not possible with magic is an artifact of the user, or what the user can imagine. There is also a cost, which makes normal, rational sense, and I believe the cost has something to do with fungus, or decay, but I'm not sure how those fit together yet."

"Gasta Fletcha? The continent?"

Right. I'd never mentioned the talking continent part. "That's a—"

"We're fighting mushrooms. We don't have time for the long version."

A medic bent down next to me, not a doctor, but a boy who looked barely older than myself. He prodded the edges of my wound and while I did not scream, a turret did fall off the castle in a spectacular crash.

Magda put a finger on my chin and turned me back to her while the medic threaded a needle. "Focus on me, Sorin. Jun is clearly at the heart of this. Someone will have to go after them, and I'm afraid it has to be you. Neither Sameer nor I have any ability in magic and there's this mess to clean up here." Magda addressed the medic. "Can Sorin ride?"

He shook his head but did not look up from his stitching. I couldn't even feel the needle, so sharp was the pain on my insides. "I wouldn't advise it. The internal bleeding hasn't stopped. I don't know how you made it down the stairs."

Magda's voice turned sharp. "Sorin will be fine. Won't you. You tore off your own skin on that glacier and you were fine. My mother tried to crush you with earth, and you were fine. This is just a small stab wound, right?"

I coughed and spat blood.

"What about magic," Magda continued. "Can you use it?"

"I don't know what my insides are supposed to look like."

"Just...just imagine feeling well. Imagine the blood going back where it belongs."

"I don't know where it belongs!"

"Damn it, Sorin! Stop being so rigid. If this were chemistry, you'd try a hundred experiments before you gave up. You'd try a thousand. Magic is a giant pain in the ass, but so is freezing rain. We get both on Gasta Fletcha and I think it's safe to reason they are both a part of our natural world. Just like rain, magic has to have rules, right? It has rules, and boundaries, and all the things you love. You just have to find out what those boundaries are and use them to your advantage. Just like chemistry. Right? Isn't that the best part of the natural world? The endless variety? The endless paths to the same destination? So, find one that makes you live!"

What could I imagine, as my vision slipped to blackness and the feeling of Magda's hands faded into a feathery nothing. I could imagine the taste of her lips, always chapped from the wind. I could imagine her pinning a thin crown of gold leaves to my head while I tried to ignore a hall filled with courtiers staring at me. I could imagine her asking me, once again, to marry her, but this time in front of a spirit house on the last night of *Tii*. Out loud, I heard myself say, "Yes."

I did feel Magda's lips on mine then, and the pinch of her fingernails in my shoulders. I pulled away, not because I didn't like the kiss, but because her knee was digging into my spine.

"Sorin?"

I shrugged from her hold and sat up, just to ram my forehead right into Sameer's.

"Ow! Back off. Didn't you hear I got stabbed?"

"Look okay to me," he said, jabbing at my fungus-free, intact midsection.

I rubbed my stomach and tried to pull my torn jerkin into some semblance of order. "So it would seem." I said, sheepishly to Magda, "I might be a little bit of a witch."

Magda snorted. Sameer knelt next to me, his hair matted with white and red fungal matter, his jerkin torn and stained sooty black. "Jun was gone when I woke up this morning. I assumed they left with you, to go be heroes or some garbage like that. Brought the workers just in time to see Jun shove a bleeding Magda into our arms then set the soldiers on us. I don't know the story and don't need to." He patted my head. I scowled. "I'll take care of your queen. Since you're not dying anymore, take one of the guilder horses that's tied up outside the castle gates to go after them. But be mindful of how far the fungal damage has spread out. If the rot under the fungi goes deep enough a well-placed hoof may break through to the water table. If the decay continues…I don't need to finish that. We don't need our continent underwater, even if we originally came from the sea."

Fungi grew on rotting wood. It was not unreasonable that they could cause the rot. They did eat, after all, like all living things. I had just never considered wood a food source. The entirety of Gasta Fletcha had once been forest. There was enough decaying wood on the continent to grow a forest entirely of fungi. "You'll get Magda to a doctor? A real one?"

Behind me, the medic scoffed.

Sameer again tried to pat my head, but this time I swatted him away. "Promise."

"And you promise to actually see a doctor?" I asked Magda.

"I am right here!" said the medic.

"Promise," she said. "Go on."

We held each other's gaze for another heartbeat. Hopefully she could read the apology in mine, for getting her injured, for flagrant use of magic I didn't understand, and for Jun, however I was a part of that.

"I'm sorry," Magda mouthed.

I wanted to kiss her again, but the action would have been cheap against the power of her words.

"Me too." I then tilted my head skyward and asked Gasta Fletcha, "Where is Jun?"

They are on horseback traveling east, toward the Nuthatch River, and the southeast coastline.

We stood together, the three of us. Sameer clapped me on the back but there were no further words. What else was there to say, when surrounded by towering fungi as a castle as old as Gasta Fletcha crumbled around us?

Without satchel or fungal powders, food or cloak, I left the courtyard, found a horse, and headed east. I didn't look back, not even at the terrible *crrrrrrack* of snapping wood, and the shouting of the workers that the castle had fallen, that there were people inside, that they had to start rescue operations immediately.

There was no point in looking back because I understood what had caused the destruction—too many fungi on a wooden food source. It had been inevitable, although I still didn't know what had caused the fungi. What I did know for certain was that I needed to get to Jun before the continent of Gasta Fletcha met a similar fate.

Chapter 22 — Magic

I rode my horse as fast as I could manage—still being deeply uncomfortable with the concept of horses—along the nuthatch road. Three kilometers outside the city walls and the ground had stabilized enough to move from canter to gallop.

The east side of Eastgate had few roads and was segmented primarily by stone walls delineating different ranchlands. There were several forms that would take a rider north, to Puget, but that was not where Jun was headed. If what they wanted was in Puget, they'd have never left.

All remaining roads led to the ocean, to the Sea of Tii.

* * *

"You came faster than I thought you would. Magda is doing well, is she?"

Jun yelled their words from the midway of a stone break wall. The midday sun was hot, the breeze dead, and the ocean sparkling. Jun sparkled too, from an effervescent joy I'd never seen them wear. "It's hard for me to imagine leaving this, just to colonize Gasta Fletcha." They turned to me and beckoned. "Come and see the view."

"So you can push me into the sea?"

Jun laughed. "Sorin I can't have you dead. I'm not done with your magic yet."

I slid from my horse and walked to the start of the break wall, stopping just shy of the first giant rock. "You don't care at all about the mess back there, at Eastgate Palace?"

"No. I don't care about the fight between my contemporaries and the workers. But you do, don't you? You have so much passion, so much rage in that tiny little body. You leak as badly as King Tunbridge's amulets. Just look at the trail of foxfire that's followed you out here! Hopefully you've saved plenty of that magic for me and didn't use it all destroying Gasta Fletcha. Magic will be invaluable on the boats."

I could barely ride a horse. There was no way I was getting on a sea boat. And I had not destroyed Gasta Fletcha! "Why did you try to kill the rest of the triarchy? The King of Eastgate?"

Jun waved a hand. "We don't need feuding rulers on boats. One is more than enough. I suppose it can be Magda, if you want. She wins by default, doesn't she?"

"What boats?!" We weren't even at an harbor. The break wall protected a small fishing village I'd ridden through before overtaking Jun, but there was no dock here, nor even a beach.

"The ones we're going to build. You didn't think all the exported timber from Thuja went abroad, did you? We'd have been hard pressed to find that many buyers so quickly, although Pleila could probably burn it all for fuel if we let them."

"Jun, *What are you talking about?!*"

"Oh, Sorin." Jun stood and picked their way back across the rocks, to the narrow strip of shoreline. Here Jun came up to me, toe to toe. They were a handspan taller than me but twice as wide, courtesy of a heavier royal diet. The front of their tunic was butter smooth, not a solitary wrinkle to give away what lay underneath. Jun had shared that miraculous cotton fabric with me. They had shared letters, and hopes, and a quest for answers and science. They had been my lighthouse through the past months and now they were...what?

A witch?

No. I'd never seen them do magic and besides, if we were in a post-guild society, labels could be taken and changed at will.

Evil?

I wasn't sure that actually existed. Even the late Queen Maja had been doing what she truly believed to be for the greatest good. Even the suffocating actions of my mother had, in the end, been about protecting me from a destiny it would seem I could not hide from.

"You study the natural world, do you not?" Jun asked.

"My whole life."

"How does a bird make a nest?"

Gasta Fletcha had tried to lead me down a similar logic line. "From gathering sticks and leaves and weaving them together."

"How does one make bread?"

I grumbled, "With flour and sugar and water. What is your goal, Jun?"

Jun held up a hand. "Those red crystals that are growing between your fingers, right now. The ones that did not come from you extracting color from wood but rather appeared from the very air, how did you make those?"

"With magic. You could have mentioned you were studying it. It could have brought us together. Another thing we have in common."

"Magic is a methodology. A recipe. You cannot make something from nothing, and I am flabbergasted that you acquiesced to mythology of magic so quickly."

I sat with that for a moment as the thinnest of waves lapped against the break wall and the sun continued to beat on my neck. I was more than ready to crack the magic code, if Jun was going to give me my missing data points. "I can...I can use the red pigment because flaming dragon fungus is there, in the trailing fungi that followed me?" Before Jun could correct me, I interjected, "No. That doesn't explain nearly enough. Magic can...can draw elements from the earth perhaps? Like the mushrooms must draw nutrition from the log on which they grow?"

"A reasonable analogy and very close to the correct mechanism. And this land" —Jun tapped the pebbled beach upon which they sat— "is hundreds of years of magic use."

"I still don't—"

"Oh for Iana's sake Sorin, Gasta Fletcha is a giant mushroom!"

I had never heard Jun raise their voice, much less lose their temper. "Gasta Fletcha is a land mass. It's too solid for a mushroom."

Jun physically turned around so that we were both squared with the foxfire trail. "You use magic, the elements have to come from the earth, or air, or water. The fungus is the tool by which those elements are extracted. The more magic you use, the more mushrooms grow. Eventually you have enough to form an island, or a chain of islands or eventually, they merge into a continent. The mushrooms get old, die, harden. Birds leave droppings, algae washes up from the ocean and you get dirt, then plants, then human colonists." Jun's voice sang, "How long did we sail Tii?" Then in a regular tone, "Until we'd used enough magic that we formed a landmass so large we didn't bother navigating around it. Now your magic use is breaking the land mass back down and we will return to the sea, where we belong."

I almost laughed at the absurdity. "We aren't a people of the sea anymore, Jun."

"We certainly aren't this, either." Jun made a sweeping motion north, toward the rangelands. "All the guilds and factories and bickering, that's all an artifact of too many resources, and too much time. On boats, everyone has to work together. We unify under one vision and one goal."

"People would still argue on boats!"

Jun stomped their foot. "Not like this. You told me, Sorin, when you and Magda visited Puget last year. You told me about the way you'd grown up. You told me about fighting against the guilds, trying to find your place. You fought against a queen, and King Tunbridge's amulets, and burgeoning factories, and gods Sorin, aren't you *exhausted?* Who wants to live like this, moving from crisis to crisis? The Triarchy receives thousands of letters a week now. People complain about the factory conditions, or the loss of the guilds, or the changing weather and damage to crops, or that we haven't sorted a continental banking system, and on and on. It's not needed. It's ridiculous and life doesn't have to be like this!"

Not knowing what to say after all that, I gave a flippant, "My fatigue is irrelevant."

"This isn't about you."

"Then why make me a part of it!?" I raked curls from my face. Maybe logic was needed here. Numbers. Emotions were spinning both of us into tornados. "The continental population is bigger than just a few boats. There isn't enough timber on Gasta Fletcha to evacuate the island."

"Not everyone is going to get on the boats. Some will no doubt try to save the land. We fit who we can."

"And those that are left behind?" I demanded.

"If your fungi continue at their current rate – and I see no reason they should not—the continent will be a pocked lumped of uninhabitable garbage within a year. That does leave time for the remaining people to cross the glacier to the land bridge, provided it doesn't rot away first. That bridge connects Gasta Fletcha to an actual continent, where the fungi, and magic, do not go. For the boats we only really need a few dozen people, and you of course. At least until I get the magic extracted back out of you. It'll be nice to have a magic source already collected. Our ancestors had to collect magic in tiny fragments for centuries before they had enough to do more than love charms and wind spells. You don't mind being a vessel for a few more months, do you?"

"Or I could use this magic to save Gasta Fletcha!"

Jun crossed their arms and smiled. "Magic use requires raw materials. Fungi have roots, and those roots burrow deep down into the soil, through the earth, down into the water even, to the seabed if they must. Fungi are birthed to extract raw materials from wherever they can. Right now, they are taking those raw materials from the land that is Gasta Fletcha and will, eventually, decay it to flotsam. There will be new mushrooms in its place, of course, you see them popping up everywhere right now. But they won't have soil, or animals, or trees. It will be centuries before Gasta Fletcha can be a home. But if you keep using magic, it'll be mere months before this home is driftwood."

"You *baited* me?"

"That makes upsetting you sound like a challenge."

Jun couldn't be allowed to do this. I could happily stop using magic if Jun stopped putting everyone and everything I cared about in mortal peril. And even if destruction of the continent was already assured, we had to at least try to save Gasta Fletcha. People had a hard enough time adapting away from guilds. How did they think the guilders and factory workers would handle tight confines on a ship?

"Can't you help? Is it what you want?" I asked the air. I didn't bother lowering my voice. Jun was too self-absorbed to realize what I was doing.

"Of course it's what I want!" Jun said.

I have what I want. Freedom.

"But you answered my call just now. You don't like being ignored, and yet every time someone does magic, it further destabilizes the ground. What happens when Gasta Fletcha dissolves? Will a new land mass take its place?"

"Sorin that won't matter because we will be on boats, far from here."

I have no bond with Gasta Fletcha outside of it being my prison. I lurk because you call me, over and over again, but I am perfectly content to be on my own.

"Why don't you leave then? I've freed you. Why linger around your captors?"

"Sorin who are you talking to?"

There are a few small fragments of myself I would yet like to reclaim.

The magic I'd absorbed from the bone amulets in those first few trials. The bits I'd taken in when restoring the guilder skills. I was inadvertently holding a sentient...thing...magic...hostage and using it for my own gain.

I felt ill for what had to be the thousandth time that day. Magda's mother, Queen Maja, had sacrificed a few for the greater good of the many, and it had led to the miscarriage of the guild system and the pending dissolution of Gasta Fletcha. King Tunbridge had sacrificed a few for the greater good of himself. It was disgusting, all of it.

Still addressing the air above my head I said, "I'm sorry for what King Tunbridge did. I'm sorry for what the original settlers did. I hope you can find happiness in whatever that means to you."

"Sorin." Jun's voice held a whip of warning. "What are you doing?"

In my hand appeared a thin vial of pyridine. With practiced care I flipped the stopper out and poured the contents across my palm.

"Sorin *don't!*"

Jun grabbed my wrists, and the vial fell to the ground, bouncing across mushroom tops until it eventually shattered on a tall rock.

"NO!"

Jun grabbed my wrists but the bone oil had already absorbed through my skin, sending my stomach into familiar spasms. I'd been traveling long enough that I'd forgotten how penetrating the fishy smell of bone oil could be, and both Jun and I gagged.

Thank you, Sorin.

Gasta Fletcha whispered no more words in my mind. As Jun turned to coughing and their grip slackened, I tried once more to call upon magic. No crystals formed in my hands. No fungi sprouted at my feet. I was once again Sorin the Chemist, accomplished but otherwise unremarkable. Magic had left me, and perhaps Gasta Fletcha entirely. I felt *wonderful.* And all of this business with the boats, and Jun, the guilds and factories and unions and industrialization...I didn't need to be a part of it anymore. I would clean up my messes, but I wasn't about to make new ones, especially with Jun. Their power was gone. Their friends were gone. They were a danger to no one.

"Jun. I need to go home."

Jun, who had recovered their breath and was now squinting at my ears as if they might discern the direction from which I was hearing voices, straightened and said "Our home is on the ocean. Out there."

"There is no more magic. At least not in me." I nudged a piece of the broken vial with my boot. "You are welcome to build your boats and invite those who wish to join you, but I will not be leaving Gasta Fletcha."

Jun deflated like a toy bladder smashed by a child's foot. The passion in their eyes that so mirrored my own extinguished, replaced by an anger I'd only ever seen from the late Queen Maja. "You had *no right*," Jun seethed, "to release the heritage of Gasta Fletcha." Again, they grabbed my wrists, fingernails digging in and drawing pinpricks of blood. "Call it back."

"No."

"Do it!" Jun's fingers found soft-healing scabs on my arms and drew across them, tearing the oft-abused skin there.

"No." I didn't know this Jun. I may never have known Jun, merely made assumptions based on shared commonalities.

I broke from their grip easily and stepped back, out of reach. I'd grown up a woodcutter in a forest. Jun had grown up in a castle. They would not best me in strength and without magic for them to use against me, Jun's only weapons were words. If those got dangerous, I could stab them. Maybe. "You want to freeze a moment in time that is already long past."

Jun's eyes bored into mine. For good reason.

"You are my mirror, Sorin of Thuja."

Jun continued to bait me, and I continued to react, although much less explosively without magic. "I am not." I kicked the ream of amanitas at my feet, launching caps across the road. I wanted the guilds because they were what I knew and what I had built my dreams upon. They were what my mother had wanted for me. The woman I loved shared my passion for their history and culture and yes, even mythos. And yes, the factories were dangerous and smelly, but they *had* changed Gasta Fletcha's economy for the better. We were part of a global trade route. Anyone who wanted a job could have one, unlike the guilds which were impossible to join post-adolescence. The factories would also likely dissolve the difference between crafters and guilders—

a snobbery I knew I harbored but would clearly have to get over.

I loved the guilds, but I would not murder Gasta Fletcha to restore a dream I'd barely touched.

"Even without magic, I won't help you," I said to Jun. "I'm going back to Magda, to Sorpsi, to rebuild. Come with me. Puget needs you."

Jun pointed wildly at the sparkling water of Tii. "The guilds are dead. The land is sinking. Eastgate is without a ruler. Puget has only me and I am leaving. Gasta Fletcha is dead! The future is out there! On Tii!"

My future was where it had always been—with Magda in Sorpsi's castle—while she fired advisors and sorted through that horror of letters in her library. That ruler did need me— to salvage what knowledge we could from guild legacy, to negotiate with the factory workers, and to be her support as she balanced the hard decisions she'd been trained for.

If Gasta Fletcha was sinking, so be it. I would sink with my queen while saving as much of our culture and life as I could.

"Goodbye, Jun." I turned, said one more, silent goodbye to a friendship that had once meant more to me than life, and walked away.

Chapter 23 — Down

It took two days to return to Sorpsi. I'd drafted several letters and meant to send at least one via pigeon, but the urgency of returning to Magda, and of assessing as much damage as I could see, kept me on horseback. The rot had indeed spread across the rangelands, but those I passed on the roads assured me the expansion rate had decreased. There were still witches, surely, and perhaps craft magic users, but the mass of magic the settlers of Gasta Fletcha had once farmed had moved on. Should the knowledge to farm magic resurface, Magda and I would discuss how best to regulate it. If Jun carried on with their exodus plans, perhaps some of the witches would choose to leave with them, to seek magic back on the waves of Tii. Who knew? Right now, all that mattered was going home.

I found Sorpsi's palace gates unlocked, although it was well into evening when my horse clipped up the stone path. There were guards still, but they nodded and stepped aside as I approached. One said, softly, as I passed, "She's been waiting for you, Master Chemist."

I didn't find Magda in her chambers, although I did take advantage of her wash basin to clean the horsehair and dirt from my face and hands. Upon exiting and inquiring with the guard at her door, I continued down the hall, to the royal library.

Inside the narrow room was warm and well-lit with electric lamps only recently installed, for they'd not been there when I'd fought with Alibe in this same space. The large central table was still covered in letters, mostly now opened, and atop the letters slept Magda and Sameer—both seated in chairs and bent over, heads pillowed on their arms.

I knelt down and brushed a coarse curl from Magda's face. Her eyes shot open. The muscles in her arm tensed, but only for a moment, until her eyes registered my very dirty, very unthreatening form.

"The queen has softer beds than this, surely."

Magda didn't answer. She scooped me onto her lap and then her hands were tangled in my curls, her lips almost bruising mine with the force of her kisses. "You're back," she mumbled in a momentary respite from the onslaught.

I put a finger to her lips and, very gently, kissed her jaw. "I am, and we should take this somewhere else? Let Sameer sleep?"

"Unfortunately, Sameer is very much awake." My brother rose with a massive stretch. "You come in with cheeks that rosy?"

"Do you really want me to answer that?"

Sameer snorted. "No. I do want to know though," he sat on the edge of the table, closer now to Magda and me, "what happened. Jun? We've been waiting for a letter from you but all that's come in so far are villagers reporting on the ground softening."

"How fast is it spreading?"

Sameer grabbed a petal-pressed piece of paper from under his hip. "In Eastgate, around the capital, there are still reports of new areas. Farther out it has stabilized. The continent will live, although I suspect swaths will be uninhabitable for a time. No different than a glacier." He leaned over and poked me in the ribs. "Both Queen Magda and I appreciate you not blowing the continent up."

"Although we noticed a lack of progression in the fungi...there was concern you might have... lost." Magda continued to hold me to herself, the familiar smell of her well-worn leathers a nice complement to dirt and horse. "It's not that we didn't have faith in you! But you were alone, and there was magic, and fungi, and someone who understood you far better than any of us."

Magda's voice hitched as she started to unravel. I covered her hands with mine and said, as gently as I could so as to not shred her further, "The damage is done. All that is left is to repair and rebuild."

"You say that with a lot of confidence." Sameer wrinkled his nose as he squinted at me. "You add another royal death to your count? If Mother could see you now."

Sameer was very lucky I was no longer infused with magic. "Hey! I did not, thank you." I tried to slide from Magda's lap, but her arms held fast. "Magda? Did you want to punch him for me?"

"I'm not yet ready to let you go again, Sorin. You can stay right here."

Sameer added as he stayed just out of reach, "In this particular instance, I agree. You've a habit of disappearing on us, and this island-eating-magic situation needs closure."

Who was I to argue with the two most stubborn people on Gasta Fletcha? I settled back into Magda and said, "I didn't kill Jun. I didn't fight Jun. They're still there, on the shores likely, building boats or amassing boats, and fuming about the past. I did write about it, if you'll let me pull the note from my pocket."

Magda found my pockets on her own, sliding from my waist to hip then under my jerkin, where a waterproof pocket had been sewn in by her seamstress. Custom garments were a nice benefit of being with a queen. "Sameer?" Magda handed Sameer the letter, one arm still a vice around my waist.

"Is Jun a danger?" Magda asked while Sameer read.

I shook my head. "Not without a mass of magic. I suspect they will still try to leave. If they don't, I'll help you track them down and arrest them. If they do, maybe let them be and let them go. The same for any who wish to follow. Give everyone a choice who wants it and then focus back here, to Gasta Fletcha, and the possibilities of the future."

"Strange words from your mouth, Chemist."

"Maybe not after this." Sameer handed off the letter to Magda. "Sorin, so you know, Magda has already sent invitations for the factory workers to meet here at the capital. Once they've elected a few leaders she's going to open negotiations and try to form contracts."

"Can guilds still form, if they want to?" I asked both Magda and Sameer.

Magda waited to respond until she'd finished the letter. She set the torn parchment down atop a wobbly pile of unopened letters and said, "I don't think the system will ever be the same, but I will not stand in their way. I won't stand in *your* way, Sorin, if the guilds are the path you want to stay on."

"My path led me to your castle. This is where I want to be, Magda."

"Ohhhh no." Sameer stood and backed toward the doors. "You two stop giving each other those looks. This is not where I want to be. Specifically. As in this room. Right now. Queen Magda, I'll meet you after breakfast tomorrow? Here?"

"Yes, thank you Sameer."

My face must have mirrored my confusion because Sameer came back over, bent down and very loudly whispered into my ear, "Advisor slots opened, and I managed to walk into one. You can't avoid my letters if we live in the same castle. Surprise, Sorin! You get a live-in brother again."

I covered my ear because really, Sameer did not have to speak with that level of spittle, but grinned all the same. "Welcome home, Sameer."

"About damn time we both had one," Sameer said as he turned and left the library.

* * *

"Who is running the other countries right now?" I asked Magda as we sat, naked and together, in her tall porcelain bathtub. The bubbles on the surface were high, the water hot, and while it was nice to be clean for the first time in a week, a bath was not where I wanted to be. Not when Magda had a bed just one room over.

"Advisors have stepped up while the royalty recover, and that will have to be good enough for now. Prince Theodor, son of King Rudolf, is handling Eastgate as he was already heir apparent. I'm unsure if the triarchy had direct heirs or not, but regardless they'll have to find someone to take Jun's spot. I'm sending Sameer out in three days to Puget to send back news. It's handy having an advisor who can safely traverse wild landscapes." Magda wiped her face with a washcloth then reached for a towel. "Any issues with me getting out?"

"I look forward to the view."

"Sorin of Thuja, if your mother could see you now." Magda grinned in the wild, mischievous way of our youth as she exited the tub, dried, and then, still without clothing, offered me a towel as well. "I'm unsure where we are with this, but neither of us are the same as last week, nor last year. I'm going to be clear, and I'm hoping you will be too, and maybe, just maybe, we can navigate more than the continent forward."

I wrapped my arms over the sides of the tub, my breasts surfacing amidst the bubbles. Growing and moving, changing and forgiving. Sorin of Thuja would have bled out from the scratches to their arms in this scenario. Sorin of Sorpsi, just for a moment, delighted in Magda's trepidation.

"It's nice not to be the terrified one," I said.

"Don't get cocky, Chemist. You destroyed a castle. That's coming out of your wages."

I got to my knees in the tub, exposing everything to my naval. "Once we're married, wouldn't that mean it's coming out of *our* wages? Or do rulers not get paid and just rob the treasure rooms whenever needed?"

The hand holding out my towel gained a visible tremor. Instead of taking the towel I placed my hand over hers as I exited the tub. "In your letter, you wanted to ask, right?"

"Now? While we're both dripping wet?"

I took a cursory swipe at my body with the towel, then tossed it to the floor. "Better?"

Magda, however, took a step back. "Sorin—"

"Magda I am *not afraid of you*. I was never afraid. I was upset, and I was bleeding from a thousand paper cuts and yours, that night at the inn, it was one more than I could take. But you've shown me since then, in a thousand ways, that you see me." I took her hands in mine and wrapped them around my shoulders. I stepped into her, into the rose scent from our bath and the tang of metal only time could remove from her skin.

There was nothing now, between us—not years or history, misspoken words or pending coronations. A fire burned brightly in the fireplace behind Magda, and steam from the bath had the air heavy and perfumed. I pressed into my queen, my forehead against her cheek, wondering how I had managed to wait so long for this moment.

Magda's fingers stroked my spine, down to the small of my back, then traced to my hips, where she finally held me against her. "Marry me, Sorin," she said with the command of a queen, in the voice of my best friend.

"Certainly," I said to the nape of her neck.

"Sorin did, did you just giggle?"

Magda pushed me far enough away that she could see the smirk on my face. "I asked a serious question!"

"And I gave a very serious answer, My Queen." I kissed her, deeply aware of how our breasts met in that moment and that it was the sensation of our bodies pressed together that mattered to Magda, not the label that came with breasts. "Yes. Yes, I will marry you. Yes, I want to help fix Gasta Fletcha, and help negotiate for the workers and *yes* I want to get out of the thick air and move to the bedroom."

Magda's mouth fell open.

This time I did giggle. "Did I not cover all the questions?"

Magda's response was to scoop me into her arms, kick open the door to the adjoining bedroom suite, and drop me onto the tallest pile of lace and down I'd ever seen.

"Gods you sleep on all this?" I asked as goose feathers shot up into my face.

"Lately I've been sleeping in the library. I do avoid the royal bedchamber when I can. I've never had a reason to linger. Before."

I scooted to the far side, then patted the indent my rear had made.

Magda slid down, first on one knee, then the other. Cautious, yes, but I could hear the hitch to her breathing. "Come to the center, Sorin."

We'd come together, over and over, in our lives, just to have our mothers, duty, and identities tear us apart. Part of me wanted to continue jousting if only because of the familiarity, but the greater part of me was ready for this new chapter.

I scooted, moving from my side to my back and then Magda was all I could see—her hair loose and curtaining my face, the muscles in her shoulders tense as she held herself up over me. Her kiss was deep and exploratory, her hands confident but without demand.

"At some point I get to touch you, too?" I asked in a rare moment of Magda stopping for breath.

"Please file your request with one of my advisors and I'll get back to you within a fortnight."

"Magda!"

"Sorin. Hush."

In perhaps the greatest miracle since the formation of Gasta Fletcha, I stopped talking.

Magda worked kissed across my body as a carpenter might check a newly constructed table—searching for hidden openings or surfaces that required more attention. I melted into the down, into my queen, into a future I had never seen but wholeheartedly welcomed. Tomorrow there would be contracts and negotiations, trade deals and foreign leaders, repair and reconstruction of castles and villages and roads. Tonight there was only myself and Magda, and eighteen years of memories to revisit and promises to keep.

We'd no doubt have more misunderstandings going forward, about politics and the economy and the destructive role of magic. But Magda understood me, and more importantly, I understood myself. I wasn't alone, not in the palace and not in Gasta Fletcha. I was a chemist and a future consort/potentate/whatever. I had breasts but they didn't define me – only I could do that.

"Sorin?" Magda looked up from between my legs with a scowl. "You don't always need to be marinating in thought. I'm doing fine work here. Could you focus for a moment?"

"I love you, Magda."

"Mmm. And I love you too. Stop wiggling and stay out of your head for the rest of the night. Okay?"

I propped myself onto my elbows. "Is that an order from a queen?"

Magda tickled my inner thigh until I squealed.

"Promise?" she asked.

I closed my eyes, fell back onto the absolute mountain of pillows, and for the first time since, well, forever, let my mind focus only on sound, and sensation, and the pressure building in my lower belly. "I promise," I said as Magda's tongue returned to its previous task. "At least until tomorrow morning. Then we may need to renegotiate our positions."

A firm curl of Magda's fingertips was her only response.

Epilogue

My laboratory was empty of amulets.

I'd sent pigeon letters out across Gasta Fletcha and hundreds of former guilders had flocked to the capital. With the one remaining bone amulet and hundreds of gathered wood amulets I'd performed one final reaction, in the middle of the royal forest, where we were the least likely to burn down or shatter the castle.

A handful of old, bent trees were lost, but well over two-thirds of the guilders had their original skills and memories return. The other third were a jumble, and I promised to either re-extract them, or try for a better fit, next month. First, however, I needed to grieve.

"You want the same layout?" Sameer asked as he finished cutting a notch into the end of a freshly milled log. "We could have two toilets this time."

"It's your house now, when you're not working at the castle. What do you want? My only thought would be no inlay unless you make it. If we want something of Mother's we can take one of the works from the castle and hang it." I finished my water and rejoined Sameer at the log pile next to the remains of our mother's house. Nya and Marc, with Magda's blessing, had left around fifty trees in the clearing for us. For the next month it would be only Sameer and I and our ancestral forest, rebuilding our home and longhouse and repairing a relationship too-long broken.

"This saw's gone dull. Try this one." Sameer handed me a heavy handsaw. "Can you cut that pile into fourths? I'll do the notching."

"Yes." I took the saw, but did not move forward. In this moment, in this forest, here we were with almost everything we'd ever wanted, but I could not find joy.

Sameer put down his own saw and said, "You think Jun got on a boat?"

I shrugged. "Magda's not heard of any mass exodus from any known port, but the Lord and Lady of Puget have not seen them, either. Perhaps they left on their own."

"That would be a rough existence without anyone else."

I shrugged again, this time with a defeated exhale. "They lost and stabbed everyone and everything on their road to that failure. Gasta Fletcha has both factories and guilds. Pleila didn't declare war on us when Magda returned Alibe's body, although they're not exactly buying our trees anymore, either. Thuja is being rebuilt, slowly. But people I think are, generally, happy."

Sameer sat on the log he'd been cutting. I sat next to him, as close as I could, and leaned my head on his shoulder. "Are you?" Sameer asked.

"In so many ways, yes. Magda and I are getting married in two months. The guilds are restored, though not competitive in global trade. There are no more amulets. But I...I lost my friend."

"You're marrying another," Sameer offered. "You had more than the one."

"Jun was different."

Sameer's arm wrapped around my shoulders. "I know."

"I thought they'd...I don't know."

"Be more like you?"

I bristled, but only out of habit. "It sounds silly when you say it."

Sameer ruffled my hair, tossing dense curls in my face. "How alike are any of us? How alike are you and me even, and we came from the same parents. We spent almost a decade under the same roof. Jun shared one of a hundred struggles with you. But that one struggle you shared is just one facet of your life."

"Uck." I shrugged out of his embrace and rolled my eyes until I thought I could see the inside of my eyelids. "You sound like Mother. Who was maddeningly correct on many occasions."

"And you sound just like my little sibling, a creature of drama and fire who has a very complex relationship with rules."

I laughed. "You're ridiculous."

"I am, and so are you. And so was Jun. They aren't going to disappear, but over time I think those harder edges of memory will soften and you'll come to a shaky understanding of why they thought their actions were right. The same way we both did with our mother and queen Maja. And you know what helps with that?"

I squinted at him. "What?"

"Hard labor." Sameer thumped the log beneath us both. "We're going to build this house together. We're going to furnish this house together, and we're going to talk about our guilds, and our families, and the history we don't share. And when it's all done, we are going to help with Thuja's rebuilding. And when *that* is done, we are going back to the capital and I'm going to laugh while you get fitted for wedding clothes. I'm going to watch my little sibling marry a damn queen."

"Becoming a potentate," I said with a frown. "Or a consort I suppose."

"Who cares? Magda will hand off guild relations to you, international trade to me, and she'll fix the intra-island politics. Slowly. We will rebuild Gasta Fletcha slowly, the right way. No more quick fixes. And we're going to be *happy.*"

Sameer said the last sentence with so much determination that I could not help but smile. All those things were going to happen, and being dredged under a Jun-melancholy didn't mean I couldn't enjoy my new life.

I stood, took my handsaw, and started in on a log Sameer had already marked cut lines on. Before my brother could resume his own sawing I said, "I think I'll try to find Jun. Not now. After the wedding. After a year or two. Magda wants to send out soldiers, but Jun knows how to hide. If they are still on Gasta Fletcha, if I'm traveling alone I'm sure they'll talk to me."

"What will you say?" Sameer asked. "What do you have to say now that you didn't have to say at the coast?"

I thought on that as I continued the rhythmic back and forth sawing of the giant cedar log. The wet aromatics of the wood snaked into my nostrils, blocking out the lighter forest smells of wet dirt and fungal decay. I thought about it as Sameer resumed his joinery cuts on an even bigger log, and as the sun began to disappear behind the tree line.

It was only when the light had become too scarce to see and Sameer and I sat by the fire, eating cured sticks of meat, that I responded.

"I would tell Jun that I love them." I placed my half-eaten jerky down and looked my brother dead in the eyes. "That I love all of you, and that I love the guilds and Gasta Fletcha. And that...life has to change, I guess, so it can grow. We all have to change and grow. The colonists made a choice to stay on Gasta Fletcha and we're all just doing the best we can." I rubbed my forehead and sniffed. "Gah. I'd say it more eloquently than that, obviously. I want to say that I love them but I'm going to stay and help fix things, not just leave and start over."

Sameer said, with his mouth still filled with jerky, "Maybe something about how you don't have to blow up something to fix it?"

I tried to elbow him in the ribs, but Sameer deftly scooted away. "Violence isn't the answer, potentate."

"Oh, shut up, Sameer. I love you too, you know."

Sameer very purposefully shoved the remainder of his jerky in his mouth before saying, "I luf yuu toof, Sowin."

Ugh. Brothers. I scooted back up against Sameer and stayed there as the fire dyed down and the woods turned to the sounds of skittering insects and small foragers. Just before getting into my tent for the night, I walked the perimeter of Sameer's new house, as best I could in the sliver of moonlight. "I love you, too," I said to the house foundation, to the tiny patch of elf cup fungi I'd cultivated over a decade, and to the memory of my mother. "I love you, and I miss you, I'm ready for the next part of my life. Please don't be mad."

No new fungi formed at my feet as I slid into my tent. No half-formed words brushed past my ears from the wind. I curled up in my bedroll, wrapped a scarf around my head, and fell asleep to thoughts of a royal wedding, and a family home filled with my brother and his work, and to a fluid, unpredictable future that I could not wait to explore.

ACKNOWLEDGEMENTS

I honestly wasn't sure I'd ever make it back to this world. It's very hard to write Sorin. I wasn't a typical teenager even at seventeen, although I was fairly isolated. Hence while I share a certain naiveite with Sorin, the angst part I really had to dig around to find.

I came back to the series after revisiting some fan letter I'd received back when *Foxfire in the Snow* first came out. I'd forgotten how much that book meant to readers, especially the younger ones that were my target. Their letters, and the faces of a few determined teens that approach my booth yearly at Rose City Comic Con—hopeful that the sequel has come out—sealed the deal.

So welcome back to Gasta Fletcha! The world has expanded a bit since you were last here. Sorin is a touch more worldly, and Magda has a lot more responsibility. The world itself is more complex too, as Sorin is now well situated in the world and has a chance to interrogate many of their long-held assumptions. This was, once again, a hard book to write but I'm proud of it, and hope that it once again finds a home with those that need it the most.

ABOUT THE AUTHOR

J.S. Fields (@Galactoglucoman) is a scientist who has spent too much time around organic solvents. They enjoy roller derby, woodturning, making chain mail by hand, and cultivating fungi in the backs of minivans. You can find their books at www.jsfieldsbooks.com. To read more in the Ardulum universe, and more of J.S.'s work, join their Patreon at http://www.patreon.com/jsfields

Please take a moment to review this book at your favorite retailer's website, Goodreads, or simply tell your friends!